OVER THE COUNTER

A Year in the Village Shop

SHEILA TURNER

Over the Counter

A Year in the Village Shop

Illustrated by Edward Norrington

HOLT, RINEHART AND WINSTON

NEW YORK   CHICAGO   SAN FRANCISCO

To Phoebe and Bob

In this book I have tried to present a true picture of certain aspects of English village life, but I feel it is only fair to tell my readers that they will search in vain on the Ordnance Survey for the parishes of Upper and and Lower Barley.

S.T.

1 September

When I first told my brother that I wanted the pair of us to set up as village shopkeepers he was amused and sceptical.

"I don't think we could do it, Mary. We don't know the first thing about the job and we haven't got much money to play with either. Suppose we made a mess of it?"

"Suppose we did. So far as that goes, we might make a mess of anything. At least this wouldn't be a mess on a big scale, like farming for instance."

"Farming's definitely out as far as we're concerned."

"All right. We should both love it—but I agree. . . ."

"And there's probably much more in keeping a shop than you imagine."

"Maybe there is; but if old Mrs. Winchcombe at home could make a living out of it for herself and her great, fat, lazy son and his wife—it can't be too difficult. After all, the old woman could hardly read and I remember people nearly always had to add up their own bills for her."

Jim laughed. "Times have changed, I expect, since we were children in Devonshire."

"Not in the real country they haven't—at least, not much. Now listen—and I'll tell you all about it. . . ." and I settled down to describe the place and to outline my plan.

I'd found a little general shop in Lower Barley, a tiny village in the Wiltshire Downs, and I believed it was the very thing for us. Jim had spent four years of the last war as a prisoner in Japan and then two years more in hospital. He'd lost a leg and nearly his life and, although he'd pulled through at last, he was still a sick man—not so much sick in body but sick in spirit, for after he'd left hospital he'd acted for some time as a kind of un-paid agent to our very disagreeable Aunt Grace, who has a biggish place in Somerset. He'd hated his time there, and cer-tainly it did him more harm than good, and what he des-perately needed now was independence, peace and quiet and some kind of work which he could enjoy.

For myself—well, my husband had been killed early in 1945 and I had a half-grown daughter to bring up. My own income was very small indeed and Jim's pension nothing to get excited about; but we had definitely decided to set up house together, we were country people through and through, and here, I thought, was a ready-made job for us both. If we couldn't farm—and Jim was right, of course, it would be madness even to try it without plenty of capital—why not keep the village shop?

We talked about the idea for a whole evening and the next day we borrowed a friend's car and drove down to Wiltshire.

Jim liked the place at once and, although I pretended carefully to consider the pros and cons, I had made up my mind the first time I saw it.

The house was charming, at least it could easily be made so— very small, of course, and very old. It had three bedrooms, oak-beamed and with gently sloping ceilings—and I chose for myself the room from which one could look across the orchard, now carpeted with brightly painted apples, to the sage-green velvet downs. The red and purple heavily patterned wallpaper, hung with texts in maple frames, the brown paint-work and the huge, brass-knobbed, double bedstead made the room pokey and dark, but, in my mind, I could see cream walls, apple-green paint, chintz curtains and my own furniture. I itched to get to work on it.

The other bedrooms were a little bigger than mine and their decoration just as hideous, but they would yield to kindly treatment.

The present owner was a middle-aged, foxy-faced widower whose name, Jacob Fenton, was painted in black letters over the shop window. He had bought the place during the war and was now longing to get back to Southend.

When he had shown us upstairs he led the way into a big sitting-room with an open fireplace and windows set in walls at least two feet thick, and then, through a square hall, painted dark green and stacked with empty boxes, into a very pleasant sunny kitchen. Here, he announced proudly that the house had "all mod. con.", meaning telephone, electricity, hot and cold water but no proper drainage.

Jim unwisely asked what happened to the bath water, etc., and Fenton muttered something about "a stream at the end of the orchard and there'd never been no trouble so far", and changed the subject.

I caught Jim's eye and shook my head. Like many things in the country, this was clearly a matter it was better not to go into, so long as "there'd never been no trouble so far".

There was no need for me to be shown anything else, for I knew that the place was exactly what we wanted; and I left Jim to bargain with the owner while I poked about outside. First, I went out into the road and looked across the Green. Some geese were paddling at the edge of the pond and, on the far side, a boy in blue jeans was hanging over the little grey stone bridge. The village was beautiful and sleepy in the afternoon sun, and I felt at home in it at once.

It was September and, as I turned back, I saw with pleasure that there were bronze chrysanthemums and a few red and yellow dahlias alight against the garden fence, and I began to plan what I would do with the garden itself. Then I explored the sheds at the back and beyond them the orchard, which was neglected and quite small but which would do very well for a few chickens and perhaps a pig . . . perhaps we could have baby pigs . . . and, if there was a stream, we could have ducks and . . .

I was brought back to reality by Jim's shouting that he was ready to go, and when I said goodbye to Fenton he told me that, if we bought the place, he was willing to move out at once and lodge in the village so that we could start doing it up. ". . . Not but what it's in very nice order," he added hastily.

I thought this an excellent plan and I could see, as we left the village, that Jim was excited and pleased and more definitely interested than I had dared to hope.

"We'd better stop at the agents' in Marlborough," he said presently, with an air of false calm. "I wouldn't trust that chap a yard. I'll let them have a cheque on deposit and get the thing fixed up as quickly as possible."

I knew better than to seem wildly enthusiastic, but already I could see the little house repainted and furnished with our own things; Bumble, my sheepdog, his huge paws and head like great shaggy white chrysanthemums, asleep on the sun-warmed bricks outside the back door—and Barbara, home from school, excitedly weighing out little packets of sugar and tea.

There proved to be a good deal more to it than that—but everything went smoothly and it was not yet October when the decorators moved out and we moved in.

We had stayed overnight in Devizes so that we could take over at ten o'clock as arranged. The early morning was brilliant, too brilliant, and before we reached Barley the rain had begun and soon settled into a steady downpour.

The shop was shut for the day, to give us a chance to get

settled; and, pushed against the newly painted shutter, two bulging dustbins (Fenton's presumably) spilled their disgusting contents on to the pavement. The village was deserted, the pond swollen and pocked with rain, water streamed off the un-guttered roof on to the doorstep, and inside the house Jacob Fenton was impatiently awaiting our arrival.

His hired car was in the road, his belongings had already been taken away by lorry and, rather unwillingly, he paused as we stepped indoors.

"You don't have to worry about the stock," he said glibly, "this here'll tell you everything," and he offered me a tattered Grocers' Price List. "Whatever ain't marked on the shelf, you'll find on the proper page. Is there anything else you wanted to know before I buzz off?"

"Well——" began Jim, who felt, like I did, that there was absolutely everything to know—"Well——"; but before he could say more the car driver sounded his horn, Fenton flashed a set of pearly teeth at us and, muttering "Bye-bye, all the best," dashed out of the house. The front door crashed behind him in the wind and we were left on our own.

The house was as clean as a new pin, for which I gave full marks to the decorators, and almost unrecognisable in its new dress. I went from room to room, gloating over their changed appearance, but I had only just come downstairs again when our furniture van, unlike any other I have ever known or heard of, arrived before it was due and its doors were quickly flung wide open to the driving rain.

Everything got wet. The men tramped mud up the stairs and into every room and a very beautiful chest of drawers, left to me by my grandmother, couldn't be persuaded into the house at all and had to be dumped in an outside shed among garden tools, a wheelbarrow and Barbara's bicycle. But the men were friendly and obliging and quick and, when they had gone, although the house was in an appalling muddle, the fire I had lit in the kitchen was burning strongly, the kettle was singing, Bumble had spread himself on the hearth to dry, the cat, wide-eyed, stared at us from the settle by the fire and Jim smiled at me cheerfully.

"This'll be cosy presently," he said and, with the rain battering against the glass outside, we settled down very contentedly to our first meal.

After lunch we investigated the shop and found it very small and narrow with a big bay window and a scrubbed wood counter.

It looked to us, when we first went in, like a miniature Army & Navy Stores, Harrods and Selfridges combined, and we thought, "how amusing and delightful."

After we had poked about for a time, we were not quite so sure. The shelves were packed with stuff, but there was clearly no kind of method of arrangement and I wondered anxiously how we should ever find anything. Oranges and bananas jostled chocolate, cheese and cold ham. Soap flakes, starch, sausages, hammers and nails, ties, socks, bundles of firewood, cough mixture, toothpaste, packets of tea, coarse white china cups and saucers, tins of treacle, piled pots of jam, soap and brilliantly coloured sweets in glass jars were jumbled together anyhow. The arts apparently were not catered for, but certainly most material needs could be satisfied—even my need for a dustpan and brush and a frying pan, all of which I found hanging from the ceiling.

"I suppose we ought to get down to making some kind of catalogue," said Jim, rather half-heartedly, but I felt that we must concentrate first on the house itself. It was as well that we did, for by the time we had cleared up some of the mess made by the removal men, laid two carpets, sorted out the furniture, made up the beds, unpacked china and books, secured the chickens in a temporary enclosure (and, thank goodness, it stopped raining early in the afternoon), fed all the animals and ourselves, lost and found the cat three times and persuaded Bumble that he was not to enter the shop in any circumstances

—we were both worn out and could think only of hot baths and bed.

As he limped into the bathroom, Jim turned and yawned.

"I shouldn't be surprised," he said, with the easy optimism engendered by warmth, fatigue and a pleasantly full stomach, "if this shop business is far easier than we think. After all, if old Mother Winchcombe could do it, so can we."

"Yes," I said, and "Goodnight"—but in my mind's eye I saw a crowd of angry women muttering and even shouting to-morrow morning about "amateurs what don't know their business" while we fumbled ineffectively among the tins and bottles on the shelves.

2 October

The next morning was a Saturday and, punctually at nine o'clock, we unbolted the door, took down the wooden shutter and nervously awaited business.

We did not have to wait long.

Almost at once the old-fashioned door-bell clattered on its bent wire and in came three women, followed by a bald old man with a wooden leg.

I felt as panic-stricken as a young actor on a first night for, as they stood looking at me, I suddenly realised that we had no idea where to find anything nor of its price when found. I felt hot and flustered but, far from shouting angrily, as I had imagined, our customers patiently helped us to find what they wanted and then priced the things for us.

"No, dear," said the stout, elderly woman in a man's cap and curlers, "you're doing yourself. 'Tis only one and three for the flour," and, "Up there, missus, on the top shelf under they boxes, you'll find 'un," advised the old man.

Even with their help, it seemed to take us hours to carry out the simplest order and, before long, I felt like snatching things from the shelves and simply giving them away. And we had no time in which even to collect ourselves, for on that first morning I believe every inhabitant of Lower Barley who could walk had, from sheer curiosity, visited the shop by noon.

Everybody was kind and friendly but Jim said to me later on that he had never felt such a fool in his life. We'd had no idea at all of how little we knew. The shop, tiny as it was, apparently stocked hundreds of different kinds of things, hardly a single article had a price on it and, if the customer didn't know how much it cost, one of us had frantically to flick over the pages of our list while the rest of the company stood and waited and stared, and perhaps offered well-meant, but useless, advice.

The hours flew by and, except between one and two o'clock, the place was never empty. I concentrated on the general business of the shop and left the Post Office affairs to Jim—the Post Office, which in fact consists of a high desk on legs, such as one sees in the outer offices of old-fashioned solicitors. Inside the desk we found stamps, postal orders, various forms and an ink pad and a stamper with which I very soon saw Jim satisfyingly banging stamps on parcels.

He said, before we arrived, that, with only very slight experience of Civil Service affairs, he was sure we'd be better off without the Post Office at all—but I felt that the village must really need one. So in spite of his misgivings and of the tiresome instruction which we were to receive on Monday from some G.P.O. official, we decided to give it a trial.

As the afternoon wore on I began to gain confidence and I knew where to find the more ordinary things—but when we finally locked the door at six o'clock I was utterly exhausted. In fact I felt far too tired to cook—so for supper we simply ate out of tins.

"Eating up the profits," said Jim gloomily—for he, too, was worn out—but although I didn't say so, it seemed to me that one has to get food somewhere, so why not off the shelves?

It was on the next day, Sunday, that I decided to try to keep —not a day to day diary—but some kind of record of our life here—and this is a beginning.

I remember that we decided, after an early breakfast, really to get down to arranging the stock properly so that we should not suffer another day of muddle like our first; and, while we were sorting the stuff and throwing away the rubbish, we came across some very peculiar things indeed, including a small, striped, black velvet cushion with the letters ER 1909 picked out in coloured pin-heads, and a cupboard full of patent medicines of distinctly Edwardian vintage. The bottles were either leaking or solid and some smelt horribly. There was a tremendous lot to do but by midday, although we were both filthy, the job was nearly finished.

Jim had a hot bath before lunch, which I was determined should be good—for above all things I wanted to keep his spirits up—and I gave him an omelet (in spite of the move our hens had laid four eggs), some rather good cheese from the shop and perfect coffee (brought with us).

Jim sank into a peaceful sleep afterwards but I felt that I couldn't waste an exquisite autumn day entirely, so I called Bumble and together we set off for the Downs. When we were half-way up the nearest hill, I turned and looked about me. The lower slopes were patterned with pale stubble and new plough, and the beechwoods in the valley were spectacularly dressed in orange, yellow, green and red. Here and there I saw, with disapproval, wasted and blackened straw still smouldering, for I have very old-fashioned ideas about harvesting and don't believe that I shall ever, ever be reconciled to combines; but some fields were already ploughed and the fresh-turned earth deepened in colour against its neighbouring stubble.

Later in the afternoon Bumble embarrassingly put up a covey of partridges just as an elderly man emerged with a yellow labrador from a near-by spinney. There was no possibility of avoiding him, so, with Bumble well behaved and at heel, I put on a very casual face and hoped for the best. I received only a cold stare and no comment, so slunk past and turned for home, fairly sure that this must have been Mr. Davenant, the Lower Barley squire. I had already been told that, except for occasional shooting, he is a withdrawn character, interested in nothing later than the Bronze Age.

I tried half-heartedly that evening to drag Jim to church but I was, in fact, myself rather shy of going, so I was relieved when he wouldn't even think of it. Instead, I went out on to our front doorstep and looked, with satisfaction, at Lower Barley.

The village is quite unspoilt and nearly all of it rings the Green. There are a few thatched cottages with wattle and daub cream-washed walls and crooked beams, and the rest are of mellow rosy brick beneath golden lichened weather tile. We look straight out on to the Green; and beyond the elms which fringe its far side rises the squat grey tower of the little Norman church. Behind the church one can see a corner of the Vicarage and beyond it again are the tall beeches which flank the Manor drive.

But the heart and centre and core of the village is the pond— the pond which lies plumb in the middle of the Green, and is fed by a fast-moving stream which runs through the Manor park and under the road and reappears at the bottom of our orchard —the pond, half empty now and its edges poached and rutted; the pond, old as the village itself and perhaps older.

I stared at its smooth, polished surface and wondered how many unharried cattle have, through the years, dawdled there to drink and cool their legs as the teasing flies buzz and hover . . . how many great horses, their shining coats patched darkly with sweat, their kind faces nodding as they feel the cool mud round their fetlocks, have gratefully sucked up the water and stood there contentedly letting it dribble from their velvet lips . . . how many generations of children have turned somersaults over the faded white railings on the west side and how many little boys have fallen into the water and fished and sailed their boats.

The village is very compact and the total population is probably only about three hundred; but we were assured that this is enough to make the shop pay—and Jacob Fenton told us that the weekly takings should be at least a hundred and thirty pounds. Jim, who admitted that he thought the man quite unscrupulous, assured me that he went through the books very carefully before we moved in but I doubt if he was any sort of a match for Jacob.

We found that it didn't take us very long to sort out the villagers by name, and by the end of our first week Jim seemed to know everybody: but there were two women, a Mrs. Piggot and a Mrs. Babbage, whom I simply couldn't tell apart. They were not, in fact, exactly alike but I invariably called one by the other's name, which was unfortunate, for they detested each other—something to do with cheating over a goose at a raffle in 1931.

The bald, old man with the wooden leg is always referred to as H. Potter and is gardener at the Vicarage. He fought at Jutland as a stoker first-class in the first world war, and still has a distinctly nautical air, with his wooden leg, his high-necked blue jersey and short blue coat and, when he covers his bald head at all, his greasy yachting cap. I like him, for he is a friendly old man, and since he discovered that Jim is a retired Commander, he calls him "sir" even when he is paying down money for his tea, bacon and tobacco. His sister, who does nothing of the sort, told me that he and Jim should have a lot in common and be "company for each other like". They've each lost a leg and served in the Royal Navy, so I dare say she's right.

The elderly woman who came in on our first morning, and who wears a man's cap stuck through with two formidable hatpins, is a very determined character, Mrs. Root by name. Within two days of our arrival she confided to me that she hadn't spoken to her next-door neighbour for five years.

"She come pokin' into my place one day—with no excuse nor nothin'—just to see what we was having for dinner—and I told her off, see? And we ain't spoke since."

As we expected, we have been having a trying time with the Post Office. On the Monday after we moved in, a bumptious, pompous little man, with a striped blue suit, black hat, heavy horn-rims and a madly irritating manner, arrived—to teach us how to sell stamps, I suppose. Actually there was quite a lot that we should have been glad to be told, but Jim is not very good at being patronised or treated as a half-wit and I was so afraid of an explosion that I don't think either of us took in much of his instructions.

When, at the end of the day, the little man had teetered away in his shiny little black car, I comforted Jim with grilled cutlets (the travelling butcher calls twice a week, as Bumble and the cat are already well aware), garden cabbage cooked in butter, biscuits and cream cheese—the last a gift from H. Potter's sister who works in the farm dairy. I also opened one of our few bottles of sherry. Jim grumbled but was pleased, and the tiresome memory of the G.P.O.'s visit was properly effaced.

The squire's wife, Mrs. Davenant, came into the shop soon after we had settled in. I felt a little uncomfortable as I remembered my encounter with her husband but the matter was not mentioned. She is an enormously fat woman, about five foot five and weighs I should say quite fifteen stone; and, so far, I have seen her only in a thick, purple tweed suit and a rather manly felt hat, worn tilted well forward and with a fine diamond clip in the front. She was evidently surprised by us but soon became very friendly, and when she discovered that Jim was at Dartmouth with her eldest son our stock rose.

She told me at once that our foxy predecessor was very much disliked and that the village is full of Communists and not what it was—children pampered and women spend their time gawping at television.

I have noticed that people often talk like this to strangers, but let the stranger criticise their village (or their families) and the fur flies. Anyway, I rather liked her, for she has honest, wide-apart brown eyes and, although her false teeth are inclined to slip disconcertingly, she has a genuine smile.

Another member of the gentry came into the shop during Mrs. Davenant's first visit, and I was astonished to find that they entirely ignored each other, which seemed to me extraordinary in so tiny a place as Barley. "Not speaking" is evidently not confined to one class in this neighbourhood.

One of our most frequent visitors is a Mrs. Lacey. She is fortyish, plump, pretty and brown-haired, and seems to be typical of the best sort of countrywoman—still bakes her own bread and cakes, makes jam and bottles fruit and vegetables— and is in fact a war refugee from Coventry. She has a large family, three girls by her first husband and two boys by her second. She was first married to a man called Boot and now to Albert Lacey. Her children are therefore either Boots or Laceys —to the constant amusement of the rest of the village. They are a lovely family, all of them fair and rosy and good-looking, but when they are all in the shop together the noise is terrific and no one else can get inside it.

Then there is Bessy Hinton, who has agreed to "oblige" me daily with the cleaning of the house and the shop. She lives quite near and wears large, pale pink pearls and very tight, rather short slacks. Jim thinks she is frightful but I am sure he is wrong, for she is a good worker, *very* respectable, good tempered and already devoted to Bumble and the cat. Her old grandmother, Mrs. Rous, has children and grandchildren all over this and the next two villages; but Bessy's father and mother were killed in an air raid on Southampton where he was stationed just before the end of the war. Although Bessy is in her twenties and married and presumably keeps house for herself, her grandmother waddled into the shop only today and said that she always liked to pay Bessy's bill with her own at the end of the week. I wish somebody would do the same for us.

The Red Lion is kept by a man called, absurdly, O. Beery, but is really run by his wife, Kate. He, I am told, is a tiny, wizened old man and he is said not to have stepped out of doors for the past thirty years. I cannot believe this is true, but it is a fact that I have never seen him yet. Kate Beery is quite the opposite, and is in and out of the shop every morning and out in her garden at most other times. She speaks very fast and has a rather vacant expression, wears her skirts short and her red legs bare, and usually a little pale blue knitted cap is stuck insecurely on her grey head.

One evening last week she gave me a basket of Bramley Seedlings over the wall. "You're welcome," she said as I thanked her, "but I mustn't stop . . . I've got to let me fowls out."

"Why do you keep them shut up all day?" I asked.

"Why indeed?" She winked and her head began to nod excitedly. " 'Tis because last winter me neighbour used to boast she had six or seven eggs a day. Nothing in that you might say—but, seeing as she only had the one hen, it seemed a bit funny. But I don't like an argument, so I didn't *say* anything. I just keeps mine shut up till they've done laying. That's all."

I began to laugh, but saw at once that Kate was not meaning to be funny so hastily corrected my expression.

"There's more to it than that, too," she went on, "for 'tis just as awkward in the summer. You see Miss Grogan's only got the one hen, like I told you—Fanny its name is—and Fanny used to like to come over the gate calling on my birds. Well then, along comes Miss G. and opens the gate to fetch her little hen, clucking and dropping corn as she goes. Fanny hurries home after the feed, of course, and my fowls goes with her— and they find theirselves shut up quick with Fanny in the hope they'll lay. Of course I used to see through it all—anyone would—and I just pops over and lets 'em out again. But I never *say* anything."

"Doesn't Miss Grogan ever say anything either?"

"No, we don't speak—nor ever have since she kept emptying her slops into my ditch."

This last news left me speechless myself, but Kate evidently has a sixth sense which tells her when it is opening time and, jerking her head towards the house, she was away with long strides up the garden path before I could think of any suitable comment.

Barbara's last letter from school contained the following: "Please could you send me some chocolate because it was Pat's birthday and we pooled our sweets. How nice—it won't cost you anything now." I thought this would amuse Jim and, as the shop was empty for a moment, I turned to read it out loud. He had disappeared, however, and I found him in the kitchen trying to unclothe a large cheese. The thing arrived, weighing half a hundredweight, in a kind of keg and tightly swathed with thick muslin which was embedded in the cheese itself. Jim was sweating and swearing over it, and half an hour later the job was still not done. There *must* be some proper method, and he agreed that we should have to consult the grocer in the next village.

When I returned to the shop, the vicar was waiting to buy stamps. He is simply too unreal to be true, a complete edition of the conventional stage parson, frail, white-haired, blue-eyed, slightly deaf and very vague. He welcomed us very kindly, for this was the first time we had met, and asked a great many questions—but I don't think he listened to any of the answers.

As soon as he had gone, the "man from the G.P.O." marched in again, but Jim was still involved with his cheese so I refused to call him. "Very well, madam," he said huffily, and he began to pour out a stream of rules and instructions and to take out buff form after buff form from his brief-case. I am afraid that I listened with even less than the vicar's attention, for we were constantly interrupted by customers whose entrance he seemed to take as a deliberate insult. At last it dawned on him that there was no likelihood at all of a long peaceful session and, pathetically deflated, he stopped talking and, banging his papers on the counter again and again to ensure their perfect alignment, he put them away carefully and said a cold "Good day".

I felt very mean at not offering him a cup of tea but, if I had, we should never, never have got rid of him.

I had no idea before we came here that we should be so constantly busy. I think both Jim and I pictured ourselves working in the garden or even sitting in the orchard doing nothing half the day, to be recalled to the shop occasionally by the tinkle of the bell—but we were quite wrong. There seems always to be someone in the shop, often chiefly to gossip but usually to buy as well. At first we thought that it was just natural curiosity about newcomers, but in fact we are so handy for everyone that the villagers just pop in and out all day from habit.

The Red Lion is on one side of us and on the other is a tiny thatched cottage in which Mrs. Crabtree, who is over eighty and was born in the village, lives with her son, Tom. She is very bent and her thick black serge dress, bound with black velvet, is stretched tightly across her rounded shoulders and touches the ground as she walks. Her faded blue eyes peer shrewdly from behind their steel-rimmed spectacles, and her white hair is scraped back tightly.

This morning she came in to buy "a nice thick rasher" and to tell me of an accident which she had on Sunday. She'd made a pudding, "very sweet and three eggs in it," a giant of a pudding, and, as it cooked, she dozed by the fire. Waking suddenly, she started to lift it from the stove but it was too heavy and the whole boiling pudding tipped right over her.

"Right over my dress and in my slippers—oh, dear, what a mess! But my blisters are nearly gone now," she said, showing me the scalds on her old hand. "Such a shock it gave me, and my boy Tom was upstairs and couldn't hear, so I gets over to Lucy (her married grand-daughter) somehow—and then I went off."

But she seems none the worse, and was even laughing this morning about her lovely pudding gone and all the mess.

Not only does this brave old woman write beautifully (her father was a surveyor and she used to make his notes for him), but she has the curious accomplishment of being able to write backwards. I don't remember how I discovered this, but several times I have persuaded her to do it in front of an admiring crowd and then held the writing up to the looking-glass.

Mrs. Crabtree is Barley's oldest inhabitant and she told me that our cottage was once the blacksmith's shop. "And the bellows blew," she said, "and the great horses stood stamping in that liddle room where you has that bit of a fire now."

At the end of our first week two travellers arrived and spent over an hour with Jim. He seemed to be ordering a great deal of stuff—but I thought it best not to interfere.

The result of this was that on Saturday morning when the women, with the men's weekly wages in their purses, crowded in to stock up their shelves and we were almost worked off our feet, the wholesaler's van arrived with an enormous load of tins and cases. There was, of course, nowhere to put the stuff, so it had to be dumped in the hall of our cottage—to which Bumble greatly objected. He is the gentlest fool of all dogs, but his bark is in proportion to his size and the van-men were extremely nervous. In fact, I doubt if they had ever worked faster.

We were so busy that we hardly had time for lunch and could not even begin to deal with the pile of stuff cluttering up the hall until after we shut shop at six o'clock. Then at the end of a long day we were faced with the unpacking and stowing away of it all, and poor Jim's leg was hurting him so that he looked white with tiredness. He finds this unaccustomed standing rather trying; and so do I—but with less reason. Like Kate next door, he doesn't *say* anything—but I can tell: and I felt very sorry for him that night. He can be short-tempered but he never moans about his own troubles.

When at last we had finished, we saw the little autumn fair arrive on the Green. It was the smallest I have ever seen, a tiny, hand-turned roundabout with miniature pale blue horses, a coconut shy, two or three small stalls and four scarlet-and-gold swing boats. As dusk fell, the lighted scene was exquisitely

gay and fairylike, it might have been a stage set really, and Jim
and I stared at it, fascinated and charmed.

All this month, so far, the open weather has held and, on
Sunday, when Jim was finishing off the permanent chicken run
in the orchard, I managed to tidy up the whole of the front
garden, although I was not sure that I ought to have done this
when everyone else was going to church. Mrs. Root stopped
on her way by, to pass the time of day, and I barely recognised
her—no man's cap, no curlers, but, instead, a very handsome
pale green hat, and a full-skirted, plum-coloured coat with little
embroidered darts at the waist.

The Boots and Laceys, all five, are in the choir. They
marched by on the far side of the Green looking unnaturally
smart and sedate, but I noticed the youngest but one, David,
walking wetly at the edge of the pond and the littlest, Boosey,
following in his exact footsteps.

Presently H. Potter, who is no church-goer, arrived with a
gift of wallflower plants. These were almost certainly pinched
from the Vicarage garden, but I could not be expected to know
that and they will look lovely in front of our house next spring.
H. Potter seemed inclined to linger, so I handed him over to
Jim and was pleased, later, to see him getting to work with a
spade.

Jim spent the evening doing the Post Office accounts, which
did not come right, and I retired to the fireside to sew. But the
day's work was not finished, for at ten o'clock the front door
knocker crashed, Bumble barked furiously and I opened the
door to young Tom Craddock, a tractor driver, from a near-by
cottage.

"The wife's taken one of her fits," he said calmly. "Would
you please ring up Nurse?"

"Yes, of course," I said and asked him in but, as I telephoned,
I wondered what sort of fit he meant and supposed it must be
physical or Nurse wouldn't do.

"Could you come over, Missus," he asked then, "just till

Nurse comes? The kids is awake and yelling and I only got the one pair of hands."

I followed him, inwardly reluctant—for if the woman were crazy I should be terrified—but he revealed on the way that his wife is epileptic. Luckily the worst was over when I arrived, and by the time Nurse Ames drove up I had managed to calm the two small boys, who had been bawling their heads off. Nurse Ames is tiny and capable, with a comical Irish face, and she winked at me in a friendly way as she marched upstairs.

I wonder what happens if Mrs. Craddock has "one of her fits" when Tom is away at work.

Mrs. Davenant rushed in and out of the shop early yesterday to ask me to go to the Women's Institute meeting in the afternoon. I was very reluctant but, when she had gone, Jim said that I must.

I arrived five minutes early and found the village hall cold and dank, with the usual varnished wood walls, spotted lithograph of the Queen and small stage whose curtains don't quite meet. I also found about twenty members standing about, most of whom I already knew—except the President, the vicar's wife, to whom unfortunately I at once took a mild dislike. She is a tall, big-bosomed, large-featured woman with a pale thin mouth and her grey hair is dragged back into an untidy bun. That day she wore a brown tweed skirt, a blue silk blouse, its "V" filled in with net, and a grey cardigan a good deal longer in front than behind. She was not friendly and clearly despises anyone in trade.

I said to Jim afterwards that as she is Lord Somebody's daughter she ought to know how to behave; but Jim retorted that Lord Somebody was in trade himself (on a rather larger scale than we are) so one shouldn't expect too much.

"Good afternoon," she said to me coldly, when I arrived. "You must be the person who has taken the shop." I agreed and was about to say something civil but she turned away and left me standing.

"Never you mind her, ducks," said kind, plump Mrs. Lacey, a young Boot on each side of her, "stuck-up cat. She's his second wife, you know. Married the poor old gentleman when he wasn't looking, as you might say, and she's worn the trousers ever since."

"What's the lecture?" asked old Mrs. Crabtree, nodding at a wispy, anaemic-looking woman on the platform.

Her grand-daughter, Lucy Rous, leant forward and whispered, "How to make gloves."

"How to make love?" The old lady giggled. "I bet *she* don't know much about it."

Well-stewed tea and buns followed the "talk", and I took the opportunity to slip away and relieve Jim in the shop.

It was nearly closing time when I got back and I found the place full of little boys leaning over the counter and peering fascinated at something on the other side. For a moment I was very puzzled, and then I realised that Jim had found an easy way to their hearts by showing them the mechanism of his tin leg.

His success with the young had happy repercussions this afternoon.

It is still ten days short of November 5th but, for the past week, bangers and fireworks have been let off outside the shop every evening and Bumble, who is very gun shy, has suffered tortures. We felt that it was useless to protest and that we should just have to bear it but, after school today, a crowd of boys arrived, dragging behind them an ancient tub cart, borrowed from the blacksmith's dump. They were collecting in it fuel of all sorts for a giant bonfire, and Jim cleverly traded a great heap of boxes, cardboard, shavings, paper and half a dozen firelighters for a general promise that there should be no bangers let off, from now on, within a hundred yards of our house.

H. Potter, who was buying his daily two ounces of tobacco at the time, said morosely, "They boys' promises don't mean nothing." But he was wrong.

Directly after they had gone, the woman who wouldn't speak to Mrs. Davenant came in to buy stamps. She has red hair and fine eyes—and is rather good-looking in a massive sort of way, fiftyish, overdressed for the country, and very much made up. She was very off-hand until Jim appeared, and then her manner altered entirely and she asked him a lot of personal and rather impertinent questions, to which she got exceedingly short replies.

When she had left, we were told that she is a Mrs. Frobisher-Spink who lives at Lower Barley Lodge, down the lane beyond the Red Lion and opposite Barley Farm.

I asked if she was a widow, and old Mrs. Rous, who was paying Bessy's weekly bill at the time, laughed so much that all her bulges wobbled from the chin downwards.

"Not as I knows of," she said at last, "though he's been gone I don't know how long. Cleared off he did—and," she added darkly, "not alone neither. I used to work there Tuesdays and Fridays and sometimes it was a rare carry-on, I can tell you . . . not but what he hadn't got something to put up with, poor man, for she likes her drop and always did . . ." and Mrs. Rous raised her elbow significantly.

I was sorely tempted to pursue this fascinating subject, but Jim's shout for help with yet another huge cheese saved me from myself.

It is chilly now in the mornings, and when I feed the hens before breakfast the grass in the orchard is wet with frost. The elms and beeches shed their leaves silently in the still air and the children scuffle to school through drifts of palest gold and brilliant orange.

"Badger" Rous, the road-man, is kept busy with his broom and shovel and the new-fangled three-wheeled cart with rubber tyres, and he grumbles at every passer-by because the leaves fall faster than he can sweep.

Autumn is here, the dahlias in the garden are black, a cool mist creeps along the fields as dusk falls and the pheasants "rock-cock" in the park as they settle for the night.

Mrs. Davenant asked us to tea on Sunday—but I felt loath to waste a fine, free day and was searching for a reasonable excuse when I was saved by the unexpected arrival of friends from Oxford. We walked all afternoon over the Downs in misty sunshine and, as the gold turned to pinkish grey and the chill evening air spread across the weald, we returned, pleasantly tired, to a cosy tea at home; and ate thickly buttered crumpets from the shop by a pungent applewood fire.

Monday is evidently the quietest day of the week in the shop because, I suppose, people are either at home doing their washing or simply finishing up the stuff they bought on Saturday. Quite often we get at least an hour without customers but yesterday, just after I had unbolted the door at two o'clock and was hoping for at least a short time in which to write to Barbara, the door opened and, borne on a mass of scarves, veils, bangles and home-woven tweed, entered an exceedingly arty-crafty woman—a complete stranger. She was in her fifties, I suppose, and very intense. A long, inquisitive nose, jutting from a pale face, only just divided a pair of snapping black eyes, and her greying, shoulder-length hair was tied back with "art" ribbon. Attached to her wrist by a long lead, were three minute dogs of a breed unknown to me.

She stood staring at me for a few moments and then said plaintively, "I've been waiting for *hours*,"—which was quite untrue, for there was no one outside five minutes ago—"you must be Mrs. Braid. I've heard such a lot about you already, though I've only just come home. I've been away over a month you know." She paused, as if she expected that I must indeed know, but as I had not even heard of her existence until now, I could only say apologetically that I was afraid I didn't know her name.

"We're the 'Weavers' " (she spoke in inverted commas and capitals) "my sister and I. We have a little nest on the Badgerford road—people come from miles to see it. We weave and keep goats and breed my dear little Fairies."

She looked vaguely round the shop. "*So* wonderful of you to do this, but *so* tiring I should think—all this standing, I mean, when one isn't used to it—or have you done something of the kind before?"

"No."

One of the dear little Fairies bit its neighbour and the air was filled with yelps and squeals; but presently they calmed down and their owner asked unexpectedly, "Are you musical? I do hope so."

I admitted that we are not musical and immediately she snapped on to the "we".

"Oh, yes—your brother, of course. I've heard all about him, too. An Air Force type, as they used to say, isn't he?"

She showed her long teeth, slid on to our high stool and rested her unsupported bosom on the counter.

"He was in the Navy," I answered shortly.

"Oh, how funny——" she looked at me doubtfully as if perhaps I didn't really know everything about my own brother— "I heard he was a flying officer."

"No, he was a sailor."

"*Really?* A war-time sailor, was he? Such a wonderful experience and so broadening for them, I always think—after civilian life I mean."

"My brother was in the Royal Navy for twenty years," I announced finally and realised, as I did so, that this woman was already bringing out the worst in me. Why should I want her to know that I had never kept a shop before; why should I care what she imagines about Jim?

She looked round her and gathered together several tins. "I want these," she said, "and a pound of sugar and rice and sago and·a bottle of tomato sauce and two tins of EATIT-UP for Fairy Frivolous . . . she just won't eat anything else, will you, darling?"

She paused and made encouraging maternal noises to her charges while I collected a considerable pile of groceries on to the counter.

Then, "Oh dear! I'll never, never be able to carry all that," she whimpered in a baby voice, "I wonder—I wonder if your brother could possibly bring them up?"

"I'm afraid we don't do any delivering. My brother doesn't walk a great deal——"

"Oh, but he should. A man needs plenty of exercise I always think."

"My brother has an artificial leg."

"From the war? Poor, poor man . . . I *must* get him to tell me just how it happened. I'm sure he's had hundreds of thrilling adventures."

"I expect I could get one of the village children to bring these up for you," I said hastily, and, flustered, began to add up her bill.

When, at last, she had gone, Jim burst in from the back of the shop, where he had been lurking.

"What the hell did you want to discuss me for with that old hag?" he shouted angrily.

"My dear, I couldn't help it——"

"Bosh! Telling her I was in the Navy, telling her I'd got a tin leg. What's it got to do with her?"

"I'm sorry, Jim—I *couldn't* help it. I couldn't let her call you an Air Force type."

"Weavers!" he snarled, his face as red and scowling as it used to be when he got into a temper at the age of ten. "Be damned to them! And to you, too," he added most unfairly and banged out into the garden.

I sympathised with Jim but felt unjustly treated, and was not at all soothed at having to bribe one of the small Laceys with a shilling to deliver the groceries.

Mrs. Lacey told me afterwards that the Weavers' name is Brown, Miss Phyllis and Miss Emily.

"They must be a nice pair," I said sourly; but Mrs. Lacey shook her head, saying that the younger one, Miss Emily, is quite different. "Not that you'll ever see her," she added, "unless you go there. She's hardly ever allowed outside the door."

It's odd how, for weeks on end, perhaps, everything in one's daily life seems to go pretty smoothly and then, all of a sudden every single thing goes wrong. It began yesterday afternoon when that Brown woman upset Jim—and me, too, though he apologised later in a rather off-hand way. Soon after she had left, the bacon man arrived with our weekly order but brought eight pounds of sausages short. They were sold very quickly and Mrs. Root, who came in late, had to go without.

I tried to explain what had happened but, "Some folks must have got their favourites already," she muttered angrily, her face flushed and her cap wobbling insecurely as her head shook, and she stalked out of the shop, slamming the door so that the bell tankled furiously and an iron saucepan hanging behind it fell heavily into a box of dessert apples. I hate people being annoyed with me, and find it specially disagreeable when it really isn't my fault.

Later, I fell over Bumble, who had sneaked into the shop, attracted by the smell of the Fairies, and dropped a case of eggs which I was carrying in front of me. Twenty-one were broken or cracked.

And then, when I was hot, flushed and untidy and in the middle of clearing up the disgusting mess, Mrs. Frobisher-Spink had to come in to say that something had gone wrong with her wireless and would Jim perhaps come down and have a look at it. Of course, he wouldn't and I had the tiresome job of saying so . . . and, from Mrs. Frobisher-Spink's manner, she seemed to think that it was I who wouldn't allow Jim to come.

The result of all this was that I felt fed up with the whole thing and, when I had put supper ready for Jim and fed the animals, I retired miserably to bed with a few tears.

This morning I woke to discover the rain pelting in at the open window over my bed but, in spite of that, I felt un-accountably cheerful.

Downstairs, I found Jim up early, the kettle singing, bacon sizzling in the frying pan, the coke brought in, the cat lapping milk (this morning's of course—last night's jug still in the safe!) and a letter from my Mama enclosing a cheque for £25.

Jim, with a half grin, confessed at breakfast to one of his appalling fits of depression during the last twenty-four hours, which had happened to include the time of Miss Brown's visit, and dear Bumble sidled up to me, smiling and with an eggy beard.

I prepared for a pleasant, easy day ... and so it has turned out.

3 November

Lower Barley takes Guy Fawkes Day seriously, and when, soon after daybreak, a wet mist drifted down off the hills everyone gloomily forecast a complete washout for the bonfire; but the weather changed completely as the sun went down and, with a great wind roaring through the gathering dusk, the children rushed out of their houses, shrieking with joy and excitement; and presently a crowd of boys in the light of our shop window shoved a wobbling guy and a couple of cans of petrol into a barrow—and, followed by most of the village, pushed it, singing as they went, across the Green.

About a quarter of a mile along the Badgerford road is a small piece of common land and on this, throughout the past week, a huge pile had risen—the result of the boys' hard work and cadging. Now it was enormous, at least fifteen feet high, and in the blowing darkness, lit only by fireworks and a few torches flaring and dipping in the wind, it seemed twice as big.

The common was crowded with people, and just before seven o'clock we joined them to see the fire lighted. A minute later two of the men, their torches held high above their heads, shouted something about "The Guy-the Guy" and, stooping, pushed their blazing staves into the petrol-soaked tinder.

The crowd gave a great yell, and with one huge hiss of terrifying flame the whole pile roared and crackled gloriously—lighting up the people, the hedgerows and even the distant village.

Jim and I stayed for a time to watch the sparks drifting high in the wind and then went home to comfort Bumble and the cat—but rockets and wheels rushed across the sky, and shouts and laughter and the hiss of fireworks were borne to us on the wind long after the Red Lion emptied and until well after midnight.

On our last half day, when I was walking through the village, I made friends with the blacksmith, Amos Rous, a short, square man with the correct huge shoulders and arms of his calling, thick black hair and vague blue eyes. I wanted our fire-screen mended, and found him idle and talkative and a most gentle and melancholy man. There's very little horse work now, he told me sadly, except racehorses, of course, and that's a specialist's job. It's mostly farm tools and implements nowadays and, he added almost shyly, sometimes a bit of gatemaking. I persuaded him to show me a sample of his wrought-iron work, which lay tucked away in a shed at the end of his garden, and discovered a piece of beautiful craftsmanship with an exquisite design—all his own. He said that not many people can afford iron gates nowadays—but I decided that if ever we come into money he shall make me one.

The wild wind of Bonfire Day dropped the next morning and brought behind it a teeming rain which has gone on now for a week or more, and the cows which slowly tap along the road to and from the farm have made the surface a slur of slime. Every woman who comes into the shop grumbles, though I should have thought they would be used to it, but they hate to have mud brought into the house.

The vicar's wife is one of those who complain most about the mud, and she went on and on about it when, the other day, her telephone was out of order and she came in, still rather patronising, to send a telegram. At last she wrote down her message and handed it to me and I consider it a great tribute to my self-control that I never even glanced up at her figure as I read these startling words: "Bust collapsed. Suspect too dry. Send instructions immediately."

With expressionless face, I took her money, agreed that the day was unpleasantly cold and the cows a nuisance, and said a calm "Goodbye" as, without a smile or the smallest attempt at explanation, she sailed out.

Most improperly (and Jim would have been very angry with me if he'd known) I simply could not resist reporting all this to Mrs. Lacey who came in a moment later. Luckily for my sanity, she was able to explain and, in a gust of laughter, did so. The vicar's wife is apparently taking a correspondence course in sculpture ". . . And the mess she makes in what used to be the poor vicar's study is something awful. Dabs of clay and such on the floor, so it treads all over the house for me to clean up . . . and sopping cloths draped over the most dreadful things you ever set eyes on. 'Bust dropped' indeed—it's a pity she don't drop the whole thing. She hasn't got a spot of talent nor nothing like it—and that's the truth."

Albert Lacey followed his wife into the shop at this point, for he had cut his hand and is off work. I had never seen him before and was a good deal surprised. He is quite old, at least sixty and immensely tall, with drooping grey moustaches and weak blue eyes which water all the time, so that he keeps on wiping the tears from his cheeks with a red-spotted handkerchief. He seemed to me to be a very unexpected kind of husband for his quick, little, plump sparrow of a wife and, later, I asked old Mrs. Crabtree what he does and where he works.

"Poor fella, he goes off to one o' they nursing homes every day," she said seriously.

"Nursing homes? What on earth do you mean?"

"Why, one o' they Government places where they keeps stores or summat. Nothing to do all day but put their feet up and drink tea—till they gets fetched home by bus. There's four of 'em goes from here and a proper rest cure it is."

I had really believed that she meant "nursing homes", and the old woman was delighted at her success in pulling my leg. She did have the grace to add though that "Albert ain't as bad as some. His eyes is queer through the war and he can't do no proper work, see?"

The day hounds met on the Green, Mrs. Davenant, looking stouter and shorter than ever with a heavy tweed overcoat on top of her purple suit, insisted on our shutting the shop and coming out. Jim agreed very willingly—any excuse to get out of doors being welcome—but there were dark looks and mutterings from several young women with prams who were waiting by the shop door when we returned.

When they had rather disagreeably taken themselves off, H. Potter's sister said kindly that you might have an empty shop half the day long and then sure enough if you shut it for a minute there's a crowd of young women grumbling at nothing. "Some people just likes an excuse to find fault," she said, and went on to ask why we don't get our milk from the farm instead of pale, bottled stuff from the Badgerford dairy. "We got a proper fine Guernsey herd, you know, the ones you sees go by every day, besides the Ayrshires what grazes the park but I reckon I can work it so as you has the best milk and a drop o' Guernsey cream as well."

I realised that the farmer probably keeps his Channel Island milk specially to sell to the Milk Marketing Board, but did not like to reject Kate's kindness. After all, I said to myself, it is for the farmer to mind his own business without interference from me—though presently, on reflection, it occurred to me that perhaps this kind of life is not exactly improving my character.

Mrs. Frobisher-Spink and Miss Phyllis Brown keep on finding excuses to visit the shop, and I am afraid they both have an eye on Jim. I had forgotten, when we came here, that there are always a lot of spinsters and unattached women in villages, and he is only forty-five and, I suppose, not at all bad looking— thin, dark and blue-eyed, with high cheekbones and a longish upper lip. Certainly he is very popular with the cottage women, and, from the beginning, our Bessy kept his room much better than she did mine and polished his shoes and brushed his coats far more eagerly than she polished the floor and brushed the stairs.

Miss P. Brown is really a terrible type, and I can't blame him for loathing and avoiding her; but sometimes he is blatantly rude to her and, poor thing, it is like smacking a jelly with a wooden spoon. You can see her spirit wobble and shake and struggle to resettle itself.

Mrs. Frobisher-Spink, of course, is a very different cup of tea, and I wouldn't mind if he *were* rude to her; but unfortunately she amuses him. It is not, I am sure, Jim in particular she is after. She is a rich woman, used to getting her own way, and she simply wants a man. Presumably, at the moment, she hasn't got one. Anyhow, I feel that it is all rather annoying and could easily lead to trouble.

The weeks fly by and, as Kate next door says unromantically, " 'Tis no sooner Sunday than it's dustbin day." Incidentally, the dustbins are collected only once a week and if the bin isn't put out into the street before 9 a.m. the cart and its very arbitrary attendants just rush by, and one is left with another week's rubbish and nowhere to put it.

As time goes on we find ourselves more and more at home in the shop and Saturday mornings hold no terror for us now, for we know everyone, we know our stock and, nearly always, its price. Both of us still find the work very exhausting, but we are beginning to enjoy it and to feel that a lot of the village people are our friends. Mrs. Root continues rather haughty though, for the sausage incident still rankles, but I hope that she will soften before long, for she is a great one for news. On this score, I have begun to realise that extreme discretion is essential to our job, for we get in here the most exaggerated and un-truthful reports of what goes on, and if we cared for gossip we could set the whole village by the ears at any time.

There are still a few local people whom I have not yet met—Colonel and Mrs. Halahan at the Old Mill House, who are away, Mr. John Carrick, who owns Lower Barley Farm (about 1,500 acres) and is said to be a morose widower whose wife died tragically of cancer a few years ago, and a few of the cottagers who, for one reason or another, do not patronise the shop. Oh yes, and old General Sir Roger Blade, V.C., D.S.O., etc., who lives with a deaf housekeeper in Lower Barley's only bungalow—unhappily named "Pixies' Playground". I said to Jim that the General could surely have changed its name but Jim thought that, perhaps, at eighty, it is hardly worth while.

By far the most important event of the month was the dramatic incident last Thursday of Lucy Rous's Letter. Break-fast that morning was forgotten, the shop opened late and the newspapers sorted in muddled haste.

First, it must be explained that there are four postmen who take it in turns to serve the village. They all seem much the same to me except that one of them is a real stickler for rules. To tamper with Her Majesty's mail is, to him, sacrilege, and only last week, when H. Potter had left his postal order out, he wouldn't let him have his Pools envelope back, and another time, when old Mrs. Rous had forgotten to put the address on a letter, he wouldn't let her touch it. Once a letter is posted, it's posted—and quite right, too.

But on *Thursday*—at about eight o'clock in the morning—came a knock at the door and there stood Lucy Rous, red-eyed and breathing heavily. She is a rosy-cheeked, brown-eyed girl in her twenties and is married to one of the Rous men, a mer-chant seaman, and in her hand she clutched a letter.

"Oh, Mrs. Braid, m'm . . ." she began, but the words choked her and the tears brimmed over and ran down her cheeks.

"Come in, Lucy," I said, and took her into the sitting-room. And there she sat on the edge of an upright chair, twisting her handkerchief in her scrubbed hands and just weeping.

"What's the matter, my dear? Come on, tell me or I can't help you."

She gave a great gulp and then it all came out. It seemed that her husband had promised, when they married three years ago, to leave the Service and go back on the farm; but he hadn't kept his word. Now, he had been away nearly a year and in the last three months she hadn't even had a letter.

"I want kiddies of me own and a proper home," she wailed. "I'd never have married him if I'd thought he was going to leave me like this."

For a moment she looked like her grandmother, Mrs. Crabtree, and I could see she had the old lady's temper.

And now there was a fresh complication; a smart young builder from Upper Barley was after her and she'd promised to go away with him and make a fresh start somewhere in Sussex.

"And I wrote to Joe last night," she sobbed, "and told him I was fed up wi' it all and I was going with Bertie and I was sorry and I loved him but I couldn't stick it any more. If he'd only even written it wouldn't have been so bad, but he might be dead for all I knew and I was going wi' Bertie and I'd made up me mind. I wrote it all in the letter and Bertie helped me and, before he went home last night, we posted it."

She began to weep again. "And this—this came this morning," she moaned, and she held out to me the letter which had lain crumpled in her hand.

"Dear Lucy, my Love," I read, "I been sick of one of they fevers they has out here and missed my ship and had a rough time. Still pretty middlin but got a ship now and sending this air mail and coming home as fast as she'll make it. When I gets back I'm going to chuck it for good and back on the old farm like I said and we'll set up and have a lot of kids like you want and so do I—your loving Joe."

"You want him back, Lucy? You do love him?"

" 'Course I do. I told you."

"How about Bert, then?"

A sort of half-smile creased her swollen face. "Oh, he ain't nothin'—only I was so fed up and ... and ... lonely like ..."

"All right," I interrupted, "we'll have to stop that letter somehow."

"Oh, Mrs. Braid, can you? If Joe gets it, I'll die! But it's that fat, snarky chap on duty this week and he'll never let me have it back, never. You know what he's like."

"Yes, I know," I said, "but you go home and leave it to my brother and me. That letter shan't go, if we have to burn down the shop to prevent it."

Lucy embarrassingly fell on her knees and grabbed my hand, and I had a job to get her out of the house; but at last she was gone, with my promise to help her, and I returned to the kitchen to tell and to consult Jim.

Jim is no supporter of petty rules and regulations, and this was a job after his own heart. "We'll manage it," he said, grinning, and I could see that he could hardly wait for the ten o'clock collection.

Punctually at 9.55 a.m. the little red van drew up outside and the fat postman squeezed himself through its door. Importantly he jangled his keys and importantly, glancing at his watch, he opened the post-box which is set in the wall of the shop. Then he came inside and began to stack the letters into a neat pile on the counter while I fetched for him any parcels which we had taken in for post.

It was while this was going on that there was a sudden crash from the back of the shop. Jim, who had been standing on a step-ladder, had stepped backwards and, with one skilful sweep of his arm brought down with him about twenty square empty biscuit tins (put there for the purpose) and, I think by mistake, an entire shelf of saucepans and kettles. The noise was terrific and Jim, as he yelled for help, lay on the floor almost hidden by the debris.

The fat postman ran to his rescue and, while his back was

turned, I raced through the pile of letters. Like a fool, I had never asked Lucy the shape and size of her envelope and I thought I should never find it. Jim and the postman were crashing and banging about but I knew it couldn't last much longer—and then I found it, pale blue and written childishly in green ink.

In true melodramatic style I stuffed the letter down inside my blouse and, as the fat postman lugged Jim to his feet and returned to his duty, I remembered to show some concern for my poor brother.

"Sure you're all right, sir?" asked the fat postman kindly—but he was looking at his watch and I knew he was itching to be gone.

"I'll see to everything," I said, "and thank you—thank you very much."

"Thanks," said Jim, and the fat postman straightened his cap, snatched up the mail and darted through the door. A minute later his little red van was out of sight.

I turned to Jim, standing among the wreckage.

"I got it," I said proudly. "Is your leg all right?"

He nodded. "Jumped back on the other one," he said with the slow, pleased secretive smile of intense amusement which I remember so well when he was young. His thin, drawn face was transformed by it and, for a moment, I felt as happy as I knew Lucy would be when presently I should cross the road to her cottage.

Old Mrs. Crabtree has rheumatism in her knees and she came slowly and painfully into the shop the next morning.

Lucy swore on Thursday to keep our secret but I think her grannie knows. As I gave her her morning paper, she laid her worn, rutted hand gently over mine and I looked up to see her eyes wet with the easy tears of old age—but, like Kate next door, I didn't *say* anything.

The vicar's wife has decided that we are not much beneath her socially after all, and she has become gracious and almost friendly; but I still don't like her, for I think she is a snob and a gossip.

She knows, as unfortunately people always seem to know when I don't like them, although I always try to be particularly polite, and also I cannot look at her ample figure without remembering the fascinating telegram which she entrusted to me a little time back. This recollection brings me always, in her presence, to the very edge of helpless laughter and so, rather naturally, she thinks me a very silly woman.

Last time she came in she said there was to be a jumble sale next month in aid of church repairs, and would I let her have any old clothes. I replied flippantly that I always wear my old clothes myself, but she was not amused and I quickly promised to look out something. After she had gone, I thought that perhaps this would be a good opportunity to get rid of the most disreputable of Jim's coats and the oil-stained flannel trousers which he says he keeps for gardening but usually walks about the village in.

After a wet beginning, November has brought mild and open weather—a few roses still nod in the front garden and some small bronze chrysanthemums can still be picked from the border. Jim and H. Potter have, between them, finished the digging somehow (though neither of them can push the spade with his foot), and nearly all the autumn clearing up is done, so that the place begins to look well cared for.

I was standing in the front garden on our last "half day" and putting on Bumble's collar for a walk, when I realised that strangers were looking over the fence and smiling at me. They were Colonel and Mrs. Halahan and I liked them both on sight. They asked us for drinks on Sunday evening and I shall like to go, for they seemed very much our sort.

Bumble and I spent the afternoon on the Downs and came back, for the first time, along the Badgerford road. About a mile short of our village, I passed The Weavers, an olde worlde cottage with a spinning wheel painted on the plaster between the beams. I quickened my pace when I realised how near I was to the Browns but it was no good, for I had evidently been observed, and a moment later Miss Phyllis Brown was at the gate calling to me to come in.

I turned back reluctantly and told Bumble to stay outside and, as I was shown the cottage and the woven tweeds, a crowd of minute dogs yapped persistently at my heels.

I was rather surprised to find that some of the tweeds were very nice indeed, with lovely colouring; and the house, too, was a curious mixture, partly arty-crafty, string stools, raffia mats and hideous pottery and partly sound old furniture and some good water colours.

Presumably the sisters' tastes differ greatly; and I looked round with some interest for the younger one—but there was no sign of her until I was just leaving. Then we met, face to face, in the hall and Miss Phyllis reluctantly introduced "my sister, Emily".

Mrs. Lacey was quite right, and Miss Emily is certainly very different—small and plumpish, with soft brown hair, lively blue eyes and a rather sweet expression. She was very quiet and, in fact, said nothing at all except "How do you do" and "Goodbye".

On Sunday, friends from Marlborough fetched and took us over to see Barbara. She looked well and ate the unbelievably enormous luncheon and tea which children usually tuck away when they escape for a few hours from school. Apart from the pleasure of seeing my young daughter, I enjoyed the change.

Later that evening we went up to the Halahans, who live at the Old Mill House not far from Mrs. Frobisher-Spink. They are sixtyish and were very friendly. Their house is too big for them but they love it and so did I, for it is built of mellow red brick, with fine Elizabethan chimneys, and part of it spans our stream which meanders through their garden. Inside, there was an air of comfortable shabbiness, some good pictures and a great many books. She is a small woman with clear grey eyes and the same kind of sense of humour as we have. Her father was a history don at Balliol and she seemed very intelligent—but not frighteningly so—and also often bubbling with laughter, a state of affairs which suits me very well.

He is short, red-faced and blue-eyed, barks rather than talks (but very gently), and clearly admires and adores his wife. He seemed to take very kindly to Jim, and I was particularly pleased at this, for Jim badly needs some congenial company. Their elder son was killed last year, testing some kind of aircraft, and the younger one, Philip, is at home "trying to write". A fair, effeminate young man of perhaps twenty-two, he appeared just as we were going and I was shocked and saddened to see the kind of boy he clearly is.

We have at last had a friendly visit from old Mrs. Root. I had hoped she would come, for she and her husband are very fond of faggots—a kind of meat ball sent to us every week by a wholesale butcher—and yesterday, having heard that she was laid up with a cold, Jim took her usual order down to her cottage. This gesture was plainly a success because, still very snuffly and wearing three cardigans and a high-necked jersey, fastened at the throat by an enormous Woolworth diamond brooch, she strode smiling into the shop this morning and demanded some of the patent cough lozenges beloved by all the village. As she turned to go, she beamed at me and winked at Jim, so the unfortunate sausage incident is evidently over and forgotten.

Her departure coincided with the arrival of Miss Phyllis Brown who makes some excuse to come in every single morning. She seldom manages to get Jim alone and when she does I am afraid he is rude to her; but I suppose this must have a stimulating effect for she appeared again this afternoon to ask us to a cocktail party. I accepted, because it was impossible to do anything else, but Jim was furious with me.

Mrs. Halahan came in, too, and was also asked to the Browns' party. She, too, accepted and was discreet enough not to refer to it after Miss Phyllis had departed. Instead, she said that she wanted to arrange to send away a parcel of groceries.

"It's the boys' old Nannie," she explained, "at least, it isn't her, for she's quite comfortably off, but a niece she wrote to me about who is in trouble. Nannie says the girl's husband left her a few weeks ago with three young children, the smallest of them only a baby. I thought perhaps we could send them a monthly parcel."

Mrs. Halahan smiled rather diffidently. "I don't want you to think I'm advertising this very small charity; it's just that I thought it would be nice to get the things from you. I know you'll understand and help me choose."

She was, of course, quietly doing us a good turn as well—and together we chose suitable groceries.

When she had gone, I reflected on the kind of things different people buy—nearly always an indication of their characters. The shiftless, out-of-work type, think nothing of taking home expensive tinned fruits, sliced bread (to me an absurd extravagance), chocolate, sweets and cigarettes. The respectable people are far more careful. They buy only what they can pay for, usually necessities, and if their children want sweets they have to get them out of their own money. I notice, too, that the most reluctant payers are by far the most extravagant buyers, and suppose that this isn't only peculiar to villagers but applies, too, to the outside world. So far as that goes, village life is an exact reflection of larger life. Birth, marriage, death, love, hate, seduction and betrayal, kindness and brutality, greed and generosity, they are all here. It is just that our world is on a smaller and more intimate scale.

For my own part, November ended with my paying a long visit to old Mrs. Crabtree next door.

"I hope you won't think it an impertinence, dear," she said, as she checked over the groceries in the brown canvas shopping bag which she always leaves with her weekly order, "but I thought it'd be nice if you stepped round for a cup of tea Thursday—if you hadn't nothing better to do, of course."

"I'd love to come, Mrs. Crabtree. May I bring Bumble too?"

Her old eyes sparkled with pleasure, as I'd known they would.

"Indeed you may," she answered. "I can't abide cats, as I've told 'ee before now, but dogs—that's different and a more beautiful creature than your Bumble I never did see. I loves all dogs."

"Even Miss Brown's Fairies?" I asked rather indiscreetly.

"Bah!" said the old woman. "Them ain't dogs—rats we always calls 'em in the village. Not but what they may have nice natures," she added fairly, "same as other beasts if they're treated proper. See you tomorrow at five then, and we'll have a good talk before Tom gets home."

At five o'clock exactly I walked up the little cobbled path and, before I could knock, the door opened and Mrs. Crabtree, in her best black dress and a pale blue woollen shawl, smiled up at me and drew me inside.

"Sit down, dear," she said, indicating an armchair, covered in American cloth and containing two fine red satin cushions, "while I wet the tea."

I sat down, and while the old woman bent over the stove and tilted a small iron kettle into her brown, china teapot, I looked around me. No modern gimcrack furniture here, no "contemporary" patterned carpet and Woolworth china—but a couple of armchairs, solid and worn, two strong Victorian upright ones, with stuffed seats, and a round mahogany table, its red plush cover nearly hidden by a white tea-cloth, beautifully embroidered at the corners. Sensible, big willow-patterned cups and saucers stood on a scrubbed wooden tray, and some little cakes, with pink and white icing, were clearly home-made for the occasion. Over the mantelpiece, on which stood Tom's jar of pipe-cleaners, an alarm clock and two monstrous china dogs, was a big framed photograph, presumably, from the clothes and the mutton-chop whiskers, of Mrs. Crabtree's father. The other walls were nearly covered with photographs, too, including a half life-size likeness of a soldier in the puttees and high-necked tunic of the 1914 war and various wedding groups, stiff, unsmiling and carefully posed. There was a small dresser on the far side of the room and on it, beside bits and pieces of china, lay a Bible, a bottle of ink, a pen and a cheap writing-block. On the floor was a threadbare carpet and a rag-rug. The window was tightly shut and the room darkened by the pot plants which flourished on its ledge. The fire, in the old-fashioned kitchen stove, glowed redly and the room was warm and cosy.

"It's nice here, Mrs. Crabtree," I said. "How long have you lived in this cottage?"

"Since I were first wed," she answered, "and that's a tidy time ago. I've buried three husbands, you know."

A little startled at this information, I said, "No, I didn't know."

"Aye, there was John Battle what brought me here when I were just seventeen——"

"Brought you from where?" I interrupted.

"Oh, just from the place where Miss Grogan lives now, t'other side o' the Red Lion. That's where I were born—I were just going to tell 'ee," she said severely. "Shepherd to Barley Farm, John were, and killed by lightning one summer—and his collie, Nell, wi' him." She looked down at Bumble. "Not one o' they sort—but a real collie. Come from Wales, she did."

Mrs. Crabtree seemed to be remembering old Nell more vividly than her first husband and, as she poured out the tea, her veined hands shaking as she used them both to hold the heavy pot, I asked her just what had happened.

"Oh, I forgets now, dear, 'tis a long time ago—but he were the best husband I ever had—and they brought him home, poor lad, in a dung cart and his clean smock all mucky and Nell beside him. They said 'twas his crook had done it."

As she spoke I could clearly see the young man alone on the hill with his dog and the huddled sheep and the great lowering clouds piling up from the west, changing the pale greens and golds of the downland to dun and olive, and then the sudden wind tearing up from the valley and the blackened sky split with light as the thunder crashed—and the frightened flock scattering, when the storm had passed, with no one to guide them and nothing to stop their crazed flight.

"Ten years I waited afore I wed again," said Mrs. Crabtree, as she offered me the plate of cakes, "and then Tom—well, he needed a man, you know, he were that unruly—though he's a good enough boy now and bides at home with his old mother of an evening. He never seemed to take to women, though I used to fear he'd be off after one some day."

I reckon that Tom must be at least sixty-five, so I should think she is fairly safe now.

"Tell me about your second husband," I said.

"Oh, Albert—he weren't a bad sort of chap; but it didn't last long. Off to the trenches he was a year later." She pointed to a flat gilt box, tied with red, white and blue ribbon. "The King gave him that you know—not just Albert, of course, but all the boys in France—one Christmas, I think it were. But he never came back—only that little old box and a beautiful letter from some colonel or something; but it weren't no good to me nor didn't mean nothing with Albert gone and me second housemaid at the Manor and Tom on me hands again and a baby on the way."

"That would be Lucy's mother?"

"Yes, and a right good girl she were, and her husband, too, but they be gone now, same as Albert and a lot more."

"And your third husband? You must have been very pretty. It isn't everybody who's so attractive to men."

Mrs. Crabtree took my cup to refill it and, as she put it on the table, she eyed me shrewdly. "You needn't lose heart, dear," she said kindly, "there's plenty of fish in the sea yet and you ain't so old nor so plain ye need worry."

I was annoyed to feel myself blushing, but she went on serenely. "And it isn't always for the best neither, for I can tell 'ee, Crabtree weren't no good. I'd been in service at the Manor for years and I'd got a nice bit put by and I were gone sixty when he asked me; but he only married me for me money and a nice place to put his feet up. Well, I saw through that pretty soon and in six weeks he were gone."

"*Dead*, do you mean?"

"Dead? No, of course not. D'you think I murdered him? No, I just told him he could get out and he went. Took up wi' a widow over Devizes way soon after—but it didn't last long. I reckon she made him do some work and, in the end, it killed him. Anyhow, they brought him back to Barley, for he were Martha Root's brother, you see, and I buried him here in the Yard, along of his mum and dad. But I didn't grieve and I didn't make out I were sorry—for I weren't. Have another little cake, dear. I made 'em for 'ee specially."

"Tell me about the village, Mrs. Crabtree, things you re-member about it."

The old woman smiled. "There's a lot of things I remember which nobody else don't," she said proudly. "You're feeling settled like, you and the Commander?"

I told her that we were very settled—and happy, too.

"Very different you are to the last lot," she remarked.

"And who had the shop before Fenton?"

"John Rous, of course—that was Lucy's father-in-law, you know—and *his* father before him. It's always been a Rous at the shop so long as I can remember."

Bumble had edged silently forward and laid his head on Mrs. Crabtree's knee, and now she looked down at him fondly. "The lamb!" she said and gave him three lumps of sugar and a pink cake.

He took them very delicately and eyed me sideways with a mixture of shame and defiance, for he is never fed at meals. Then he lay down.

"Go on, Mrs. Crabtree, dear," I said persuasively, and as I spoke I could hear myself as a little girl begging some grown-up to tell me a story. "Tell me more about the village."

"Not about the folks in it I won't," she retorted sternly, "for I don't hold wi' gossip . . . it don't do no good to nobody."

"I don't mean that, I want to know what it was like here in the old days."

"Much better. We didn't have no wireless, nor no telly, nor no buses, nor motor-cars, nor tractors—and a good thing, too, if you asks me. Why they used to have thirty horses up at the farm and, if we wanted to have a jolly we'd go dancing on the Green. My dad was the fiddler when I was a youngster and he used to play at the harvest homes. My! They was something to remember. I never seen such food and drink and goings on."

"But has Barley itself changed much?"

"No, not really, though there used to be some great big barns where the old general has his bungalow. Before the fire, that was."

"What fire?"

"A whole stack yard—and the Dutch barns crammed wi' wheat and five ricks as well—all burnt to the ground."

"How awful. When was this?"

"Oh, I dunno—but a long time ago. At night it was and the harvest just finished. The flames seemed mountains high and the village were full of smoke and fire engines. I were only a bit of a girl then and I remember one of the farm hands, a big man with a beard he was, standing there crying, and I asked my mum about it and she said he weren't weeping exactly for all the corn that were lost but for all the work they'd done for nothing.

"And I remember when Squire's son, the wild one that were always drinking, drove straight into the pond one dark night and the dog-cart turned over on top of him. The mare struggled out all right but he were pinned under it and drowned and not a soul knew nothing until the morning."

"Good heavens! What a ghastly thing to happen."

"Aye—but maybe it were a judgment on him for his evil living," said the old woman relentlessly; and then she went on,

"I mind the time, too, o' the great snow when we were cut off from the world for ten days and nothing going in or out ... and we run out o' flour at last and some said as nobody outside cared what happened to we in Barley. But Mr. Rous at the shop (he were the village baker, too) and a-twenty o' the men and lads stirred theirselves up and swore as they'd dig and fight their way to Badgerford before they'd see the women and little 'uns go short: and so they did. 'Tis true we'd got our own milk and bacon and meat, if need be, but bread be the staff o' life, as it says in the good Book.

"And I mind how they set off wi' their picks and spades and shovels, and how Mr. Rous shouted out for every one of us to keep their fires going and the bakehouse, too, for there'd be flour in the village before morning. And sure enough they was back in the middle of the night, and they'd got four sacks o' flour and a keg o' whisky and they come roaring and singing over the snow so the noise got us all out of our beds to meet them. And the stars was shining overhead and we was so excited we didn't feel the cold, and every cottage started baking and cooking all the night through—just dough bread, you know, not setting it proper like. My! That were a rare do."

"Tell me some more."

"I dunno what else to tell 'ee, except when the King come through the village once on his way somewhere. Poor little Lucy cried her eyes out because she never seen him and she wouldn't believe he hadn't got no crown on his head."

"Which King was that?"

Mrs. Crabtree's old eyes stared vaguely at me.

"I don't rightly know," she said uncertainly and, all of a sudden, she looked very old indeed and very tired and her lips trembled.

Ashamed at having worn her out, I quickly got up to go and thanked her for all her kindness.

But she didn't move from her chair. "Thank 'ee for coming, dear," she said softly, "I think I'll just wait now till Tom comes."

She smiled but, as I opened the door, already her head was nodding and her eyes shut.

As soon as I got home I called to Jim, for I was longing to repeat all this to him; but he was busy making a meat safe, an absurdly gigantic thing, like an old game-larder, and so, while it was all fresh in my memory, I wrote it down here instead.

4 December

The mild, open weather continued into this month and there is still no sign of a change. Most of the ploughing seems to be finished and the winter wheat pricks the silver earth with a million tiny green spears. I have not yet set eyes on the owner of Lower Barley Farm, but there is no doubt about his being a good farmer. His cattle look splendid, the land clean, the fences sound and the ditches clear. Several of the village gossips have told me that, since the tragedy of his wife's death, he has taken to drink; but, by the way his own men speak of him, I should think it most unlikely.

The early part of December seemed to be all bits and pieces—nothing special to write about but something happening every day.

First there was the cocktail party at The Weavers, to which I had almost to drag Jim through the one wet evening we have had this month; and it was then that he began to talk about how awkward it is having no means of transport at all and how he wishes he could pick up a second-hand scooter. It is true that we are completely immobile except for the once-a-week bus, and he said that the modern machines will carry two people, so that a scooter would certainly be useful, if not luxurious. I said that it would be better to wait for the spring and warm weather; but he is very impulsive, and if anything remotely suitable should materialise I am afraid he would snap it up at once.

Meanwhile, we trudged through the rain to the Miss Browns' party, and very unrewarding and pathetic it was. Miss Phyllis was at her worst, gushing and girlish and when, after about half an hour, I asked for her sister, I was told that she was unwell and had retired to bed.

It seemed odd to me that, if she were ill, they hadn't put off the party altogether; but Mrs. Davenant, who looked about half her usual size in a bottle-green woollen dress instead of her usual purple tweed suit, whispered in my ear that Miss Emily was probably locked in her room.

"Oh, no!" I exclaimed, genuinely astonished, "Why on earth should she be?"

"Just jealousy," replied Mrs. Davenant complacently. "She's never allowed to go anywhere or meet anyone if Phyllis can help it. The poor woman's fiendishly jealous, and Emily hasn't got the courage to stand up to her. It all goes back a long time, for Emily used to play the piano exceedingly well and Phyllis never had a talent of any kind. Emily was engaged at one time but I'm afraid men usually run a mile when they see her sister—and I suppose they always have."

"Engaged, was she? What happened to her young man, then?"

"Killed in some climbing accident or other—I forget exactly: but it was years ago and it knocked poor Emily out completely. Since then she's always been absolutely under the other one's thumb."

"Who's under whose thumb?" asked the vicar's wife eagerly. "I hope you're not giving Mrs. Braid a wrong idea of us all, Margery."

She turned and looked down at me as if I were some interesting and rather unusual specimen.

"I can't understand," she said, "how it is you're not worn out with all you do, standing all day long and taking orders from the village people. Don't you find them very exacting and irritating?"

"No," I answered truthfully, "I like the village people very much."

The vicar's wife gave a kind of smile—but not with her eyes, which were cold and slatey behind their spectacles—"We all like the village people very much—but liking them is different to having to wait on them. Still, if you're content, that's as it should be . . . just as it should be." She saw her husband at her elbow. "Isn't it, Charles?"

The vicar looked vague and uncertain as usual. "Of course, my dear," he agreed and then, suddenly recognising me, "dear me, you're Mrs. Braid . . . and I've scarcely seen anything so far of you and your husband. You must come up to tea—yes, that's an excellent plan. You arrange it, dear."

"Very well," said his wife, without enthusiasm, "we must fix a day."

She moved away and, as she went, Jim came up to me and muttered that we must go.

The party consisted only of the Davenants, the vicar and his wife, a roundabout, tweedy little woman from Upper Barley, ourselves and our hostess; and I felt that we could not possibly go so soon. But Jim was determined and obstinate, and when I had finished my glass of Empire sherry, which in fact wasn't at all bad, he took my arm and, under my protection, said good-bye to Miss P. Brown with such charm that the poor woman literally blushed and wriggled with pleasure. I felt intensely embarrassed and sorry for her and furiously angry with Jim.

The next bit of December news was that the fish and chip van from Badgerford which every Wednesday afternoon spreads an odour of hot fat and frying fish all over the village did not turn up on its usual day. This caused general consternation and anxiety because people eagerly await its coming and, directly the smell first drifts along the main road, they rush out with plates and pie-dishes at the ready. Now it seems that the van was completely burnt out last week about ten miles from here and goodness knows when another will replace it. The women of the village have been lamenting its loss all day, for their husbands will grumble at being done out of their weekly treat, and the children are glum with disappointment because the fire didn't happen under their eyes, here in Barley.

Last week, we decided to have a sale of our predecessor's rubbish and we filled the window with oddments—"nothing more than sixpence". It proved to be a wonderful clearance for us and a lot of bargains changed hands. The vicar's wife bought a green-and-black sponge bag with a large stain on it and said that they all think us so dashing and original!

While she was here the dustmen arrived and one of them announced, as he tipped our rubbish into his repulsive-looking cart, that he'd left Mrs. Frobisher-Spink's unemptied, "for he couldn't wait all day for people what was too high and mighty to touch a thing for themselves". His real reason, we afterwards discovered, was that Mrs. F.-S. has just sacked her housemaid for suspected stealing. The housemaid is the dustman's niece and also a Rous and, after the dustcart had been driven away, Grannie Rous was seen waddling down the road "to have it out wi' the old bitch". We never in fact heard the result of this interview and very likely Mrs. Frobisher-Spink was perfectly in the right, but Grannie Rous is a formidable old woman and I should not care to be in her black books.

Apropos of Mrs. Frobisher-Spink, I have at last solved the mystery of the feud between her and the Manor. The Halahans took Jim and me to the cinema in Badgerford last night and, when they came in for a hot drink on the way home, Eleanor Halahan told me all about it. The solution is quite simple; about sixteen years ago Mr. Frobisher-Spink went off with the eldest Davenant daughter—though his wife naturally says that the girl went off with him. She won't divorce him and they live apparently fairly happily—and in sin—about twenty miles away.

I asked what Mr. Frobisher-Spink was like and Mrs. Halahan laughed and said gently, "Terrible. Quite honestly, the worst sort of bounder and that's partly why the Davenants feel so bitter. I don't think they'd have minded quite so much if he'd been their sort. As it is, he lives on their daughter's money and I'm afraid that's what he did with his wife's. She's a rich woman and, in my opinion, it's a great pity she doesn't give him his divorce and marry someone herself."

As I listened to this, I remembered, uncomfortably, Mrs. Frobisher-Spink's expression when she looks at Jim—but, naturally, "I didn't *say* anything".

Our Bessy came to work late this morning and almost unrecognisable. She has had her rather nice brown hair "permed", so that it stands out all round her head in a dull fuzz, and her tight slacks have been exchanged for a black satin skirt with an extremely close-fitting yellow top. Large earrings have also been added to the pink pearls. She told me, in explanation, that Bert read a piece in the paper about its being fashionable to look feminine.

She is a well-developed girl and what she is wearing under her yellow blouse is uncertain, but she now comes at you sticking out in front like a ship with a kind of double prow. I thought Jim would be horrified when he saw her, but, instead, he was very much amused.

Unfortunately, the three-inch heels which complete the new ensemble were literally her undoing, for, during the morning, I heard a crash and rushed in from the shop to find her fallen from top to bottom of our steep, narrow stairs. She was basically unharmed but her new skirt was split and, as might have been expected, her rather tatty pink knickers very much in evidence.

Poor Bessy wept for her bruises and damaged finery, and I grieved for a teapot and two broken saucers.

I have been rather disturbed to see no mention of cream on our weekly milk bill from the farm, and yesterday I tackled H. Potter's sister about it; but she brushed the matter aside.

"Two or three little drops now and then," she said grandly, "we don't miss it—nor never will."

I am glad to get cream, for Jim's sake, but "two or three drops" is probably half a pint a week.

"It's very kind of you, Miss Potter," I said, "but we really must pay for it."

"You can't do that, missus," she retorted anxiously, " 'tisn't put down nowhere and you'll get I the sack. We always takes a little bit when we wants it and nobody none the worse neither. ... I thought as I was doing you a kindness," she added a little resentfully.

This is what comes of letting things slide, and now I don't know *what* to do. But I did say firmly that I *must* order and pay for the cream properly in future—and Florence Potter marched out of the shop distinctly hurt.

I started to moan about all this to Jim but he was absorbed at the time in the Post Office accounts which, as usual, would not come right. "We're short again this week," he said angrily. "That means we'll have to put in over £2 of our own money. It's getting beyond a joke." He then accused me of mixing up the money, which I hotly denied but, as a matter of fact, I dare say he is right—and I only wish we'd never had anything to do with the Post Office.

On Sunday all the other events of the month faded into nothingness and excitement rushed through the village like a bush fire, for it was rumoured that a local syndicate (old Mrs. Crabtree, her son Tom, Amos Rous (the blacksmith), old Root and our Bessy's husband, Bert) had won something big on the Pools. Rumour increased their probable winnings hourly but by Wednesday it was known definitely that, *if* they had filled in their coupon properly *and* enclosed a postal order *and* posted it in time *and* the whole thing had been received *and* not lost in the post *and* they were not all completely mistaken—then, between them, the syndicate had won £500.

On Friday they got their money and their neighbours reacted exactly according to character.

Some of the comments made in the shop were:

"Old Mrs. C. and her stuck-up son. What do the likes o' they want wi' £200 and only theirselves to look after."

"And look at old Amos . . . I reckon he's got enough put by already, a single man, too, and us wi' families to keep and hard put to it to make ends meet."

"I don't hold wi' gambling nor never did—but we could do wi' a lot o' new china and some better chairs in the Hall, if anyone was minded to spend some o' their money on others."

"Good luck to 'em all, I says, and I hopes as they spends some of it on a jolly, like we used to have in Barley, and don't put it all by for a rainy day what mayn't come till after they're dead and gone."

I look forward greatly to hearing how they *do* spend it, for a hundred pounds each is quite a lot of money . . . and all day long people were in and out of the shop and could speak of little else.

It was a long and exhausting day, and just before closing time, a tall, black-browed, scowling stranger stamped into the shop and asked if I was Mrs. Braid.

"Yes," I said, surprised, and he informed me that he was John Carrick of Lower Barley Farm.

"It's come to my notice, madam," he said angrily, "that we've been supplying cream to you without its being booked. I've dealt with the matter at our end but I'd be obliged if you'd give a written order in future and pay for what you have."

I felt my face burning and began to try to explain; but he took off his cap and, with a very curt "Good day", interrupted my floundering and stalked out, banging the door.

I was terribly upset, but although Jim was quite sympathetic when I tearfully explained the situation he said it was really my own fault and that there was nothing whatever to be done.

All the same, I decided later to write a brief note of apology to Mr. Carrick, and I enclosed a cheque to cover any possible extras we could have had.

Then, tired out, unhappy about this stupid occurrence and hating everything to do with the shop (for I cannot bear people to be angry with me, and this time I was certainly in the wrong), I went to bed and cried myself to sleep in a very silly and childish way.

The jumble sale was held in the village hall this week but I didn't go, partly because we were too busy and I couldn't leave the shop and partly because we simply cannot afford to buy things we don't need or want. I didn't succeed in giving away Jim's coat and trousers, for he caught me packing them up, but I let them have some of Barbara's outgrown stuff.

It was just as well I didn't go out, for on that day two cases of toys, ordered by Jim, arrived and had to be unpacked and put out on shelves and tables at the far end of the shop, so that the grown-up customers could buy or reserve their Christmas presents unseen by their children. Woolly animals, puzzles, games, drums and shiny trumpets, mouth-organs, cowboy outfits, trains and model aeroplanes made a fine show.

The very next day we sold a lot of these toys, and I was surprised to find how many of the women have put aside money especially for this purpose.

Mrs. Davenant's kindly visit to our new "toy shop" nearly ended in disaster. She must weigh a good fifteen or sixteen stone, the shop is narrow and, to make room for the toys, all our other shelves are bulging and overcrowded. Mrs. Davenant walked carefully but her ample shoulders dislodged some boxes. She tripped over one of them and, in trying to right herself, grabbed at the shelf above her. Unfortunately, in doing so, she upset a six-pound jar of "Hundreds and Thousands", and the little coloured sweets cascaded over her like confetti, filling her hat brim and running down her neck and inside her shirt.

Luckily, there was no one else in the shop at the time and, good temperedly, she stayed to make £2. 14s. od. worth of purchases—which was good of her, for she must have felt pretty uncomfortable.

As she left she met in the doorway Mrs. Lacey and her three youngest, who are all away from school after 'flu, and the whole party stared at her in astonishment as "Hundreds and Thousands" trickled freely from her person. In fact, one Boot and two Laceys followed her up the street, scrabbling on the ground behind her—but she went serenely on, quite unconscious of the unusually feudal scene she was helping to create.

There is only just a fortnight to go until Christmas and the orders for Christmas fare are already rolling in, often only partly paid for but with a promise that the rest shall be cleared off next week.

Old Mrs. Crabtree, whose success in the Pools seems to have given her new life and cured her rheumatism, came in last night to announce her plans.

"Tom's got his hundred all right," she said, "and he'd best put it by against the time I'm gone—but I be going to jolly mine. And," she beamed, and beckoned Jim and me to come close, "I'll tell what I be going to do."

She leant forward and whispered her intentions, and then stood back watching eagerly for the astonished expressions she expected. We did not disappoint her and, relieved, she chuckled with pleasure. Then, "How much do 'ee reckon it'll cost?" she asked a little anxiously.

I had no idea and looked questioningly at Jim. "Maybe forty pounds," he said, "or it could be as much as fifty or sixty."

Mrs. Crabtree, flushed with excitement, her old eyes bright and her little black hat with the pink roses slipping forward, executed the ghost of a jig. "That's nothing," she said, "nothing to me. I don't care if we spends the whole lot."

She has decided to give a party in the village hall on New Year's Eve—a party for the whole village, with a high tea and crackers and a Christmas tree with a present for every child

("Just a little something—not to cost too much, you know") and a band and, perhaps, a conjurer, and dancing for everybody—"But it'll not go on a minute after midnight," she said firmly, "for we'll see the New Year in proper with the bells and all."

"It'll be wonderful," I told her enthusiastically; but, as I spoke, a shadow of doubt flickered over her face.

"You'll help me, won't you?" she asked a little shakily. "I couldn't see to it all meself—I mean I be getting on a bit—I mean I'd like 'em to have it—but——"

"Of course we'll help you," I said quickly, "and, if you agree, I suggest we get a committee together to arrange it all. They'll plan everything and you can approve it or not as you like. I'm sure a lot of people will help."

The old woman's face cleared. "That's all right," she said vaguely, "you arrange it all, dear, and I'll pay."

The shop bell tankled and, giving us a tremendous wink and with her finger to her lips, the old woman slipped out.

I turned to Jim, when our customer had gone, and asked him what he thought we had better do.

"If we get anything like the rush we hope for in here," he said, "we shan't have time to do anything ourselves; and besides we're newcomers and people won't like it if we do. You'd better get hold of Mrs. Davenant."

Two days later a committee meeting to consider the party was held at the Vicarage, and everyone grasped at once that time is very short indeed and that there is a great deal to be done. The committee consisted of Mrs. Davenant, the vicar's wife, the Misses Brown, Mrs. Frobisher-Spink, Colonel Halahan, Mrs. Crabtree's son, Tom, her grand-daughter, Lucy Rous, and ourselves. The only absentee was Mrs. Frobisher-Spink, who had to be asked but who won't, if she can help it, sit in the same room as a Davenant.

Contrary to all my previous experience of committees, this one got to work right away and, with no dissension at all, arrangements from the start went with a bang. Within a very short time I realised that the vicar's wife is a born organiser and utterly capable. Presumably everyone else knew this already. Perhaps it is frustration of these abilities which makes her so tiresome; for she probably takes after her father, Lord Some-body, who, Jim says, started in the proper traditional way as an office boy and is now a City magnate.

Miss Emily Brown actually came forward with an offer to play the piano, although her sister frowned disapprovingly and muttered something about "it'll be far too much for you, dear"; and Jim, to my amazement, confessed to a rusty know-ledge of conjuring and agreed to perform. Although he must be very out of practice, he used to be a brilliant amateur con-jurer and should be a great success; but myself could only promise to help with the decorating of the hall, for I knew that I should be too busy in the shop to do any more. The food is to be provided by caterers from Badgerford, and the tree and its presents are to be bought by the vicar's wife.

I was asked to report all this to Mrs. Crabtree and, as she listened, her face flushed with pleasure. "When they wants the money," she said grandly, "just tell 'em to ask me, that's all."

The day after the committee meeting the news of the party was, of course, all over the village. The children were en-chanted with the idea and the grown-ups, with very few ex-ceptions (who always run down anything they can), were enthusiastic; and now someone has had the brilliant notion of asking Upper Barley neighbours to come and baby sit, where necessary, and I am told that there will be plenty of volunteers for this if transport can be provided.

Jim got out his conjuring apparatus the very next day and is already practising madly; and I am so very pleased that he offered to help, for this seems to me a real sign that he is on the road to complete recovery. Before we came here he was absolutely uninterested in any of the ordinary things going on round him.

Barbara arrived home from school two days ago. She seems taller than ever, has had her hair cut very short, which is becoming, and her blue eyes shone with excitement as she rushed indoors before we had even paid off her taxi, so that she could explore the house and the shop.

Her first evening at home was spent in putting up the Christmas decorations, mainly paper streamers, bells and many-coloured balloons; and we were just wondering what to do about holly when the shop door burst open and one of H. Potter's nephews marched in with a huge armful. He refused to take any money or to say where he'd got the holly, and although I was grateful, I remembered the matter of the cream only too well, and felt very doubtful about accepting it. I had no choice though, for the donor simply dropped his bundle on the floor, grinned cheerfully and banged out of the shop.

I had bought a little two-foot-high Christmas tree a week ago and now Barbara and I packed soil into a half keg, a gift from the Red Lion next door, and when we had planted the tree firmly we stood it on the broad shelf which follows the curve of our old-fashioned, square-paned bow window. We twined tinsel and wired silver-balls and coloured lights among its little branches and then, down the inside of the windows, we hung gold and silver stars on strings. The effect after dark was fascinating and several times we had to go outside to admire our own work, for the whole thing looked like some kind of fairyland window.

Next day at four o'clock the tree was lit up for public view for the first time and soon a crowd of little faces, none more than four feet from the ground, was pressed against the glass—and as I opened the door we heard such squeaks of pleasure and admiration that we felt well rewarded for our trouble and decided there and then to keep the tree alight every evening until after Christmas.

Miss Phyllis Brown, on her last visit to the shop, bought a packet of cheese biscuits. She then opened the packet crumbily, so as to offer a biscuit to her "dinky-ducky Fairy Frivolous" and, in spite of my protests, lifted this unpleasant little animal on to our scrubbed counter to eat it. This done, she asked a lot of silly questions about Jim's conjuring, and Barbara, who is no fool but sometimes very mischievous, sized up the situation at once and said she was sure that Uncle Jim would like to show Miss Brown some of his tricks. It was all I could do to prevent her eagerly pushing past me, but at last, very disappointed, she said goodbye and left, with little Fairy Frivolous dragging back on her lead and curtseying on the door-mat in a final gesture of contempt.

Added to Miss Brown's interruptions yesterday was the final Post Office parcel rush. Parcels of all shapes and sizes and weights were stacked high on the counter and, to pay Barbara out for her tiresomeness, I made her take over the whole job of weighing and stamping them. As it happens, she is as good at arithmetic as I am bad, and really managed very well.

Mrs. Halahan rang up last night and asked me to go there for a drink and to discuss Mrs. Crabtree's party arrangements. She said, "if you're in old clothes, don't bother to change," and, rashly, I took her at her word and went there wearing an old tweed skirt and a cherry-coloured cardigan and jersey, both wearing rather thin.

The son, Philip, met me at the door, and as we walked into the drawing-room I was exceedingly embarrassed to see Mr. John Carrick already there, laughing and talking with Colonel Halahan. I felt my face reddening and, although as we were introduced I tried to recover poise, I still felt stupidly uncomfortable and quickly turned to young Philip and asked him about his writing.

He seemed mildly pleased, a very sweet smile lightened his pale, sensitive face, and he asked at once if I'd care to look at some of his stuff. Knowing that to be asked to read his work aloud is to a young writer much the same as offering strawberries and cream to his younger brother, I invited him to come in one evening and read some of his work to me, and he accepted eagerly.

While I talked to Philip Halahan I saw that John Carrick was poring over a fishing book with his host and I took the opportunity to give him a good look over. If he smiled more often, I thought, he wouldn't be bad looking, and then I remembered about his wife and felt ashamed of criticising him. He is evidently a "gentleman farmer" and someone told me that, with the exception of the war gap, he has worked Lower Barley for nearly fifteen years.

Mrs. Halahan and I had a talk about arrangements for the party, but when I left at 7.30 very little had been settled, for we both agreed that the whole organisation is best left to the vicar's wife.

When I was half-way home I was overtaken by someone and, flashing my torch, I found that it was John Carrick, who then walked along with me and blurted out an apology.

"Please forgive me," he said, "I've the vilest temper and I'm afraid I don't always try to control it. I was exceedingly rude and I apologise. I know perfectly well how these things happen —with the village people trying to be helpful and in fact putting one in an impossible position."

I was rather taken aback at this unexpected generosity and we parted in a very friendly way as I turned in at our gate, warmed and heartened—as I always am by kindness.

The mild weather still persists and, thank goodness, there is no sign of a white Christmas this year, although Barbara tells me that she is praying for deep, deep snow. We have sold nearly all our toys and the ordinary grocery shelves are beginning to look bare. As the days go by, I find myself getting very tired but Jim, who works late every night at his conjuring, seems perfectly all right—and certainly Barbara is a great help to us both.

Two days before Christmas old Mrs. Crabtree and Lucy went off to Swindon in the local taxi to do their shopping. As they drove past the shop I saw Mrs. Crabtree sitting on the very edge of the seat with a large black handbag, presumably containing some of her Pools winnings, held tightly in her lap.

They were evidently off to buy themselves finery for the party, and I thought how lovely it would be if only Lucy's husband were home in time for it.

Then, on Christmas Eve Mrs. Davenant came in to say that she is having a large party of grandchildren to stay at the Manor and to ask Barbara to go to tea on Boxing Day to meet them. Naturally I was anxious, when Barbara first met Mrs. Davenant, that she should be at her best; but, in the maddening way children have, she was awkward and shy, which specially annoyed me because the one thing she really has got is good manners. However, Mrs. Davenant is a nice woman and has, I believe, five married sons and about ten grandchildren, so surely she must understand the young.

When she left, it was nearly closing time and we were thankful, for from the way the villagers went on all day one would think that they were preparing for a siege. We had no time to stop for lunch or tea and the little shop was bursting with people all day long, so that when at last we put up the shutter Jim and I could only sink exhausted into armchairs by the sitting-room fire. Ten minutes later, though, the front door bell rang and I had to drag myself to my feet to answer it, for Barbara was busily making tea for the three of us.

On the steps stood a small boy, who handed me a large square parcel, giggled and ran off into the darkness. I thought tiredly that perhaps it was some kind of joke, but inside the wrappings was almost the biggest box of chocolates I have ever seen and enclosed was this note:

'Christmas Eve. For your young Miss. A little some-thing in return for what you done for my girl. Yours respectfully'.

There was no signature; but no one else in the village can write in this manner and I was greatly touched and somehow consoled for all our hard work by the feeling that we are now almost part of the village.

The family and animals were fed quickly and rather sketchily that night and, when the others had gone to bed, I fell asleep by the fire and woke at midnight only just enough to enable myself to wrap up Barbara's and Jim's presents.

Christmas Day started very snugly for me, with breakfast in bed brought by Jim and Barbara—scrambled eggs, coffee and toast and butter, all most elegantly presented. My daughter had knitted me a many-coloured woollen scarf, which is quite wearable and must have taken her hours and hours to make, and Jim somehow managed to get for me a huge bunch of roses, which must have cost him a great deal but which I love. . . . and he knows that I like to be given flowers more than anything else.

He and Barbara seemed very pleased with their presents, and Jim actually had one from our great-aunt Grace, with whom he stayed so unhappily after he left hospital. It was a black, watered silk tie, but whether it was sent as a token of mourning for his personal sins or for the sins of the world I do not know. I cannot feel charitably towards her, even at Christmas time, for she is a horrid old woman and was very unkind to Jim, simply exploiting his illness and good nature for her own benefit. I seldom actively dislike anybody—but I consider one of the best things Jim ever did was to throw her unpaid job back at her and escape; for she expected him always to be at her beck and call and to be fawningly grateful for her hospitality. Now, after only a few months of being on his own, he is already a different man.

We were rather surprised to find that there was no morning church on Christmas Day, but we share our vicar with Upper Barley and this year it was our turn to have a service in the evening.

I had managed to get a small turkey from Badgerford and also to snatch a plum pudding from the shop before they were all sold, so we had a fine luncheon and afterwards walked it off on the Downs. The bare, lacy trees, smooth hills, neat, grey-brown plough and pale green winter corn looked beautiful on this soft December day, and I think we all felt very happy.

After tea we walked across the Green to Lower Barley's little stone church. It was built in the twelfth century and is practically unchanged and, on Christmas night, it was very cold and only about half-full. Half a dozen little boys, two of whom read the lessons, composed the choir, the hymns were pitched painfully high and the music came from a wheezy harmonium —because the organ is sick through the damp and neglect of years. In spite of, or perhaps because of, its shortcomings, the little church gives a sense of stability and peace and, as we stepped stumblingly into the dark churchyard, very genuine greetings were exchanged; and our little party, at least, went home to its cosy fireside the better for coming out.

After supper I remembered to look at Philip Halahan's typescript. I was astonished to find in his work real literary quality and strength, and some of his poetry had fire and beauty— although I should say it would be quite unsaleable.

On Boxing Day Jim found on the doorstep an anonymous present. It was a handwoven tie; and, very embarrassingly, Jim refused to thank Miss P. Brown, saying that technically he doesn't know who it's from and wouldn't he look a damn fool if, after all, it was from old Mrs. Root or even the vicar's wife. Both possibilities seemed to me very unlikely—but he wouldn't budge.

The Boxing Day meet was in Badgerford market square, and hounds came our way and found in the Manor Park. Hunting is as old, and older, than England and aesthetically very satisfying; hound work can be a joy to watch and, in remote places such as Westmorland and Cumberland, probably only real country people hunt at all—and that, I think, is as it should be. Here though, when I see a field of perhaps fifty, many of them hard-faced, loud-voiced women, perhaps sixty horses, fifteen couple of hounds, a mass of excited children and a crowd of townsmen on foot, car or bicycle—all having a day out at the expense of one small red fox—I believe even Dame Juliana Berners would disapprove of hunting as much as I do.

Barbara, who caught sight of Charles James slinking along a hedgerow, came home weeping for him; but I assured her that with all these people about it was most unlikely he would be caught.

"I don't *mind* them catching and eating him," she wailed. "It's when he's so frightened first I can't bear it."

But her morning tears were long forgotten when two of the Davenant boys came down to fetch her to their tea party and she returned at about 7 p.m., flushed and happy and having picked up some new slang words which she still uses every other minute.

The day after Boxing Day was a Saturday, and trade was fairly brisk in spite of all the shopping done on Christmas Eve. There was a committee meeting in the evening at which everything continued to go smoothly, and it was decided that the drinks at the party should be beer, cider, orange squash, coffee and tea.

On Sunday morning the family again spoilt me with breakfast in bed—but "It's the last time, Mummy. You needn't think you're going to get away with it every Sunday," said Barbara, grinning and sitting cross-legged on the end of my bed. "I like Peter and Molly best," she went on, apropos of nothing, "but George is *clever*. Do you know he can do practically any sum in the world in his head?"

I supposed she was talking about her Davenant chums and heard myself say in a repressive parental voice, "I hope you're not pushing yourself in there too much, darling. You must wait until you're asked, you know."

"I have been asked and if it'd only freeze we could skate and toboggan, but actually we're going to take a boat down and dredge the pond for treasure. Molly's coming to fetch me at ten."

"Why do you have to be fetched?"

Barbara grinned again. "Because I'm shy and you mightn't

let me come by myself and I'm a decent kid. I heard Peter say that."

I decided that Barbara was able to manage her own affairs.

Kate Beery enjoys what she calls "a nice chat" over the wall, and this morning she had a lot to say about Mrs. Crabtree's party and finally begged me to tell her what I was going to wear. I have genuinely no idea at all and said so, but she didn't believe me and said, with a very knowing wink, "Want to surprise us all, I suppose. Well, I shan't tell you neither."

She also said that she did wish Oliver could go, even for a little while. For a moment, stupidly, I couldn't think whom she meant—but she was, of course, speaking of O. Beery. She said that, even with everyone up at the Hall, he can't and won't shut the pub. "Besides," she added sadly, "he won't go outside of the house never; I've tried but he's that obstinate . . ."

I waited anxiously for more but, before she could explain, Fanny flapped squawking up on to the wall and Kate was off at once, shaking her apron at the little grey hen and shouting, "Shoo! Shoo!"

The evening before the party, I went down with Lucy, H. Potter's sister Florence, the vicar's wife (domineering but efficient) and Mrs. Lacey, to decorate the room. Mrs. Crabtree had ordered a mass of flowers, and with them we hid the bare front of the platform and filled huge pots to stand at its edge. The bleak, varnished walls and plain, dreary windows were partly covered by decorations, and altogether the effect was very gay. Barbara blew up quantities of balloons and looked pale green when she had finished. I asked Lucy how her grannie was getting on and she reported that the old woman was in fine fettle and had bought herself a complete new outfit for the occasion.

New Year's Eve was wonderful and I shall always remember it. The party began at 7 p.m. and from three o'clock onwards the village was deserted, for everyone was indoors getting themselves ready—except Jim and Barbara who were absorbed in conjuring affairs all day and had to be driven upstairs to change at six-thirty.

It was in fact only just after seven when we arrived at the hall, and I was rather disturbed to find the place less than half full and the people who were there were standing about uncomfortably awkward and shy. I began to wonder what could be done, and then the vicar's wife took action. Entirely against the decision of the committee, she produced from somewhere one strong, short drink all round, and the effect, naturally, was almost instantaneous. The people in the hall began to laugh and talk and, as soon as the news filtered outside, the men and boys who had been hanging about in the dark crowded eagerly through the doors to get their share.

Then Mrs. Crabtree arrived with Lucy and Tom. She was dressed in black taffeta, with a scarlet and green silk, fringed shawl, the usual big cameo brooch (enclosing a lock of which husband's hair?), and a double chain of jet beads. She looked exactly right and seemed very pleased with herself.

Mrs. Root swept into the room, magnificent in blue satin, her hair (which we had all seen in curlers for several days) screwed into tight and even waves, and her old throat concealed by several rows of steely pearls.

H. Potter wore his old naval uniform. The coat was tight and he moved carefully in it—but he looked very smart, and his medals shone and clinked impressively as he stumped about the room, his wooden leg tapping on the floor.

Miss Phyllis Brown wore a kind of dressing-gown robe of deep purple, embroidered in pale blue wool. She also wore sandals and amber beads and her hair was swathed in blue net.

Most of the women had, of course, had "perms", and their hair was either standing out in a fuzz or bunched in tight curls. Our Bessy wore scarlet, very tight across the behind as usual, and all the young girls' frocks were gay and pretty. The men were self-conscious and seemed different, as they always do, in their best blue suits. The older ones had their hair well flattened and greased and often sticking up at the back, and most of the lads looked a little half-witted under their crew cuts or floppy waves.

Nearly the whole village was there, except O. Beery and Mrs. Frobisher-Spink and old General Blade, and the vicar's wife bustled about efficiently and managed everything.

The vicar himself—seeming, as always, quite unreal with his smooth, silvery hair and innocent, child-like face—wandered from group to group, shaking hands and making inappropriate remarks to all and sundry.

The Halahans, Mrs. Davenant, Kate Beery, Florence Potter, Mrs. Lacey and myself were in charge of the three rows of trestle tables loaded with food; and when the band (in pale blue dinner jackets, red waistbands and ordinary trousers) struck up, it was a signal for everyone to shuffle into their places and get to work on the pies and cold ham and tongue and jellies and trifles and cakes and drinks.

There seemed to be dozens of children in the hall, but they were fairly subdued until they had finished eating and none of them was in arms—for the arrangement for baby-sitters from Upper Barley had worked very well.

Presently Mrs. Crabtree's health was drunk and, to my surprise, the squire made a short and excellent speech to which she replied, "Thank'ee, one and all," and then sat down again, smiling happily at the friendly shouts of applause.

By now some of the men had had a good deal of beer, the din was terrific and the hall like an oven: but at last the food was finished, the tables were pulled to the walls and the chairs set in rows. Then, comfortably full, the village settled down to be entertained.

A very vulgar comedian from some near-by town was very popular, and so was Miss Emily Brown at the piano. She played very well indeed and with gusto, too, so that her audience were soon roaring out chorus after chorus.

When at last they let her go, two young married women did a kind of fairy dance which was not too successful, and their turn was interrupted by a few sardonic whistles from the back.

The dance was done barefoot, and one performer had appalling bunions, on which Colonel Halahan commented to me in rather too loud a voice.

Jim's turn came late and was, in fact, the success of the evening. The children screamed with delighted anticipation when he appeared to break a raw egg into Mr. Davenant's hat, and they screamed with even greater joy when it was seen that by accident he had actually done so. But Mr. Davenant, who seemed once more to have withdrawn into himself and to be thinking of something else, was quite undisturbed by this mishap. Luckily it was Jim's only failure, although one could feel the collective anxiety as he seemed to smash John Carrick's gold watch to fragments, and one could also hear the sigh of relief when it was returned to its owner intact. Jim must have practised his juggling a great deal in the last few weeks, for he was excellent; and, in utter and wrapped silence, the audience watched him perform to Miss Emily's soft piano accompaniment. Barbara, long-legged and graceful, acted as his stooge (I think it is called), and really looked almost pretty.

When Jim's act was finished there were a few more songs, the vulgar comedian did another turn and finally the hall was cleared for dancing.

I found myself looking anxiously now and then at Mrs. Crabtree, as the dancers swirled by her—for she is well over eighty—but the noise and excitement seemed to buoy her up and she sat there, happily beating time to the music and laughing and joking with everyone.

She had insisted that the party should end at 11.45, so that we could hear the bells out of doors; and the band stopped and the lights were lowered exactly to time, in spite of shouts from the young men that it was much too early to stop. There were a few cheers for old Mrs. Crabtree and, by some of the merrier guests, for "the bloody old Pools"—and then, gradually, the crowd trickled out on to the Green and stood about in the mild moonlight, waiting for the New Year.

In a few minutes the bells crashed out and presently the

people began to sing. "Old Lang Syne" echoed among the thatched cottages, the bells clashed (rather erratically, for the ringers had done themselves well at the party), our little Christmas tree shone cheerfully from the shop window and, barely noticed, the youngest Lacey fell into the pond.

As he was pulled out, unharmed but howling, Mrs. Crabtree was driven grandly round the Green in the Halahans' car. Twice they circled the pond, followed by cheers and laughter, and at last she and Tom disappeared into her cottage.

Shouted "Good nights" and some spasmodic singing went on for a time; a bank of cloud obscured the moon and presently, with only a few lighted windows left to show for it, Mrs. Crabtree's Party was over.

5 January

New Year's Day dawned clear and still and from the moment when people first opened their doors the party was, of course, the talk of the village. Kate told me that she heard very few grumbles in the Red Lion and Jim's efforts were given a great deal of praise.

For myself, I was interested to know how it was that Miss Emily played so exactly right for him and, when I asked him, he admitted off-handedly that they had had several practices down at the hall. I wonder what Miss Phyllis thought of that and how, indeed, she ever allowed it.

Lucy came into the shop soon after lunch and I asked after her grandmother.

"Quite O.K.," she said, "and slept like a baby. She hasn't had no rheumatics either ever since she won her hundred . . . hasn't had time to think of 'em, I reckon."

"She looked very nice last night. So did you."

Lucy patted her hair and smiled. "Nothing like so posh as I mean to look when Joe gets home. I've fixed on a new hair style already."

"When is he due?"

"Dunno exactly—any time really, I suppose. But," she added dreamily, "I just can't wait."

A car pulled up outside, as she was speaking, and the door burst open. A stocky, brown-faced stranger in a rather dusty blue suit stood staring at Lucy and, in a moment, she was in his arms. When they had gone, arms entwined and heads bent together, I went next door to tell Mrs. Crabtree that Joe was back. She seemed very perky after her late night and, in fact, just as usual, except that she had left her teeth out.

"'Twas they raspberry pasties," she explained. "Hard as nuts I thought and fair worried me gums. But it *was* a good party, wasn't it?"

"Lovely," I agreed enthusiastically, and thanked her at the same time for the wonderful chocolates.

"*That* bit o' nothing? Why,"—she chuckled happily—"I felt that rich I could a' bought the shop for 'ee."

On New Year's Day the sun went down redly and that night there was a sharp frost. It was the beginning of a complete change in the weather, and for several days now it has been very cold with a bitter north wind and an occasional scatter of snow. Barbara longs for huge frozen drifts but Jim and I do not. Bumble, who adores the cold, forces me out each afternoon but I find these walks extremely unpleasant; though the contrast, when we return, of a warm house, a log fire and tea makes it almost worth while. Even if I have to go straight into the shop, it is delightfully warm and cosy there, for we have a Tortoise stove which glows comfortably night and day.

Yesterday, when I was feeding our chickens, Kate shouted over the wall to know if I have heard the latest about our Bessy's young sister?

I said that I hadn't in fact heard anything about her, old or new.

Kate gaped at me. "You *must* know she's in the family way, Mrs. Braid?"

Again I said "no", and added that I haven't seen the girl for ages. Actually, I am not at all sure of her identity among all the seventeen or eighteen-year-olds who trip about the village in perms and pearls and high heels.

"Well, I thought you was more observant," said Kate severely. "Vicar and her Grannie been at her all morning, putting her through the second degree or whatever they calls it—and they do say as she's named Tom Crabtree."

"Tom? Why, he's over sixty and very respectable surely. I just don't believe it."

"Well," said Kate, "sixty or no, Vicar'll make un wed." And she grinned a little maliciously, for she and Mrs. Crabtree don't get on.

After tea that evening Philip Halahan came in, but Jim, when he had given him a drink, went out abruptly. I felt annoyed with Jim for being unkind and intolerant, for, after all, it's no more Philip's fault than being born with a hare lip or a stammer.

He is a good deal older than I thought, more like twenty-eight, and he was childishly and extravagantly pleased when I praised his work; but, curiously, he seemed genuinely to have no urge to see it published. He said vaguely that he didn't think he'd live in England much longer and it wasn't worth while exerting himself. I do not believe that ordinary people ever write only to please themselves, so I felt rather puzzled, and then I wondered if perhaps his work is addressed to some single individual—and felt more sorry for him than ever.

The next morning, I asked Bessy about her sister, Dawn, and, of course, the rumour about Tom Crabtree is completely untrue. In fact it is a good-looking young nephew of H. Potter's (the one who brought us the holly before Christmas) who is to blame, and they are to be married as soon as the banns are called. Bessy said that both parties were quite pleased and not at all abashed.

After I had had all this out with Bessy, I returned to the shop to find that Barbara, trying to be helpful, had filled a can of paraffin for somebody, forgotten to wash her hands afterwards and then plunged her fingers into a six-pound jar of boiled sweets in order to weigh out two ounces. The whole jar of sweets was, of course, spoilt. I spoke more sharply to Barbara than I really meant and she retired to her bedroom for the rest of the morning. When I went up to fetch her for lunch, expecting either sulks or red-eyed unhappiness, I found her lying comfortably on the floor, elbows on a clean pillow dragged from her bed, and absorbed in *Treasure Island*. The trivial accident with the paraffin had clearly, and sensibly, been put aside as unimportant.

Yesterday I was dragged to the Women's Institute monthly meeting by Mrs. Lacey, who told me firmly that I should never get to know the whole village properly unless I join in everything. I suppose she is right, although one of the charms of our job is that already (and we have been here only three months) we know every man, woman and child by name and many of them very well indeed.

The lecture at the meeting was on "Planning Your Holiday Abroad". It was quite interesting but hardly suitable for the wives of farm labourers who never leave the village for a holiday, never even see the English seaside, unless taken on some outing, and whose men spend their annual fortnight either gardening or sitting about on the wooden benches which line the further side of the green.

Toward the end of the "talk" I had noticed old Mrs. Root sleeping peacefully, and envied her abandon, but presently her mouth opened and a raucous snore coincided with the lecturer's bright, rhetorical question, "Now, wasn't that a *wonderful* holiday?" I felt embarrassed for both parties but lecturers must be used to this kind of thing and certainly this one did not seem put out.

The Social Half Hour was organised by Miss Phyllis Brown.

The cottage women really hate to stir from their chairs and like just to sit and be entertained—or, if they must move, to engage in some kind of childish romp. Miss Brown, however, had clearly no intention of pandering to these obvious preferences and had arranged a complicated paper game.

"Now," she commanded, as the members stood round her in an unwilling circle, "each of these pieces of paper represents a title of a book and you must all wear one. . . ." and she went on fully to explain the game which, in fact, hardly anybody understood. Only a few ever look at a real book—which in fact is the name they apply to the weekly illustrated women's magazines they all delight in—and certainly know no single author by name. Apart from this slight difficulty, most people had left their spectacles at home and couldn't read the bits of paper anyway.

As usual, I felt both irritated by and sorry for Miss P. Brown. She is a deplorable type and I keep feeling that I am overdrawing her, but truly I am not.

The game never really started but it didn't matter, for the company drifted back to their chairs and settled down to enjoy a cosy gossip about interesting village affairs, a gossip which was hardly at all interrupted by the tea and buns which were brought round by the vicar's wife and her helpers.

"They're hopeless," she said crossly when, later, she dropped heavily into a chair beside me. "No co-operation, no interest in anything. The committee might just as well not exist—Miss Brown and I are left to do everything."

"But you organise things so well," I said tactfully and truthfully. "I mean, look at Mrs. Crabtree's party."

The vicar's wife gave me a quick glance which seemed to indicate a recognition that perhaps, after all, I had some glimmering of sense in me. "I like organising," she said honestly, "and I detest muddle. If I didn't keep at them, the village people would just go on, day after day, doing nothing— no W.I., no sewing class, no basketry, no Girl Guides, no Shakespeare reading——"

"I didn't know there *was* a Shakespeare reading."

"That's not the point—there isn't now. We tried it on

Friday evenings last winter and there was no support—no support at all."

"Well," I said mildly, "I suppose they're tired at the end of a long day—I know I am. And probably they don't like to leave their husbands—and then, of course, there's the 'telly'."

"Telly!" This is not a word one can spit, but if she could have spat it the vicar's wife would have done so. "If I had my way, television would have been nipped in the bud and forbidden by law. It's the ruining of family life, it's . . ."

Lucky, at this moment little Mrs. Lacey came up and asked if she could have a word about the new surplices which really some of the boys couldn't manage without any longer; and I was left alone—but not before the vicar's wife had looked scornfully at me and said, as she turned away, "I suppose *you* approve of the contraption, Mrs. Braid—but then, of course, you're not really a country person, are you?"

She could hardly have said anything which I should have found more annoying and insulting and, although I do partly agree with her about television, I immediately thought of and longed to proclaim the most telling arguments in its defence.

On my way home through the bitter cold wind I met Lucy and Joe, arm in arm and looking absurdly happy. Joe told me that he has "been taken on at the farm O.K. and starts work Monday". This is not the time of year when extra hands are wanted, so it must be an act of kindness on John Carrick's part.

There was a dance at the village hall last night for which there was the usual crowd, although one would have supposed that most of the village pockets were empty after everyone's Christmas spending. I was up late, and soon after midnight, when the shouting and singing on the green had died away, there was a ring and a knock at our front door.

I imagined, naturally, that someone was ill and that I should be asked to telephone for help—but the emergency was of quite another kind. On our doorstep stood one of the village bad characters, a great barrel of a man with a mop of thick black hair, who towered over me as he stood blinking in the light from the hall.

He is a good workman, when he feels inclined to work at all, and when the mood is on him he is usually to be found up at Amos's forge. At other times he is mostly in the Red Lion.

Now, I asked him briskly if anything was wrong and, as he leant forward and pushed his face down close to mine, it was evident that he was pleasantly drunk.

Speaking with slow deliberation and very politely, he said, "I wonder . . . I wonder, missus, if you could tell me something."

"If I can."

"Would you mind—would you oblige me, mam, and tell me the way back to Lower Barley from here?"

He could not very well have been more in the middle of it—but I didn't *say* anything (as Kate would have it) nor did I laugh. He had probably turned away from the hall after the dance, lost himself completely and seen my light. How sensible of him to come and ask his way.

"Turn left out of the gate, Smith, and the third cottage you come to past the Red Lion is yours. Mind the pond, won't you?"

He took off his cap, made an attempt at a bow—but his great belly was in the way—and replaced the cap with care.

"Thank you, missus," he said solemnly, "thank you kindly. You done me a favour. It's dark, you know, and I lost. . . ." He looked round anxiously for whatever he had mislaid and then pulled himself up. "I lost me way," he ended with dignity.

Very unsteadily he walked to the gate and disappeared into the night—leaving me giggling weakly. But next morning Jim was annoyed and said that it mightn't have been funny at all and I ought to have called him before opening the door.

There was a scatter of snow again in the night but it was still bitterly cold next day, and the people who were forced out of doors to do their shopping arrived pinched and blue in the face and grumbling through their heavy scarves at the vile north wind.

Old Mr. Farrer, who farmed here for many years and had retired to a bungalow in Upper Barley, died last night and there was a great deal of talk and reminiscence about him in the shop all day. He was evidently a hard man but a good farmer, and sold out to the Carricks only because of ill health. The old people remember him with a kind of respectful affection and the younger ones, who were children in his time, tell me how they feared his stick, when they were after his apples, and spent the pennies which he was always giving them for sweets.

There have been hard frosts for the last two nights, the ground is like iron, covered with about two inches of snow, and the roads are treacherous and slippery where they have been worn thin by the tractors taking hay and mangolds to the stock in outlying yards. I am thankful that we had a load of logs delivered before Christmas and that Jim has lagged all the exposed pipes with sacking and straw.

He is so thin that he feels the cold dreadfully; but he seems well, in spite of it, and is usually very cheerful. I hoped that this kind of life would suit him and it certainly has. Everyone seems to like him, and although the village is so small that townspeople would imagine life here to be unbelievably dull, so much in fact happens and there is so much to do that we are both taken completely out of ourselves.

Barbara spends most of her day skating with the Davenant party on the lake in the park, and I have been a little worried in case she is inflicting herself on them too much; but Mrs. Davenant came in this morning to thank me for letting her go there. She seemed perfectly sincere, so I was a good deal relieved.

Two or three days ago I promised to visit little Mrs. Lacey's cottage and see their Christmas tree before it is too late, and this afternoon Bumble and I walked over there. The cottage is tiny and the living room seemed to be bursting with Boots and Laceys, and the tree on a table in the corner was almost hidden by children as well as by tinsel and decorations.

I consider that I am fairly hard working, but how Mrs. Lacey manages I cannot think. She has no "mod-con" of any kind, except a cold water tap over a shallow stone sink, and seven of them to feed and clothe and wash for; but although the house couldn't possibly be tidy, it is very clean and the whole family looks rosy and happy and well-cared for.

Bumble greatly enjoyed his visit because the children pressed sweets and endearments on him, both of which he adores.

I said something to Mrs. Lacey about how well the vicar's wife had organised Mrs. Crabtree's party but, "I don't like her and I never shall," she said grimly . . . and I realised, as I have before, how absolutely immovable village women are about their likes and dislikes.

On my return to the shop I found Miss P. Brown and Mrs. Frobisher-Spink having a shouting match, with Jim, white and angry, standing in the background. I waited for a moment in the doorway, and as soon as she saw me Miss Brown snatched up her two snarling little dogs from under Bumble's kindly mop face and pushed her way out. "Old enough to be his mother," she shrieked, as a parting shot, and stamped off up the road—but if this remark referred to Jim and Mrs. F.-S. it was quite unjustified, for she can't possibly be more than fifty-five and probably less.

When Mrs. Frobisher-Spink, very red in the face, had also, without a word, left the shop, I asked Jim what it was all about but he wouldn't say and went off into the house.

Angry noise and shouting upset him more than anything and I felt I could kill those damned women if, between them, they had succeeded in putting him back into one of his black moods. But he appeared for tea quite as usual, and although I was extremely curious I thought it wiser not to question him. Instead, I stared out of the window and saw Bumble ominously eating grass.

It was Mr. Farrer's funeral this afternoon and, because I had to visit a cottage on the church side of the green, I saw and heard everything.

The village lay quiet and cold with snow on the roofs and hedgerows and clinging to the trees.

It was just two o'clock when we first looked out of the doorway and the roadman, "Badger" Rous, red-faced, stooping and long-coated, his mittened hands turning on the worn wood of his shovel, was standing listening to the crackling scrunch of the first car as it entered the village. Soon other cars followed and the front doors opened as the women, their heads covered with woollen scarves, came out to stand and watch. Most of the older men had the afternoon off, "out of respect," and presently they began to gather on the Green, standing in groups of two or three, stamping the ground and beating their hands against the cold. Soon the bleak, sad day was filled with a kind of subdued noise . . . the slow-moving cars, the scrunch of tyres, the low voices of the mourners.

Then presently, all the strangers seeped into the churchyard and the coffin, long and narrow, was borne carefully across the slippery road. The men of Lower Barley took off their caps and the women stared. There were no flowers.

Then all was quiet again and the men shuffled their feet and stood, hands in pockets, waiting.

"We won't see his sort again, I reckon," said the old shepherd loudly. He has been off work for some weeks and is himself a sick man, and as he spoke he seemed to shrink under his long, heavy coat.

"I remember fetching un nigh on forty year ago—from Swindon it were," said "Badger", tapping his shovel on the ice.

"What d'you mean, fetching?"

"What I says. I fetched un in the old Ford what blacksmith had as a taxi. 'Twas the first we ever had hereabouts and she'd only got two gears. If you puts your foot down too hard—or too soft, was it?—you mucked up the change. Did the whole thing wi' your foot like."

"Was that when he first come here?" asked a much younger man, big, dark and fresh faced. He wore a dark blue serge jacket with his old corduroys and gum-boots—presumably out of respect.

"Anybody'd know as you was a foreigner, Bill. Why the old man were born here and his dad before him. No, 'twas when he got married. I brought un and his bride back from Swindon station meself."

"What, the old lady in there?"

"Yes, of course—but she weren't old then. She were a smart young piece, I can tell 'ee."

Both sides of the road by the church were lined with cars, and one of the women began counting.

"Thirty-five," she exclaimed. "You'd never have thought it."

"I would that," contradicted the shepherd. "He were very respected."

"Aye."

The men moved about a little and went on idly talking. A few flakes of snow drifted over their heads, and the yellow grey sky hung heavily above the church tower.

Presently the bell began to toll—loud and clear in the still, quiet afternoon, and very melancholy.

And then, at last, the churchyard filled again and the farmers, in black ties and bowler hats, shuffled decorously along the slippery flagstoned path until, suddenly, they were no longer mourners but just a crowd of red-faced people standing about and anxious to get home—but not liking to seem in a hurry.

Gradually the cars drove off, the villagers melted into their houses and, the excitement over, only the widow's Daimler (hired with the hearse) lingered outside the gate. The driver stamped his feet, as he waited in the road, and turned his head eagerly at every sound which might herald his release.

At last the vicar, the farmer's widow and her two sons appeared. At last the little mourning party drove away and the vicar turned back into his church. At last, walking carefully on the beaten snow, he too made his way home.

Only "Badger", the roadman, was left to chip rhythmically at the ice. He stooped to his work and a few large snowflakes fell, like petals, on his shoulders. The village seemed desolate and forlorn—and, alone, the dead farmer lay under the January sky.

There was a heavy fall of snow the next night and drifts up to five foot are reported on the Badgerford road. The grocer at Upper Barley telephoned that he is running short of paraffin, but so are we, for the demand has trebled since the cold weather began and we can't help him. The snow ploughs are out and all the farm hands except the stockmen have been working with shovels and picks to clear the roads. Our bread comes from Upper Barley and our meat by travelling butcher's van, and I remember rather too vividly Mrs. Crabtree's account of the great snow when the village ran out of flour. At least, in those days, they were more self-supporting than we are now.

The hard weather has spared us Miss P. Brown's daily visits, but I learnt this morning from Nurse Ames that The Weavers has been almost cut off and Miss Phyllis has been in bed with 'flu for nearly a week. Feeling guilty about her, I sent Jim and Barbara down there after lunch with comforting goods from the shop and a bottle of O. Beery's port.

They left soon after two o'clock but didn't return until nearly seven, long after I had shut the shop. I had managed to put an extra nice tea ready for them, which, of course, was wasted, and by half-past six I had begun to fuss about Jim's leg. So when at last they did return, I was peevish and irritable. I felt very sorry though afterwards—because I think it is a horrible thing to come home to a crochety welcome.

Barbara said that Miss Emily gave them "a smashing tea and Uncle Jim mended a stool for her and then we played cards. We really stayed so long," she added naïvely, "because we thought it seemed so dull for her alone, with that old bag in bed upstairs."

I opened my mouth to reject the expression "old bag" but, thinking that I had been disagreeable enough already, let it go.

The thaw has come greatly to my delight—but to Barbara's annoyance, for she goes back to school in two days' time and now there will be no more skating. Our Bessy has been helping very efficiently with getting ready Barbara's school clothes, for I have been so busy in the shop that it is hard to find time to get everything done. Our Bessy, incidentally, has seemed rather subdued lately and I am not quite sure—and hardly like to ask her—but am afraid that it is husband trouble of some kind.

A stranger with a very familiar face hobbled into the shop this morning, and only when he demanded his usual tobacco did I realise that it was H. Potter, wearing an auburn wig. I was told afterwards that he always wears it in hard weather but I found the effect startling and somehow rather gruesome.

Barbara went off in pretty good fettle and only a few tears— but it seems quiet and strange without her here. Jim took her as far as Swindon and said that, as usual, as soon as she met some of her friends she seemed to slip at once into another world.

When she had gone, I took the opportunity, as it was our half day, to go over to "Weavers" myself, for we have heard nothing more of Miss P. Brown and I felt that I ought at least to enquire after her. The snow had nearly disappeared but the roads were wet and messy and I had to walk there and back in gum-boots, which was extremely tiring.

When I arrived I found Miss Phyllis draped in shawls, veils and scarves and laid out on a sofa in front of a roaring fire. As I came in she looked hopefully past me, but when she realised that I had come without Jim my visit clearly lacked interest. She spent most of the time grumbling because her sister wouldn't allow any yapping little dogs in her bedroom, and I thought sympathetically that poor Miss Emily must have been having a pretty thin time.

Miss Phyllis was evidently nearly well and so I refused tea, and as I got up to leave offered to lend her some books to ease her convalescence. But, "Books are no good to me, Mrs. Braid," she said firmly, "I like to live my life, not to read about it."

Nonplussed by this sweeping condemnation of all literature, I said "Goodbye", and Miss Phyllis languidly saw me to the door. However, she was quickly stirred to life by an unfortunate uproar outside, due to Bumble's understandably mistaking one of the toy dogs for a rat. Bumble would not hurt the proverbial fly, nor a rat either, but he had proudly penned the little creature behind a water butt and now looked engagingly at me for approval. Shrieks from the toy and from Miss Phyllis continued until I had pulled Bumble away, and calm had not been wholly restored when we finally left. As I walked home I thought sadly that this visit, which had been very well meant, had been very unrewarding and I looked gloomily at the little patches of snow which still lurked under the hedgerows and in the furrows. "Waiting for more," as the old people say, when snow hangs about, and I am afraid they are right, for it has turned very cold again.

Tonight I have a splitting headache and feel hot, cold and shivery. It seems very like the 'flu.

6 February

It *was* the 'flu and I have been laid up for about ten days. Our Bessy and kind, efficient Nurse Ames looked after me, the former quite angelic and in and out of the house all day. Moreover she won't take an extra penny for all the extra hours she put in, which rather worries me—but I am still too frail to bother.

Luckily Jim did not catch it and Lucy Rous came in every day and helped him in the shop. He said tactlessly, when I first tottered downstairs, that they find they can get on just as well without me and I was so weak that I burst into tears. Jim seemed to think I was mad.

The Halahans have been so kind and, in spite of the bitter cold weather, Eleanor Halahan has been in every day to see me; and yesterday Mrs. Davenant brought tulips and daffodils, which were beautiful and gave me the greatest pleasure.

During the last day or so, while still penned indoors, I have had time and inclination to study the newspapers instead of just skimming the headlines as I usually do; but it doesn't seem to make much difference, for the world seems, as always, to be in a state of constant alarm and confusion, with everybody going nowhere faster and faster and a few intelligent people finding out by laborious scientific processes obvious truths known to country people for generations.

Friends in London write that they think we are mad to bury ourselves in a remote village like this—but we consider that it is themselves who are in fact buried. I feel thankful for our full and satisfying life and thankful too to be nearly well, for last week I could very contentedly have died.

On reflection, I realise that the above indicates a complete disregard for world affairs as sweeping as Miss P. Brown's wholesale indifference to literature—and I feel rather abashed.

Incidentally, it was my birthday today and dear Jim, although he has had so much to do with me away, has managed to finish and give me a very charming rosewood bookcase which he had secretly been making for some time. I also had a loving letter from Barbara and another very welcome cheque from my Mama. I wish, though, that the latter didn't live in South Africa, for there are times, even at my age, when I long for her support and consolation. I do hope that Barbara will feel like this about me in years to come.

I started work in the shop this morning and felt quite myself again. All our customers were kind and friendly and sympathetic, and Jim had the grace to admit that he was glad to have me back; although he scraped the gilt off the gingerbread by adding, "Thank God, I can get out sometimes now."

The snow and ice returned the day I "took bad", as Mrs. Root expressed it, and continued until last night; but now it is thawing fast and the blacksmith is kept on the run staunching burst pipes. Ours are intact and unfrozen and so are those in all the old cottages—but people in the jerry-built council houses, who pay three times as much rent have suffered badly.

I realised the other day that we have not heard anything of Mrs. Frobisher-Spink for some time, and when I questioned our Bessy she reported that "the old girl's gone off on her winter junket, like she always does"—meaning that she is in the South of France. I hope she finds someone there more worthy of her than Jim, who told me that he had quite enough to do, when I was ill, in keeping Miss P. Brown on the far side of the shop counter.

Upper Barley's Christmas pantomime was performed in the hall here last night. I detest even professional pantomime, and rather meanly said that I didn't feel well enough to go out at night. Jim never had any intention of going and made no excuses. In fact, the show ("Puss in Boots") was a great success —although Puss's tail caught fire on the footlights. I was told that Mrs. Root, who was helping with the refreshments, acted promptly and saved the situation by throwing a jug of coffee over his tail; but Puss seemed unreasonably annoyed and left the stage in a dudgeon.

Jim says that we *must* get rid of the Post Office. Every week-end he wastes hours over the accounts and they never come right, the pay is tiny and the bother just not worth it; but I can think of no one in Lower Barley who would take it on, and the village definitely needs somewhere to buy stamps and Pools postal orders. Jim said that that's all very well and why can't they walk to Upper Barley—but he had heard that there is some kind of simplified Post Office in many small villages, where you don't take telegrams or pay pensions and where the accounts are childishly easy—so if we can change to that kind of Office, he'll keep on with the tiresome job.

Mrs. Frobisher-Spink is back, and since her return wild and fascinating rumours have trickled into the shop, varying from "They do say as she's married a foreigner, a Count or summat, wi' a huge castle and thousands of acres" to the more likely "She's brought one o' they giggly boys back with her".

Since the Rous housemaid got the sack and old Grannie Rous had it out with Mrs. Frobisher-Spink, no one from the village works for her; so all our speculations are based on very roundabout news, conveyed by one of the postmen who gets it from his married sister in Upper Barley where Mrs. Frobisher-Spink's chauffeur lodges. Everyone is agog for a sight of the "foreigner" and, gigolo or not, I must confess that so am I.

Our Bessy's young sister, Dawn, is to be married on Saturday, "But," says Bessy, "just quiet like, with only Grannie and Grand-dad and me and Harold's folks, seeing as how things are."

Since the affair of Dawn and H. Potter's nephew came to my ears, I have often noticed her in the village, and it is true that things certainly "are". I should say there will hardly be time for the honeymoon.

It seems strange that the villagers, who rarely go to church at ordinary times, still count on it for the major crises of their lives. Every child is baptised, every wedding is held there and every funeral attended with curious respect. None of them, even in Dawn's shape, would think of being married in a register office.

Incidentally, I was amazed at our Bessy's reference to "Grand-dad", for I had firmly believed all this time that Grannie Rous was a widow, and indeed I have never seen or heard of her husband before now.

When I asked Mrs. Crabtree for an explanation, she smiled a little sourly. "'Tis me only brother you're speaking of," she said, "and why you ain't heard of him 'tis because he don't live here—that's why. A little bit of a chap he is, like me, but he give Kathie (Grannie Rous, I suppose) fourteen kids and then got sick of it and cleared off. . . . He's a master carpenter," she went on, proudly, "and he's always done nicely and never kept Kathie short, never."

"But Bessy said he'd be at the wedding."

"Aye—he always is. Soon as one o' his folks gets wed he's over like clockwork wi' a fine china cabinet or summat like that, made wi' his own hands, and a frock coat and all. But he won't stay. He just pats Kathie on the shoulder, has a drink round wi' the family and directly the happy pair's away, so's he."

"How long ago did he leave her then?"

Mrs. Crabtree considered the matter and counted slowly on her fingers. "Fifteen year ago, I reckon, or thereabouts. But, mind you," she added, "there ain't no other woman, nor ever has been. Kathie wouldn't stand for that. It's just he found it all a bit too much—noisy like, I dare say—for he's a quiet little lad."

The "quiet little lad" can't be far off seventy and I look forward to seeing him.

Our Bessy's appearance has been going to pieces lately—no pearls, no perm, no letter-box lipstick. This, in my eyes, is a great improvement, but her housework has suffered, too, and I have felt sure that it all indicated something wrong at home.

At last, I ventured to ask her and she confessed at once that it *was* husband trouble—but not of the kind I had imagined.

It seemed that Bert Hinton (I never think of our Bessy as Mrs. Hinton—but so she is) is sick of his job, longs to be his own master and wants to emigrate to Australia. He is only twenty-five, but is crazy to set up on his own somehow and "there don't seem no chance in this country—least of all in Barley". I don't blame him for wanting to do something more with his life than he is doing at present, for he has an absurdly well paid but footling job, shifting stores and washing out cloakrooms, in one of the near-by Government "nursing homes" or depots.

"What does he want you to do then, Bessy?"

"Oh, just stay along of Grannie, while he goes traipsing off to the bottom of the world, like Joe used to, and I won't have it. Or else he wants me to pack up and us all to go and live in Australia. He says everyone makes good down there. But what happens if they don't? That's what I want to know."

"But what makes him think he could be his own master? He hasn't got a trade or any special training, has he?"

"Of course he hasn't. But we got an uncle out there and he's promised to give Bert a start and filled his head up wi' a lot of nonsense about making a fortune out of nothing."

"Would you like Australia, do you think?"

"Dunno—but I'd rather stay in Barley." Bessy began to sniff. "We always been so happy, Bert and me and the kids, and now —now we has rows every night and I'm sure he hates me 'cos I won't give in."

"Oh, no, Bessy, of course he doesn't. But why don't you give in—agree to emigrate, I mean. I know he must get good pay at this Government store place—but it's no real work for a young man with ambition, like Bert."

"How about Grannie then? I've always been the one to see to her. I tell you, it was winning that hundred pounds what unsettled him—that's all it is."

Once Bessy had begun to talk about her troubles I couldn't stop her, and for the next three mornings she followed me about, even into the shop, saying the same things over and over again. I feel that she will give way before long . . . and that, unfortunately, means that I shall have eventually to find another "daily".

The weather has turned very mild, and on Dawn's wedding day the rain poured down as, across the Green to the church, walked Dawn herself, pale and shapeless, Grannie Rous, un-smiling—and a very small stranger in a frock coat and a rather curly brimmed bowler hat, who must be the "little lad". The bridegroom and his relations, including H. Potter and Florence (in a long raincoat and a red feather toque), had already gone by and I was glad to see that the young man was not only good-looking but had a lively and intelligent expression.

Nothing of interest has happened during the last few days, except that I had a notice from Barbara's headmistress saying that she has got chicken-pox and seems to be enjoying it.

It has rained now daily for over a week and the village is almost afloat, with the pond edging up on to the road and the little stone bridges filled to the arches by the swollen stream. Our house is built on joists, supported by brick piles, and the space between the floorboards and the earth is now completely filled with water. Oddly, the house neither smells nor feels damp and the snow last month proved our roof to be sound; which is more than can be said for poor old General Blade's bungalow—Pixies' Playground. The pixies will have to learn to swim, for the garden, which was scooped out of a small hill at the back, is nothing but a lake and the roof tiles fit so badly that the general has had to erect a contraption of umbrellas and raincoats to form a kind of protective tent over his bed. The bungalow was put up by the Upper Barley builder with whom Lucy so nearly ran off, and I am now more glad than ever that she didn't count on him to build their future. Joe, I hear, has quite settled down and Lucy expects their first baby early in October.

Mrs. Frobisher-Spink has at last been seen in the village with her young man. He is indeed a "giggly", and I can't begin to imagine why she has brought him to a remote place like this. Surely such a creature can never be made to stay here—whatever the considerations.

The rain had cleared off as they walked down the road together, and a pale sun played over the young man's black, sleeked hair and his rather plump face (surely artificially tanned to that deep bronze) with its little pencilled moustache. He looked a big fellow, tall and, I should think, fairly broad under the widely padded shoulders/of his pearl grey, half-belted jacket. His legs were concealed by very wide loose trousers, a little darker than his coat, and he wore black suede shoes and a very fancy tie.

The village youths, who were leaning back against the fence of the Red Lion at the time, stared at him, fascinated, and there was a suggestion of a titter as he and Mrs. Frobisher-Spink went by.

She came into the shop with him to buy some razor blades, and I was sorry to see that he was both sulky and rude to her, while he was flashing his black eyes and white teeth at me— simply out of habit I suppose. Although I don't care for Mrs. Frobisher-Spink and think her an old fool, it is obvious that the poor woman is in for a bad time. At present, though, she goes about wearing a cat-who's-been-at-the-cream expression—and I feel sad that all this has to happen in Barley. As Jim said, when I told him about this disgusting young man, why couldn't she have stayed in France ?

Although I dislike going out to tea, I was forced this week to accept an invitation from Mrs. Davenant, since she has been so kind to me and to Barbara.

The day was soft and sunny with more than a hint of spring in it, and the aconites glowed golden under the trees that edge the Manor drive. When I came in sight of the old house I stood still for a moment and stared at it, for it is built of honey-coloured stone, mellowed by perhaps two hundred years of Wiltshire weather, and is quite unspoilt. It is not too big and it is set jewel-like in the middle of a small, green park; and in-doors it is as satisfying as from outside, for Mrs. Davenant has good taste and beautiful things on which to prove it.

I met her husband properly for the first time that afternoon, and found him pleasant but utterly withdrawn. He is a tall, thin, stooping man with charming manners, but I felt that although he talks to people quite amiably he doesn't consciously see them at all. Mrs. Davenant confirmed this afterwards and explained, half apologetically, that except for occasional rough shooting his interests are exclusively pre-historic. As she said this, I wondered how he ever came down to earth enough to marry her and give her five sons.

She could not, of course, resist asking if I had seen Mrs. Frobisher-Spink's gigolo, and remarked coldly that no one with the least self-respect would have brought him here. "It's a pity," she said, "that Mrs. Frobisher-Spink doesn't leave the village altogether and make her home in the South of France. It would be far more suitable to her."

I refused either to agree or to disagree and quickly changed the subject, saying that I hoped Barbara had not made herself too much at home at the Manor last holidays. Mrs. Davenant at once responded with real kindness, and although I tried to resist it I felt a surge of maternal pleasure when she described

Barbara as "a delightful child, with *such* good manners—and she'll be very pretty indeed one day".

Jim has become very friendly with Geoffrey Halahan, and he goes there one or two evenings a week and nearly always on Sundays. Eleanor comes to me here, more often than not, for I usually have a good many jobs on hand and we can talk as I do them.

She told me tonight that her husband is trying to interest Jim in his pet hobby-horse—the founding of a kind of country-house home for disabled ex-Service men who have some sort of creative ability (either artistic or practical) but who find it hard to compete with the general rough-and-tumble of ordinary life. I imagine that he and Eleanor want to establish something as a memorial to their son who was killed—and I suppose they must be pretty well off to be able even to think of it. Jim is going with them one day soon to look at Chalk Manor, a few miles away, which they believe is exactly what they need.

While she was here, Eleanor and I had a cosy gossip about Mrs. Frobisher-Spink—but a quite un-malicious one—and she ended by saying, "Poor thing, she's asking for trouble and I'm afraid she'll get it. You know, if only she had a decent husband at home to knock her about she'd be an extremely nice woman."

There is a rumour of foot-and-mouth disease at a farm only five miles the other side of Badgerford; but I do pray that there is no truth in it, for I have some experience, from childhood, of its horrors. Luckily the Ayrshire herd which grazed the park last autumn are moved to an off farm for the winter, but John Carrick has a wonderful Guernsey herd here of which the village is rightly proud.

Two days later, not only was the original rumour confirmed, but now there is a case on a small farm only three miles away, alongside the railway line. All cattle movement has been stopped and Evans, the head cowman, told me disappointedly that they had been getting a magnificent young bull ready for a sale and show next week. The sale is cancelled but I feel that the farm will be blessed indeed if nothing worse than this is in front of them.

Soon after Evans had gone I heard an appalling row going on in the road outside between John Carrick and Miss Phyllis Brown, who keeps goats as well as toy dogs and has this morning let the former stray on to his land. He certainly has got a temper, and she came into the shop grumbling at his rudeness; but it is simply criminal to allow beasts to wander at this time and, sympathising deeply with him, I am afraid I was very short with her.

7 March

March came in like a real lion, roaring and blustering so that our old house shook and the windows rattled and smoke belched from the sitting-room fireplace. In fact, things were actually blown off the shop counter as customers struggled with the door.

Myself, I hate wind, but it is just what the farm lands need to dry the surface after all last month's rain.

There are two racing stables in Upper Barley and several in the Downland village above us. Every morning the horses, walking sedately or dancing according to their mood and the weather, circle the village at least twice. The lads like to show off, and if the head lad is absent there is often a lot of spectacular skipping and kicking to impress any villagers, female in particular, who may be about. This morning, one of the lads from Upper Barley rather overdid it and a young chestnut, which he was encouraging to play up, put him neatly over her head and into the pond. The lad was unhurt but very wet and the filly quickly caught and calmed; but one or two of the older women, who are inclined to cower in doorways and clutch their children into safety as the horses go by, were naturally delighted.

The lads also like to buy sweets and cigarettes from the shop as they go through—and their charges, of course, expect sugar and biscuits. I like their doing this, for I love horses and love, too, their pretty looks in the pearly, misty morning sunshine.

Just before lunch today H. Potter brought in a dreadful rumour that they have foot-and-mouth at Upper Barley and the news swept through the village like the March wind. Later, though, the alarm was proved to be absolutely false.

Last night there was a darts match in the Red Lion. Jim was asked to play and he took me with him to watch. The pub, which I had never entered before, turned out to be a rather gloomy old place, with high rooms and small windows, and over all a layer of chipped dark brown paint; but the bar was well lighted and cheerfully noisy—and a considerable crowd of men and women laughed and jeered at or encouraged the players. For myself, I know nothing of darts and dislike both arithmetic and beer, so I did not greatly enjoy the evening.

I *did* discover though why O. Beery never ventures out of doors. Poor little man, he is more than wizened—his face is terribly shattered and disfigured (presumably in the 1914 war) and, even to the kindest eyes, really repulsive.

I said to Jim afterwards, "Why on earth didn't you tell me that O. Beery was like that?"

"Because you never asked me, I suppose," he answered annoyingly.

Poor Bumble is having a very dull time, for his walks are restricted to the roads because of foot-and-mouth, and often I go out and leave him at home. Today I found two primroses in the spinney and visited the sheep in the meadow beyond our orchard. They lamb late in this part of the country and in cosy pens built cunningly with straw bales. Sheltered from the wind, it was as warm as a summer's day and I stood for some time and talked to the shepherd and watched the young lambs, marvelling at their stiff, black legs, their tight-curled wool, hard, bunting little heads and loosely tied-on tails.

I did not realise until today that Miss P. Brown's little dogs are very good of their kind, that is to say, they are very valuable, for she has just sold one to the U.S.A. I was told that the price she got was two hundred guineas, but Mrs. Davenant confirmed that it was, in fact, fifty, which is still pretty good, and she also told me that Miss Brown shows the little creatures and also judges them all over the country.

A few days ago I asked Jim to put a match to the sitting-room fire before tea. He willingly did so but threw on about a pint of paraffin first. Flames immediately roared up the chimney, smoke and flames flew from the top and, in a few minutes, the chimney was well alight.

Our Bessy, who was in the shop at the time, remarked calmly that it was the best and cheapest way of cleaning a chimney; but soon a small crowd had collected outside, hoping that perhaps the house would catch fire and offering advice to prevent it. Jim said that the chimney was big and the house solidly built and there was no need to worry—so I didn't—but some well-meaning person, without asking, rang up the Badgerford fire brigade and presently the village was filled with a dramatic clanging, and a small engine, on which clung eight men and a lot of hose, came tearing up to our door.

Before I could open my mouth to protest, four of the men fell off the engine and, dragging hose after them, clattered into the shop; and Jim, with difficulty, managed to push them out again, explaining that the fire had started in the house and pointing to the black belching chimney. Six men immediately tore off indoors and, before anyone could stop them, rushed upstairs, trailing yards of hose-pipe as before. So eager were they to get to work that Jim had almost to snatch the hose away as he shouted that it was the SITTING-ROOM chimney.

This caused another stampede and, when at last they found

the offending chimney, they fairly got to work; and the amount of mess, soot, water and general dirt which they managed to spread over everything was a tribute to their enthusiasm if not to their skill.

When, after what seemed hours, they were satisfied that the place was not likely to be burnt to the ground, we expressed our gratitude, gave them cups of tea and eventually bundled them into the street.

Presently our Bessy came in to have a look at things and words failed her. "Law!" she gasped—and this more or less expressed my own feelings.

We spent most of the next day clearing up the mess and I saw to it that Jim did his share—chucking paraffin about, the silly ass!

When the place was more or less straight, I managed to snatch a brief walk. The wind was still high and the white clouds tearing across a pale blue sky, but the days are lengthening and I found the hedgerows hazed with tight brown buds—and in the distance I saw John Carrick drilling a field of oats.

These signs and sights of spring did me good, but back at the shop I felt very depressed, for everyone was talking about foot-and-mouth. It is much too near to be pleasant and it is dreadful to think of whole herds of cattle being destroyed. Two of the old men (who add to their pensions by doing casual jobs but drape themselves over the benches of the Green at other times) have been engaged for the horrid job of digging pits and burying the carcases at the farm near Badgerford, and they were standing in the shop door when I returned, reeking of disinfectant and entertaining an audience of women and children who listened with relish to a gruesome and disgusting account of their work.

I went indoors, feeling rather sick, and thought fearfully of the lovely Guernsey cattle which normally pass us twice a day (but are now confined to the yards) and of how, in summer, if they escape, they will graze the bright green meadows and stand knee deep in the stream, ears flicking, jaws just moving and their kind eyes placid and content. I thought too of the fifteen hundred gallon strain which it must have taken many years to build up and which is now in such peril.

Bill Evans, the head cowman, a very quiet and unassuming man, has recently become the centre of interest—but he says as little as possible, comes in for cigarettes, pays and goes. The other cowmen are Bill's son (a lad of twenty nicknamed "Toots") and two "foreigners"—that is to say that they are not natives of the village and have lived here only seven or eight years. They are all clean, quiet, pleasant young men who mind their own business and, except in the depth of winter, spend their spare time in their gardens.

The vicar's wife paid us a visit today and announced that she has decided to start a dramatic society in the village. Would Jim and I join? I said "Yes" for myself, with reservations, and that very likely Jim would help with lights and scenery and so on but I was sure he would have nothing to do with acting.

"But I need a man," exclaimed the vicar's wife, expressing herself unfortunately as usual, "I can't get on without one."

However, although I refused to commit Jim, who was out at the time, I promised that I would attend a meeting next week.

The vicar's wife then said didn't I think it best to aim high, begin as we mean to go on and start with scenes from Shakespeare. I was surprised that she didn't suggest a full-length Shakespeare play and have done with it, but only said mildly that I should have thought a simple one-act comedy would perhaps be easier to start with.

The vicar's wife, giving me a long and severe look, began to say something scalding in reply; but just in time she remembered that she wanted me to come to the meeting and so she just ignored my suggestion and departed with a brief and rather gracious "Goodbye".

Jim, on his return from I didn't know where, said he certainly wouldn't have any truck with this new venture. He also alleged, I think rightly, that dramatic societies are usually a seed bed of quarrels and jealousy; so we had much better keep out of this one. He then told me that he had been with the Halahans to see the place they mean to buy for their ex-Servicemen's home. From his description, it is a lovely house set in a small park, with a home farm of about a hundred acres. Since the house is too big for most people, it can be bought fairly cheaply, but it will cost a great deal to adapt and to run. Jim was very enthusiastic about the whole plan and this is certainly yet another sign of his recovery.

The shop was broken into last night, a window pane near the door was neatly knocked out, the lock forced and the bolt drawn. About a thousand cigarettes, some tinned stuff, butter, eggs, bacon and cheese are gone.

The thief or thieves must have worked very quietly, for Bumble never stirred—though in fact he and I sleep at the far side of the house.

The news spread round the village within minutes of its discovery and people crowded into the shop immediately it opened—but, with no ill-will towards us, they were clearly disappointed that our loss is so slight.

"We 'eard the shop were cleared right out from roof to floor," said Kate—and, "They said as your dog surprised them and were shot dead, poor beast," stated Florence Potter.

And then Mrs. Root, scowling at her neighbour (the one to whom she never speaks), who is also the mother of one of our village bad characters, muttered darkly, "Well, 'ee won't have to look far, missus. And I ain't at all surprised, I can tell 'ee."

The fact that the said bad character ("Lofty" Cobbett) was discovered later to have spent the last two nights at Weston-super-Mare (having borrowed some of the blacksmith's Pools winnings) with a barmaid from the Crown at Upper Barley, in no way altered her opinion—and whatever alibi "Lofty" produced would have no effect whatever.

"I've heard about they alibis," she said contemptuously, "but there's only one hereabouts as'd act that way. I knows—for I've lived in Barley nigh on sixty years. 'Tis that young Cobbett for certain."

All the same, I feel sure that the culprit is not anyone local.

We share our policeman, as well as our parson, with Upper Barley, and during the morning he arrived on his bicycle. Far from being the conventional rustic type—red-faced, slow and head scratching—he is a little weasel of a man and he was scarcely inside the door before he started flicking over the pages of his notebook, asking questions, shaking his patent pen and scribbling down information received and, no doubt, conclusions come to. I suspect that he has not been promoted before now to more wicked areas than ours because he is so much in a hurry that he hardly has time to listen and certainly not to think.

No sooner had he inspected the door, the window and the shelves on which the stolen goods previously lay, asked us about thirty-five questions and dropped his pen into a seven-pound jar of marmalade on which I was about to stick a new top, than he was buttoning his notebook into his pocket, grabbing his bicycle and, with a muttered, "It's young Cobbett—no doubt about that," pedalling down the street at, as Jim says, a rate of knots.

I felt rather breathless after all this and quite incapable of dealing with Mrs. Frobisher-Spink's young man who slid through the half-open door and said he wanted to send a telegram. I tried to make him understand that this is no longer a telegraph office and asked why he couldn't telephone his message from the house. He didn't answer, but instead I received a knowing wink and a playful pinch on the upper arm which would certainly have been applied elsewhere had the counter not been between us.

"It is private—you see. Can you not send it, just to please, if I ask you with all my heart?"

I had only just uttered an uncompromising "No", when the door was flung wide to admit Mrs. Frobisher-Spink herself.

"Ramon, my *dear*," she cried excitedly and then, to my joy, she poured over him, in French, a mixture of recriminations and endearments which she obviously believed I should not understand. Evidently this was the continuation of a row which had been going on for days, and it was only when the recriminations became too physically intimate that I felt compelled to interrupt.

I remarked mildly in French that I understand the language pretty well and Mrs. Frobisher-Spink stopped short, stared at me and turned a deep red. "Why didn't you *say* so?" she asked crossly and unfairly and, grabbing her gigolo by the arm, she quickly steered him into the street.

When they had gone I wondered idly what telegram he had wanted to send and suppose that he is already trying tactfully to escape.

Rumours of foot-and-mouth nearer and nearer at hand keep spreading through the village; but nothing has been confirmed very lately and the situation looks a little better. We are not out of the wood though, by any means.

Our burglary has set the village by the ears, for Mrs. Root's accusations about "Lofty" Cobbett have been repeated, and not only do she and Mrs. Cobbett not speak but they are now saying things about each other which can surely never be forgotten. Mrs. Root's character is described in uncomplimentary detail all down the village street and her husband doesn't escape either, for Mrs. Cobbett even followed him into the Red Lion, shouting that a jailbird the likes of him ought to know better than to let his old woman blacken an innocent boy.

There is some very faint reason for this last insult, for it seems that, when he was only thirteen, poor Root, who is now nearly seventy, was put on probation for stealing a bicycle. On the other hand, Mrs. Cobbett's "innocent boy" has been in trouble many times and spent last Christmas in jail for pinching a roll of cloth from a stall in Badgerford market. The Root supporters make the most of this and, as Mrs. Crabtree said, " 'Tis a proper do and no mistake. But," she added calmly, " 'tis only a nine days' wonder."

Within a couple of days, our window and door were mended, poor "Lofty's" alibi proved and the general excitement died down; for it was learnt that the burglars were in fact two out-of-work youths walking from London to Bristol. Ours was their second "breaking and entering", and now they have been picked up while making a third attempt somewhere near Bridgwater.

Miss P. Brown has taken to fetching her newspaper every day at 12.50, her idea being to catch Jim alone while I am in the house preparing lunch. It was a good idea but I can't think why she persists, because I know he is curt with her to the point of rudeness. She has also taken lately to wearing a very heavy scent and probably likes to think that "she leaves her fragrance behind her". She certainly does, and I suffer doubly, for as soon as she's gone Jim lights his foulest-smelling pipe and, when we reopen the shop after lunch, it smells like a cross between one of those cheap dress shops in Shaftesbury Avenue and a second-class smoking carriage. It usually takes quite half an hour with the door open to dispel this delightful aroma, and if the vicar's wife comes in before the air is clear she sniffs in a pained way and looks slightly disgusted and very reproachful —though, like Kate, she doesn't actually *say* anything.

I should have forgotten the dramatic society meeting entirely, for we have been exceptionally busy in the shop this week, if the vicar's wife hadn't peeped round the door at noon and whispered over our customers' heads, "Tonight!"

Jim wouldn't go to the meeting but said that I could tell them he would help with the lighting, etc., if it ever comes to a production—which he doubts.

It was a coldish evening and the sixteen people who composed the meeting huddled on hard chairs round the Tortoise stove which had not been lighted in time and so gave out only a mild, smoky and rather sad heat.

Only four men were present, two of them pressed by the vicar's wife and two brought by girls they are walking out with.

Almost at once an argument began about the type of play to be chosen, and I was surprised to see our masterful vicar's wife quickly defeated by little Mrs. Lacey, who said firmly, "It's no good our doing that highbrow stuff. Even if we could do it, the audience won't like it. They want something to make them laugh."

"But it's well known," retorted the vicar's wife grandly, "that comedy and farce are by *far* the most difficult things to do well."

"Can't help that," said Mrs. Lacey. "A good laugh's what they want and I shan't stand for anything else."

There were murmurs of approval, not necessarily because the rest of the meeting agreed with Mrs. Lacey (probably they had been only half listening anyhow) but because they like her and the vicar's wife is no favourite.

It looked as if there might be a deadlock—but fortunately Eleanor Halahan announced that she had brought copies of a one-act comedy specially written by a friend of hers for village actors—and suggested that we should read it aloud there and then. This was agreed to and a very good little play it turned out to be.

Parts were allotted and it was decided to make the play the evening entertainment for Barley's Glory—a kind of grand feast day which has been held here on the last Saturday in June for something like three hundred years. Unfortunately there are only nine parts for twelve would-be actors, so that trouble is already on the brew. Also there is only one child's part, for which there is sure to be a strong and bitter competition.

I agreed to act as prompter and maker-upper only; for, although I adore acting, I thought it wiser, in our position, to keep slightly aloof. I agree with Jim, who says it won't do for us to get involved in village upsets—which, incidentally, is only too easy—and we did very well to keep clear of the Root-

Cobbett affair after our burglary. Indeed, you have to be extremely careful—because if you refuse to take sides with either party you are apt to find yourself unpopular with both.

Last Sunday was a wonderful day, warm and sunny, with a high, blown sky and the hedgerows misty with buds and the feel of Spring everywhere.

Jim took Bumble walking on the main road and I decided to wander about the lanes and footpaths as yet unexplored. I picked a great bunch of earthy-smelling primroses in the spinney below John Carrick's farm, and as I approached its gates I met him returning home in his muddy, chalk-spattered jeep. He smiled as he passed and splashed his wheels through the pools of disinfectant lying just inside the yard; and then, to my surprise, he jumped down and came outside to talk.

"Thanks for keeping your sheepdog off the fields, Mrs. Braid. I wish everyone was as careful."

"Well," I said, "I'm a farmer's daughter and I remember, when I was about fourteen, we went through just what you're going through now."

"What happened?"

"Nothing. The nearest case was only a mile away—but we were all right. But my father nearly went crazy with worry."

"I'm not surprised. What sort of cattle?"

"Pedigree Jerseys," and I couldn't help adding, "rather a wonderful herd as a matter of fact."

An interested expression crossed his face. "Of course," he said, "your brother's name. The famous Betterton herd?"

"How do you know about it?"

"My grandmother was a Jersey enthusiast. She had a small herd of her own before we came here and we always kept a few about the place until she died."

"Much better than your coarse, common old Guernseys," I said superiorly, hoping to make him laugh.

He gave a half smile. "Come and have a look at them," he

said—and then his voice hardened and he added grimly, "while there's still time."

He took a spare pair of gum-boots out of the jeep and offered them: "A bit big for you," he said and smiled again, for I am a very small woman, and as I stood in his huge boots splashing them with disinfectant, I must have looked funny.

It was milking time when we walked into the long shed, the engine in the distance was humming and the machines ticking gently as they sucked the rich yellow milk into the covered buckets. I thought, as I always do when I see this contraption of rubber tubes hanging on to the cows' teats, how much pleasanter was the old hand milking and how much better too for the beasts themselves. Then one used to see an experienced man, his three-legged stool tipped forward and his head pressed against the warm, smooth flank, his hands sensitive to the least hardness in the quarter, which might herald trouble—and one knew that the last drop of milk would be safely drained away. The milking machine may be clean and quick—but it is a machine with a machine's limitations.

I said as much to John Carrick as we stood behind an old, old cow with deeply ringed horns. "She's never taken to it," he said, "and I've got three others the same; but even you admit it's quicker and cleaner, and the real point is that there aren't the number of good hand-milkers about that there used to be."

I looked down the double row of lovely cattle with their sleek coats and square, silky bags; I sniffed with pleasure the familiar sweet smell of cows and hay and cool, washed cement floors; and I heard with pleasure the clang of buckets and the ping of milk into the pail as a lad set to work on the old matron we had been petting.

Shafts of golden sunlight from the skylights burnished the beasts' golden coats and mellowed the sweet, green hay in the troughs. In spite of the machines, the shed was quiet and orderly, the cows placidly munching, and only now and then the chains round their necks clashed gently as one of them tossed her head or fidgeted.

"You don't have metal yokes, I see?"

"No," said Carrick. "Don't like them and never have. We've always tied up with chains here."

When I had admired the milking cows, he took me to see the calves and young heifers, and then the two great bulls who scraped the ground and glared at me suspiciously; but the bulls had fine big pens, their halters fixed to a running cable, and they looked well and contented.

"They're taken out every day except Sundays," said Carrick, and I could see how keen he was about his farm and his stock; for as we walked round he seemed a different person to the dour character sometimes seen in the village, and his face was warm and eager.

I liked him very much and felt sorry for his empty, lonely house and wished that perhaps he and Jim would presently make friends. As he stopped to speak to one of his men, I took a good look at him and decided that although his hair was greying at the sides and his thin face deeply lined, he could only be in his forties. He was not, I thought, in the least good-looking, but his mouth was sensitive and kind and there was a hint of humour in the blue eyes under the thick black brows.

Back in the yard, I thanked him and said that I must get back.

"Come again," he said warmly, and shook my hand. "You're probably the only person hereabouts who has the smallest idea of what we're going through—except my men of course. They're grand chaps, all of them. They don't say a word, but they're all sick with worry."

"And so must you be. Well, good luck—and I pray it'll be all right."

I splashed my shoes again and returned the boots he had lent me, and he smiled now in a very friendly way indeed; but we said nothing more and I made my way home, pleased with my afternoon and pleased to have begun to know him.

Just before I turned in at our gate, Mrs. Frobisher-Spink swept past in her Buick, her young man lolling beside her. I don't think he has ventured afoot into the village since the other day or perhaps he has not been allowed out. As I watched the car disappear, I thought unoriginally that truly money is not everything. I suppose Mrs. Frobisher-Spink is rich, at least by our standards, and good-looking too in a painted up, rather artificial way; but she can't possibly be happy.

A few days ago some men from the Badgerford R.D.C. brought a whole mass of equipment by lorry to do something to the water pipes which edge the road. The lorry had a handsome green canvas top and they removed the whole thing and set it carefully on the grass verge to form a cosy shed in which, no doubt, they intended to relax from time to time to eat their elevenses and twelveses and three o'clockses.

After a decent interval two of the men set to work with pickaxes—but not for long; indeed, back-stretching, headscratching, gossip with our roadman and passing the time of day with Lower Barley inhabitants absorbed most of their energy so that very little had been accomplished by lunch-time. The morning was fine and they ate their midday meal sitting on the Green and earnestly reading their newspapers, each one folded up very small and held close to the face. Then, at two o'clock, a sharp shower drove them into their canvas house and they settled down comfortably to cards. Some time after the shower had passed, they emerged shyly and looked with anxiety at the sky—and presently the morning's digging was leisurely resumed.

At about half-past three there was a complete stoppage, for one of them had come across an old electric cable and the foreman, who came into the shop for cigarettes, told me cheerfully that they "can't do nothing now—not till Electricity gives the O.K."

When I asked what exactly the cable was—and if it isn't in fact very old and dead—he replied, "Dunno, I'm sure—but Electricity'll have to come out. You can't be too careful with them things."

I agreed, and the foreman laughed as he strolled away. "Put

paid to any more work," he said contentedly, "leastways till Electricity comes in the morning."

It is a good job that farm men have a different idea of work or we should all go hungry.

It rained heavily all the next day and nothing was seen of the "Electricity" or of the R.D.C. men.

Our Bessy came after supper to say that she might be a few minutes late for work next morning—but really it was to tell me that she believes it's always sunny and fine in Australia and at last she's made up her mind to go there next autumn. I shall be very sorry to lose her, but I think it is an excellent idea and will probably be the making of young Bert Hinton to whom drifting from one Government job to another is doing no good.

I asked Bessy how old Mrs. Rous had taken the decision.

"Gran? She's a caution . . . why she threatened to come with us! Poor Bert thought she meant it and he didn't half get the wind up—not but what he's fond of Gran—they never has a cross word—but he wants a place of his own; and you can't blame him, can you?"

It was just after ten o'clock and Bessy had only just gone, when suddenly we heard a tremendous uproar outside. Yells and shouts for help echoed in the darkness and Jim, who ran out flashing his torch, found that the noise was coming from H. Potter, who was apparently growing out of the ground at the edge of the road.

Jim tried to haul him up, but before he would consent to be rescued he insisted on explaining how he got there. He said that as he was going home from the Red Lion (a little the worse for wear, perhaps, though there was absolutely no proof of this) a car came by and he stepped back smartly on to the verge, and "damn it if he hadn't fallen down a well or some bloody hole". The fact is that the Badgerford "workmen" had not filled in their pit properly, having only thrown loose earth on the top with no protection, and the rain had turned it into a marshy trap. H. Potter's good leg had sunk into the hole right up to the thigh, and his wooden one had snapped in half.

Jim and the old shepherd, who had also heard his shouting, pulled him out and helped him home, all of them swearing vengeance on the R.D.C.

Directly the men arrived next morning Jim blazed at the foreman before the latter had time even to light his first pipe, and then, still raging, he telephoned to the local surveyor. I assured him that he was wasting his time and that H. Potter would have to get a new leg through some national nonsense or other; but Jim was roused for once and swore that the council would pay for a nice new leg, made to order, or he'd see that they were sued for damages, shock, bruises, and a new leg and all.

Luckily H. Potter himself was in the shop (having skipped up on ancient crutches) when the surveyor arrived, and when he was asked the cost of a new leg Jim promptly intervened and said £10.

The surveyor began to argue, but Jim said, "Take it or leave it," and invited H. Potter (who came up the street nimbly enough but, since the surveyor's arrival, could scarcely stand or move without groaning) into the garden, so that the council's representative could think the matter over quietly.

The surveyor, who is, I should think, no fool—and a nice little man, too—said that he'd let them know his committee's decision, and I heard him cursing the foreman in very un-R.D.C. language when he got outside.

I suppose the "workmen" will now demand their cards and the hole will be left there indefinitely.

A commercial traveller arrived yesterday afternoon when the shop was empty and I had to deal with him; for Jim had gone over to Upper Barley to confer with the carpenter there who, he says, can make a perfect wooden peg for H. Potter. The traveller was a tiny, elderly man with thin, fluffy grey hair, badly fitting false teeth and a made-up bow tie. He had on a not-very-clean stiff collar and a shiny blue suit—and, with difficulty, he dragged a heavy suitcase from his ancient Austin

seven. Not at all the usual slick type of young man who con-
descendingly takes our orders, for if it were not for his car he
might have stepped out of Dickens.

He told me at once that he represented a small chocolate firm
near Yeovil and worked on commission only; and as there was
no one to get in his way he put his case on the floor and quickly
unloaded a mass of Easter eggs. I did not quite know what to
do, for Jim sees to all the buying, so I said that I should have to
consult my brother. But I felt that I must at least give him a cup
of tea, and soon learnt about his family, the leaking roof of his
bungalow, the size of the giant marrow with which he won a
prize last summer, the exceptional quality of his Easter eggs,
and that he must get as many orders as possible, as his wife and
he are saving up for their first holiday by the sea for eight
years.

At last, simply to get rid of him, I gave him an enormous
order, for Easter is nearly here and, after all, we did wonder-
fully well with the extra things we bought in for Christmas.

But after he had gone I had serious misgivings and meant to
confess to Jim at once—but forgot, because Bumble got a bone
stuck in his throat and I thought he would choke to death and
we had to get the vet, and, even after it was out, poor Bumble
was very unhappy and had to be comforted with sloppy food
and love.

The R.D.C. men have removed all their gear, filled in the
hole properly (but in their usual leisurely manner) and disappeared as pointlessly and mysteriously as they came. Perhaps
the "Electricity" was not co-operative.

While they were messing about outside, Miss Emily Brown
came into the shop for the first time. She has a shy and gentle
manner and is rather pretty close to—or was, until a very short
time ago. As I gave her the book of stamps she wanted, I
thought how awful it must be to live with her sister and
wondered how she had escaped today. As if she read my
thoughts, she said that Miss Phyllis had been away for two days,
judging toy dogs at Brighton or somewhere. I was just going

to ask her more about this judging and showing when Jim
came in and Miss Emily quickly left the shop.

I liked her lively and kind expression and said so to Jim—but
he only grunted in, I suppose, agreement, and started talking
about H. Potter's peg which will be ready by tomorrow night.

On Sunday we went to tea at the Halahans' and the talk was
mostly of their ex-Servicemen's place. Geoffrey Halahan is
really going to buy the house, which sounds quite perfect, and
has already had an architect and builders down to plan altera-
tions and estimate their cost.

There was no sign of young Philip, and when I spoke to
Eleanor about his work, she seemed embarrassed and unwilling to discuss it—so I asked her to show me round the garden and did not refer to him again. When we left I considered
again the old, old problem. Why is it that the finest and best
people so often are the ones who are killed and the second-best
left unharmed? Nannie used to say to Jim and me when we were
small that it was "because the dear Lord wanted the good
ones and was ready for them". I considered this a highly unsatisfactory explanation at the time and still do.

Jim said the other day, "I suppose we really ought to have
ordered a few Easter eggs—but it's a bit late now"—and the
words were scarcely uttered before a van from Yeovil, Somerset, drew up outside the shop door. Privately rather alarmed,
I watched the driver bring in two enormous packing-cases and
then, as Jim began to protest, I quickly signed for them, saying
off-handedly "I know all about these; it's quite all right."

In fact, it wasn't at all all right, for I seemed to have ordered
no less than six dozen small, six dozen medium and six dozen
large chocolate eggs. I had, of course, to try to explain to Jim
how it happened and the explanation sounded, even to me, as
unsatisfactory as Nannie's.

Jim took the whole thing fairly calmly, cleared the shop window completely and filled it to the brim with our new purchases; and they looked very attractive indeed until the sun

came out and threatened to melt the lot. We then removed them, stacked them on shelves behind the counter and re-filled the window with its usual tins. Before closing time we had sold seven Easter eggs.

On the following day we sold nine Easter eggs.

On the third day we sold twelve little eggs and three big ones.

On the fourth day I telephoned frantically to the grocer at Upper Barley and asked if he would like some chocolate Easter eggs. He said, "Yes, a dozen of each," and, delighted, I walked over with them.

We now have one hundred and forty-nine Easter eggs left in our shop.

On the fifth day I forgot these beastly eggs for a time, because it was the Grand National next day and the village was agog with excitement about a horse called Barrabas, trained near here, which was supposed to have a very good chance. Nearly everyone had put something on it, varying from Mrs. Davenant's five pounds to Kate's shilling. Myself, I had never heard of Barrabas (the horse) until last week, but I didn't want to be left out of the fun and decided to "invest" (as Mr. Vernon and Mr. Littlewood would describe it) half a crown each way. I found that the odds were fifty-to-one, so very much feared that the village was slightly over-optimistic.

Jim said superiorly and obviously that betting is a mug's game, but I discovered by accident that he himself had put five shillings on Barrabas.

After all this excitement we were recalled to reality when Mrs. Davenant came in and bought Easter eggs for all her grandchildren—no less than fourteen (eggs I mean). We were now left with a hundred and thirty-four.

Jim said, "Don't worry. I dare say they'll go next week"— but I couldn't imagine how unless we melted them down and made them into chocolates; and making chocolates is all very well, but you have to know how to do it unless you are content with untidy blobs.

Next day turned out sunny and warm, and Jim kindly said that he would hold the fort in the afternoon so that I could get some fresh air. I was sick of the smell of chocolate and, accepting his offer very gratefully, I took Bumble for a long road walk and forgot about the shop and the eggs and everything for a good two hours.

I returned to find Jim looking extremely self-satisfied and the shelves strangely bare.

"Carrick came in to buy Easter eggs for a nephew," he said casually. "He seemed to think we'd got rather a lot, so I told him what you'd done."

I suppose I didn't look very pleased at this news, for he went on rather hurriedly, "I hope you don't mind. Anyway, he said he'd have the lot. He said he'd forgotten to send a donation to the hospital and these'd do instead. I thought it a jolly good idea—and I got one of the Boot children to take them up to the farm for him."

I felt absolutely furious with Jim, but could think of nothing to say so retreated to the kitchen to make tea. How dare he let a neighbour buy our stuff out of charity, and who the dickens is John Carrick to think we can't afford to throw away a hundred and thirty-four (no, a hundred and thirty-three) chocolate eggs if we want to. I decided not to speak to him again, nor to Jim either—at least not for some time.

Barrabas fell at the first fence.

We have been very busy in the shop, for the villagers are now stocking up for Easter much as they did for Christmas—and we shall certainly have to stay open all day on the Thursday before Easter. But we shall be shut then for four whole days (except Saturday a.m.) and I look forward to doing nothing at all, at least nothing that I don't want to do.

H. Potter marched in on his new leg this morning and brought with him a letter from the R.D.C. offering to pay him £8.0.0. and he wanted to know what "without prejudice" means. As Jim and the Upper Barley carpenter have, between them, made him his beautiful new peg, at cost price, for £2.15.0., I advised him to accept "without prejudice".

I suppose that most of this unexpected profit would find its way to Kate and O. Beery, but I misjudged H. Potter who told me that he intended to take Florence to the pictures in Badgerford and to buy her a new Spring hat.

There was yet another case of foot-and-mouth over the weekend, which brings it all terrifyingly close—but March skipped out like a lamb, the green haze on the hedgerows is breaking here and there and little Boosy Lacey brought me this evening what he calls a "tossy-ball of cowslips".

8 April

The vicar's wife came in today to buy a chocolate Easter egg. She was surprised and pained that we had none, and said that we really ought to try to stock seasonal goods so that the villagers need not traipse off to Badgerford for their shopping. I agreed with her.

The shop has been full of people all day but the only rumour they brought with them was a report that Miss P. Brown has been invited to judge toy dogs somewhere in the U.S.A. If this is true, what a wonderful holiday it will surely be for her sister!

When John Carrick came in to buy stamps, I left Jim to look after him, for I am still annoyed with him about the Easter egg business. Jim looked amazed as I rushed out of the shop to fill Florence Potter's paraffin can, a job we both detest and usually try to avoid, because she always leaves a little paraffin at the bottom and so the can overflows—which means cleaning up the mess and scrubbing one's hands afterwards.

I thought there was something peculiar about Jim this morning and later realised that he was wearing a new tie, which surprised but pleased me, for I am always trying to smarten him up. Indeed, to him nothing ordinarily is wearable until it has been in use for at least a year. Later, he surprised me again by asking if I thought I could manage alone on Saturday morning. I said, "Yes, but why," and he grinned and said he'd got something to do which he'd tell me about later and he would probably be out all day. If he hadn't looked embarrassed, I should have thought he was going over to the Halahans' place at Chalk —but now I am extremely curious.

Good Friday was fine and warm. It is traditional to plant one's early potatoes at Easter, regardless of whether it falls late or early, and so, like everyone's, ours went in on that day. In fact the ground was in perfect condition, and as we worked I observed with delight that there are wild daffodils in bud in the orchard and a few in full bloom in the front garden.

I took Bumble for his usual road walk after lunch and felt enchanted with the loveliness everywhere. It is an early spring, the grassland is already a brilliant green, the arable is nearly all sown and the harrows have made the smooth, silver-brown fields look as if they had been gone over with a giant comb. The sheep were out in the park and the noisy lambs skipped about charmingly, making a kind of picture-postcard country scene.

I met young Philip Halahan on my way home and asked him if he had sent any of his work to London; but he was surly and unfriendly, just said, "No, I'm afraid not," and, lifting his cap, walked quickly away.

As I approached the village I began to think about Jim's mysterious errand, and I had a sudden intuition that he was going after a scooter; for several times lately he has grumbled at our having no means of transport and I supposed he had seen one advertised in the local paper. I felt a little disturbed about this, for I knew very well that we could not afford it even though they are said to do hundreds of miles to the gallon. But if we were going to have anything, I *did* wish that we could have managed a tiny car.

When Jim went off on the nine o'clock bus to Badgerford this morning I tried to seem quite uncurious, but I was pretty sure that it *was* the scooter, for he rushed back at the last moment for his cheque book.

"See you later. Don't work too hard this morning," he said, and went off with that very casual and rather bored air which men childishly believe conceals their excitement when they are up to something.

We were only moderately busy in the shop after he had gone and so I decided to put up the shutter at half-past twelve, especially as it was another wonderful day and Eleanor Halahan had telephoned and suggested a picnic on the Downs.

At a quarter to one, with Bumble in the back of the car, we drove up a rough cart-track to within half a mile of Saxons' Plate, a flattish depression at the top of the nearest hill, where you can lie in the sun sheltered from any wind, or poke about and, if you are lucky, find an arrowhead among the flints.

I have become fond of the Halahans, and Eleanor and I enjoyed a happy and peaceful day, getting back to their house for a late tea. I left there soon after six and walked home.

As I came in sight of the shop I was surprised to see a collection of people outside our house and also, partly hidden by the villagers, what looked in the distance like a small tram; and as I drew nearer Jim disengaged himself from the crowd and came hurrying to meet me. His expression combined both pride and apprehension, and I began to realise that he must have done something awful.

"Come and see, Mary," he said with a nervous grin.

The knot of people parted and eyed me curiously as I came up and looked with amazement at what Jim had bought.

It was not a scooter, oh, no! It was not even a tiny car, second-hand or new. It was a Rolls Royce, vintage, I should say, about 1920, and its likeness to a tram increased on closer inspection. It was, in fact, an antiquated shooting-brake with glass sides, it stood very high off the ground, the tyres were not actually solid but they looked peculiar, and the circumference of the wheels was enormous. The angle of the steering column was nearly perpendicular (*very* tram-like), the roof was flat and projected some way in front of the upright windscreen, and the bonnet, in shape rather like an old-fashioned round-topped trunk, was held down, quite properly, by a thick leather strap.

I could feel Jim looking at me anxiously. I could feel the crowd staring at me and waiting for my reactions and I had to think quickly.

"Jim!" I exclaimed, "how wonderful! Could we go out in her now, this minute?" (I nearly added, "if she'll move.")

Jim beamed. "Yes, of course," he said. "Get in."

I expected him to have to turn the handle—but not at all. The self-starter worked and the engine ticked over sweetly. Jim released the hand-brake, a curious affair on the outside of the body, and the car slid gently away, followed by laughter and shouts of encouragement from the onlookers.

The "Tram" went beautifully, all her equipment—of the strangest and, I should have thought, most obsolete type—was in perfect order, and although the fittings were tarnished they were still good. The front seat was straight-backed and I found myself nearly level with the hedge-tops—but you could tell at once that there was nothing wrong with her.

When we were through Upper Barley, I turned to Jim. "You must be mad," I said. "She'll cost the earth to run."

"Oh, no," he said airily, "she's only 20 h.p. and extremely economical for her size. I got her for a song—an absolute song."

"A big song or a little song?"

"Oh, very small indeed. Fifty quid, as a matter of fact, and taxed to the end of the year. She's a gift at the price."

Myself, I thought she would have been an expensive gift at any price—but I hadn't the heart to say so. One look at Jim's silly, proud, delighted face and I was defeated. I just sat and agreed with him as he babbled on about "the best always being the cheapest in the long run", and "a Rolls will last for ever", and "listen to the engine, she goes like a watch".

When we got home Jim manœuvred her into the cart-shed and she fitted it exactly, although I thought she looked rather undignified and would have seemed more at home in an old-fashioned coach house, painted dark green, with double doors and a weather-vane on the roof.

Jim is very happy and, thank goodness, he passed all his one-legged driving tests when he was staying with Aunt Grace, so he has nothing to worry about on that score—so what does it all matter. And his last words when we went up to bed were, "I thought we'd run down to see Barbara tomorrow and take her out," which I must say is rather a jolly idea.

On Easter Sunday we both went to early service and found the church beautifully decorated with spring flowers. I believe that Nurse Ames is chiefly responsible, and the little Irish-woman certainly has a flair for handling flowers. A persistent "cuckoo-cuckoo" from the spinney outside added to rather than detracted from the service.

We had an uneventful drive to Gloucestershire and presently I began gradually to feel less conspicuous and rather superior; but, to Jim's faint surprise, I would not allow him to drive up to Barbara's school. I know what schoolgirls are like and I did not mean to have Barbara laughed at through our fault.

So we rang up from the hotel and told her to come to lunch —which she did with great excitement. I warned her, while Jim was absent, not to jeer at the car, for, although a little old-fashioned, it is Uncle Jim's pride; but the warning was quite unnecessary, for to her a Rolls is a Rolls.

She comes home for the holidays next Tuesday, late this year because the school is in quarantine, and she was aggrieved because she will have only a bare four weeks at home. She wanted Jim to fetch her in the "Tram"—but I said definitely no.

We were home comfortably by seven o'clock and I forced myself to say firmly that we *must* only use the "Tram" very occasionally, for we really can't afford to run it. Jim agreed, but much too readily to mean anything.

On Bank Holiday I did absolutely nothing all day and thoroughly enjoyed it. The weather was too lovely to stay in bed late, so I lazed in the garden and we had cold food.

Even our village, which leads to nowhere, was invaded by cars and motor-bicycles which rushed in from the Badgerford road, circled the green, hesitated and zoomed off to Upper Barley; and I felt thankful to be peacefully inside our own gate.

Jim spent the afternoon watching six-a-side football matches, between our own and neighbouring villages, which were played on a piece of ground behind the school known as "the Recreation", as opposed to the field called the "Manor Rec", which is sacred to cricket and was given to the village by long-dead Davenants.

This football, which is always played here on Easter Monday, is, Jim says, very strenuous and extremely rough, and the tournament went on until nearly seven o'clock. When it was over, most of the players and their supporters flocked to the Red Lion and, as Lower Barley were in the final and beaten by only one goal in the very last minute, O. Beery and Kate did a fine and noisy trade all evening.

After supper I surprised Jim in the cart-shed lovingly dusting the "Tram" and I observed that the famous square front had been burnished so that I could see my face in it.

The following are some of the comments on the "Tram" which I have actually heard:

Eleanor Halahan (to Jim): "I think she's a wonderful bargain and taxed to the end of the year, too. You're very lucky." (To me): "Mary, he must be crazy—but it's no good saying so and he looks so absurdly pleased, what *does* it matter?"

H. Potter: "I'll clean her for you any time, sir—inside and out.

They old uns is worth twenty o' the rubbish they puts up now-adays—and it ain't only motors neither what's changed for the worse."

Mrs. Root: "Some folks must be making a tidy bit o' money out o' we. 'Tis a pity prices don't go down." (And I am afraid we are out of favour again.)

Mrs. Crabtree: "Too grand for the likes o' we now, I suppose——" (but she is smiling as she says it).

Kate (who has rather a weakness for Jim): "I always said as he was made for better things. 'Tis a real pity though as he can't have a new one."

Colonel Halahan: "A Rolls never wears out. Take care of her and she'll last you a lifetime; but, if you *should* ever want to part with her, my dear fellow, she'd come in very handy for Chalk Manor and I'd be glad to have her."

The vicar's wife: "Just a little ostentatious, don't you think? I mean with the village shop; but, of course, you know your own business best."

Miss Phyllis Brown (to me): "Oh, his poor leg. I'm sure a great heavy thing like that will be too much for him. Surely you could have let him get a small modern car." (To Jim): "Perhaps, one day, when I'm off to a show with my little Fairies—perhaps I could ask you——?"

Mrs. Davenant: "I wish I'd known you wanted a car. We've a 1916 Daimler which we can't *give* away. You could have had it with pleasure."

Now that spring is here, I find myself hating to stay indoors so much and I realise that this is going to be *the* real trial of the shop in summer. Jim says grandly that perhaps we could get Lucy Rous to hold the fort in the afternoon, but I am afraid that this only shows how the "Tram" has gone to his head for we have, in fact, very little money to spare.

Our Bessy's sister, Dawn, was rushed to the Cottage Hospital a day or two ago and a son was born this morning. As it is not our weekly bus day, Jim took old Mrs. Rous, our Bessy and the proud young husband into Badgerford in the "Tram". The Rous family (and, therefore, it seems, those they marry) have strong political convictions and the unhappy child is to be christened Winston Churchill. Grannie Rous wanted to pay Jim for the petrol, but, in his most charming manner, he gracefully refused. Afterwards I reminded him coldly that he is a mere tradesman and should not take up such a lofty attitude.

The dramatic society met last night and the whole affair was a flop, which it was bound to be, for earlier in the day various members came into the shop and without exception said that they hadn't even looked at their parts. I wondered how the vicar's wife would deal with such lethargy, and in the event she was admirably firm. She refused to continue the meeting at all once she had learnt the state of affairs, and said that unless everyone knew his part perfectly by Friday week she would have nothing more to do with it. This could, of course, have been taken as an encouragement to everyone not even to open a book, for she is not at all popular; but there is no one to take her place and as they seem eager to do a play I imagine they will now make some kind of effort.

Next morning when I told our Bessy what had happened, she said that there is already ill-feeling about the choice of a child for the only available part in the play; and even Bessy, who is seldom or never "difficult", said she couldn't see why Tommy Bissett had been chosen, seeing that "he's right down at the bottom of his class and teacher said he was the stupidest child in Barley".

I felt sure that the schoolmistress, who is a very discreet, very nice and very sensible woman, never said any such thing; but I also remembered that Bessy herself has a child eligible for the part. Maternal ambition has evidently got the better of her usual good nature . . . and this is another indication of the troubles which lie ahead of the vicar's wife as producer.

I asked Miss P. Brown, when she came in this morning, whether or not it is true that she is going to America to judge toy-dogs. She said, "No," adding coyly, "not that I haven't been asked, mind you, and I might accept another time—but I can't possibly leave my poor sister just now."

I asked her why and she answered, "Such a lot to do. Fairy Fantasy due to whelp in a few weeks and Fairy Fuchsia with eczema. Emily's not actually unkind to the little pixies, of course, but she takes no interest."

I reported this news to Jim later on and he seemed extraordinarily annoyed. Miss P. Brown is rather a bore to him but I don't see why he should really care whether she goes to the U.S.A. or not.

I am afraid Barbara is having rather a dull time, for there are no Davenant grandchildren here these holidays, but she seems to be amusing herself somehow and has developed a passion for gardening and for Jim's society.

She loves the village and so do I, and just now it is looking *so* pretty—daffodils and tulips in blow in all the cottage gardens, the trees misty with softest green and, behind them, the church tower cool and grey against a delicate blue sky. The pond is full and the boys now have a craze for sailing boats, which sweep gracefully on its surface or lie, sails flapping wetly, like injured birds. The grass is fresh and brilliant and H. Potter's Buff Rocks (the same colour as the new thatch on his cottage) straggle about the chalky road. New white paint gleams on the churchyard railings, and Katé has put up primrose-yellow curtains in the bar of the Red Lion.

I extravagantly sowed a double row of sweet-peas today, inspired by the beauty of our big pear tree at the back of this house which is clouded with blossom. I do wish though that dandelions would last in water—but they won't—for the road verges are ablaze with them—not a popular sight with farmers but a lovely one. Some of the children pull them for their tame rabbits and old Mrs. Weller—said to be over ninety but still very active and "keeps herself to herself"—makes dandelion wine and offers the little boys a penny for a basketful of heads.

But a penny doesn't seem much to a child nowadays and she has a job to find any pickers. Usually it is one of the small girls, idling along with her little brother in a push-cart, who earns the pence.

I really can't account for Jim's behaviour lately. Today he appeared in a new tweed coat, at least it was new when we came here last October and has never left its cupboard since. The spring and the "Tram" have really gone to his head, I think. I feel particularly dowdy myself and would love some new pretty clothes: but I must forget about it, for there is no money to spare and really no need for anything in this job.

Dramatic news of Mrs. Frobisher-Spink's gigolo has arrived by way of our Bessy, who was told by the postman that his married sister at Upper Barley told *him* that her lodger, Mrs. F.-S.'s chauffeur, has been given notice. It appears that last night Mrs. Frobisher-Spink and the chauffeur visited her garage to inspect a scratch on the wing of the Buick and found more than they were looking for. In the back of the car was the "giggly" cuddling the chauffeur's sixteen-year-old daughter who works in the kitchen there. The chauffeur, said to be an ex-Commando, pulled the girl out of the car, boxed her ears and sent her home. He then hit the "giggly" hard on the nose. When he got up, the chauffeur hit him again, and then Mrs. Frobisher-Spink intervened, gave her chauffeur the sack and "swept into the house" with the "giggly" tailing behind her, rather the worse for wear.

I should have thought poor Mrs. Frobisher-Spink would have done better to sack the gigolo, for her chauffeur is said to be an excellent driver and a very nice man.

One cannot, of course, be sure that all or any part of this is true, for the powers of invention possessed by the village have to be heard to be believed.

Fresh news arrived a little later, via Miss Phyllis Brown who rushed into the shop, her bangles clinking, and babbled breathlessly, "There's been a ghastly tragedy at Mrs. Frobisher-Spink's. Have you heard?"

"No."

"It's that appalling young man she brought back from France. The chauffeur caught him with his wife and lost his temper and hit him with a tyre lever. He split the creature's head right open and they say he's at death's door. If he dies, it'll be murder—murder in Lower Barley!"

I think I looked rather severely at Miss Brown, for I felt sure that there was not a word of truth in all this—chiefly because the chauffeur's wife is nearly fifty herself and far less attractive than Mrs. Frobisher-Spink.

"As a matter of fact," I said, "I did hear there'd been some kind of fuss—but I don't think it's anything like as bad as your version."

"*My* version, Mrs. Braid?" Miss P. Brown stood back—and I think "bridled" is the usual expression for the way in which she drew herself up in anger and reproach. "*I'm* not in the habit of spreading gossip, I can assure you. I know the village shop is where everyone comes for news and I just wanted you to have the facts as I was told them. . . . However," she added with great dignity, "if you prefer to get your information from the cottage women, pray do."

And she stalked out of the shop, forgetting to take her daily paper, so that presently she would have to walk all the way back for it.

I suggested to Jim that he might like to take it up to her.

On Sunday the Halahans took us both over to Chalk Manor for the day. Barbara didn't want to come, and grandly invited to lunch with her a grandson of old General Blade's whom she has picked up—a nice boy in his first year at Marlborough. She wished to have cold tongue and tinned peaches—and so it was arranged.

Chalk is a tiny hamlet set at the very foot of the Downs but near enough to Devizes not to be too isolated. There is a little church, a few cottages, two farms and the Manor House. The last is, as Jim had already described it to me, perfect—an

Elizabethan house of pinkish red brick, with a moat, a walled garden, a small park, several cottages and about a hundred acres of good farmland. Inside, the house is bigger than it seems, and the rooms are gracious and well proportioned.

On this perfect April day the place looked, I suppose, at its best and I can think of nothing lovelier for the purpose that the Halahans have in mind.

Jim is very taken with the whole idea and he and Geoffrey pored over plans and wandered about with foot rules and absorbed expressions while Eleanor and I sat on the wide, shallow window seat that runs nearly the whole length of the drawing-room, with the sun streaming in on us. The garden outside was a mass of different delicate greens, and some moor-hens were scuttering about in the moat.

"Do you like it?" she asked.

"I love it. If a man can't do good work here, he'll not do it anywhere."

"And Geoffrey means to have workshops and a laboratory, you know . . . it's not only for the arts. I think Humphrey would have approved—in fact, if he could have stayed in one place long enough, he'd have loved to run it. I can picture him settled down here—and married. . . ."

This was the first time she had ever spoken of her elder son and I wished she would go on, but the men came back and presently we had a picnic luncheon in the garden.

Jim and Geoffrey seemed to agree remarkably well, but I was amused to see that it was my rather irresponsible brother who did the braking when his host's wildly extravagant ideas threatened to run away with him.

I had been counting the days and believed that our area was clear of foot-and-mouth as from yesterday, so I was appalled this morning to see a Ministry of Agriculture van followed by our local vet's car, on their way down to Lower Barley Farm. It seemed utterly improbable that they could have got a case there at this last moment . . . but not utterly impossible and, distracted with anxiety, I tried to find out from Florence Potter.

She works in the dairy there but had heard nothing; and, because I had to look after our customers, I didn't see the M. of A. van leave.

Presently John Carrick himself appeared. I thought at once that he certainly wouldn't come in casually to buy cigarettes if anything were wrong; and I felt so relieved that I quite forgot the incident of the Easter eggs which had annoyed me so much.

"I thought you might like to know that we've got the all clear," he said.

Unthinkingly, I spoke from my heart. "I *am* so glad. I can't tell you what I felt when I saw the Ministry's van and the vet go down to you."

J. Carrick gave me a long look as he picked up his cigarettes and put them in his pocket.

"It was only a routine call," he said. "Thank you for minding . . . ." and he left the shop and went striding down the road to his farm and his lovely herd.

Mrs. Frobisher-Spink's "giggly" has gone. He was seen at the station, with several expensive hide suitcases, by Mr. Parker, who has a smallholding on the road to Upper Barley and also runs an ancient taxi as a sideline—and probably more profitably than the main line: for his garden produces stuff for sale only when there is already a glut everywhere; he seems unable ever to get his two cows in calf, and his turkeys die of that mysterious disease which causes turkeys to stand on one leg, their heads hunched between their shoulders, in fixed determination not to move until they die. Anyway, Mr. Parker saw him getting into the 9.15 for London and he lost no time in spreading the news.

By 11 a.m. we had been told (*a*) that Mrs. Frobisher-Spink was sending him to have his head seen to (not in the way I should think he needs it but to have the imaginary gash treated by a specialist); (*b*) that he has cleared off with Mrs. Frobisher-Spink's pearls and a diamond ring worth five hundred pounds —and (*c*) that he was meeting the chauffeur's wife in Reading and taking her to the South of France. So we can take our choice.

The vicar's wife was buying sago today (the kind of thing she *would* buy) and said that it was a pity I didn't go to the W.I. meeting this month, for there was a talk and demonstration on "How to furbish up your old clothes for the Summer", and she was sure I should have been interested.

She also said that she'd heard that Jim was going to hire out the Rolls as a taxi and added that we ought to think twice about trying to cut out poor Mr. Parker. I assured her that we had no such intention, but she went out muttering something about "if we'd only consulted her first, she could have *told* us there was no demand for a second taxi".

The weather has broken and a soft, steady rain fell all last night and is still falling. Great grey clouds hang low over the village and the Downs are blotted out entirely. The rain is needed and welcome—but the shop had not been opened more than a few minutes before someone came in grumbling, "Terrible messy weather! It don't seem like spring, do it?"

One of our hens is broody and Jim and Barbara have gone over to Upper Barley to fetch a sitting of duck eggs. He wanted to take the "Tram" and pick up some wire netting, but the battery was flat. I am afraid that it is a weak cell.

I sold a short story a little while ago and the cheque arrived this morning; it also happens to be Jim's birthday tomorrow, so —instead of spending the money on clothes—I suppose I must buy him a new battery. This is not, in fact, as generous as it sounds, for the "Tram" is a pleasure to us all these holidays and Barbara adores it.

The Badgerford garage have promised to have the battery ready charged tomorrow morning and Eleanor will pick it up, so all is arranged.

Jim was delighted, really delighted, and said that we must use the "Tram" more often so that the battery will be kept fully charged. I can see the sense of this—but it was not exactly what I intended.

Barabara said (though she might as well have saved her breath) that she could easily provide some extra exercise for the "Tram" if Uncle Jim would like to give her and her boy friend a lift sometimes; for Master Blade is interested in archæology and together they spend hours snooping round the fields or on the Downs. They usually return with chunks of stone, flints and bits of pottery—all of which have to be washed in the kitchen sink and laid out to dry, so that the house is beginning to look like a rockery. But Barbara is happy and occupied and has made friends with Mr. Davenant, who has asked the children to the Manor to see some of his collections.

The dramatic society met again on Friday at 6 p.m.—at least some people arrived soon after six and the last comer strolled in at 6.40. There was no need for the stove this time and everyone —except the vicar's wife, who kept fidgeting about, looking at her watch and peering out of the door—settled down to a comfortable gossip until the meeting was ready to start.

The play is set in a farmhouse and the chief characters are:
The Farmer: Mr. Parker, who has done quite a lot of acting before and is already inclined to argue with the producer; *His Wife:* Miss P. Brown (Jim said cattily that this is as near as she'll ever get to catching a husband); *His Sister:* Lucy Rous (but I should think she may be rather unshapely by the Summer); *Her Child:* Tommy Bissett, a good-looking very cocky little boy, who needs a clip on the ear; and *The Thief:* Amos Rous, the melancholy and gentle blacksmith. (This was the part which the vicar's wife wanted Jim for.)

All the minor characters have quite a lot to say, so there is really no excuse for jealousy.

When the meeting at last turned into a rehearsal it was soon apparent that there had been a genuine attempt all round at learning the words, and the vicar's wife, who seems as capable as a producer as she is in other spheres, got to work eagerly.

She will have a lot to do though, for the blacksmith, who is short, square and immensely strong and could easily look a villain, showed no sign of departing from his usual sad and quiet manner, and Miss P. Brown was very much "herself", only occasionally putting on a kind of Cockney accent. Lucy Rous was quite good, that is to say she was perfectly natural, but Mr. Parker, who looks a little like one of his own turkeys in decline, had very definite ideas of his own and will probably fall out with the vicar's wife before long.

Before we left, a long time was spent in fixing suitable days for rehearsals which are to be held twice weekly, for on no single day was everyone available . . . and one excuse after another was put forward.

"'Tis washing day on Monday and I be that tired . . ."

"I goes to me sister's every Tuesday baby-sitting——"

"It's my young lady's night off Wednesday——"

"'Tis choir practice Thursdays—and I reckon I couldn't get here till half-past seven——"

"Me husband wouldn't stand for being out Fridays . . . we always likes to look at the telly that night——"

"Saturdays ain't no good. Everybody goes to Badgerford and stays in to the pictures like——"

After about ten minutes of this, the vicar's wife began to look as if, at any moment, she would go raving mad, and I thought it a great tribute to her masterful character that in the end rehearsals were definitely fixed for Mondays and Thursdays. I promised to attend as soon as the actors were doing without their books altogether, and was let off until then. "Though it won't be for long," the vicar's wife threatened optimistically.

It has been real April weather this week, sun and showers and rather a lot of rain—"growing weather," as H. Potter would rightly say, and our early peas and broad beans are well up. And the Guernsey milking cows, which have been for so long confined to the yards and pastures round the farm buildings, walked down the road this morning to graze the lower park.

This gave me great pleasure and I thanked God truly that these lovely beasts were safe.

Jim took the "Tram" into Badgerford yesterday and returned with news of an appalling Philip Halahan scandal. I felt deeply distressed and hoped that it might not be true; but Eleanor telephoned after tea and begged me to go up there.

Jim had heard that it was a police matter and I felt dreadfully afraid for them all, but Eleanor said that the situation had been dealt with in time, Geoffrey and Philip had gone off to London and the boy is to be packed off immediately to friends in the U.S.A. and from there to relations in New Zealand.

Poor Eleanor! I have known her only as a kind and gay and unruffled person—but this has been too much for her and I found her desolate and in tears.

I stayed with her for the night and most of the next day until Geoffrey came home, and she talked and talked about her two boys. I think it was the best thing she could do—but I felt so sorry for her and wished that there was more for me to do than just to listen and sympathise.

While I was over at the Old Mill House, Barbara took herself up to the farm, made friends with Evans, the head cowman, and had a happy time with the young calves and all the small farm animals. John Carrick was very kind and friendly and gave her tea.

"He's really a very nice man, Mummy," she said, when I got home and asked what she had been finding to do, "and I think he must have made a mistake about my age; because he made me pour out tea and honestly behaved exactly as if I was grown up."

This is the most certain and shortest way to Barbara's heart, and she chattered on endlessly about the farm and its owner.

For myself, I was emotionally tired out and went to bed very early.

Dawn's baby was christened yesterday afternoon, and it was a

much more contented and settled little party that made its way
to church than when Dawn was married in a hurry. Old
Grannie Rous wore her best black satin and a black hat, decorated with pale blue ribbon bows and a small glass bird. The
young husband, Potter, looked handsome and awkward in his
blue suit and starched collar, and our Bessy tripped to church
on very high heels, wearing a large picture hat and the red silk
dress which she bought for Mrs. Crabtree's New Year party.
Dawn herself looked very pretty indeed in a blue and white
nylon frock, a little blue straw hat and white mesh gloves.

The "little lad" did not attend but there was a scattering of
Rous relations, and young Potter was supported by his uncle
and aunt.

Old Mrs. Rous had kindly asked me to the church and I had
accepted gratefully, for I thought it very friendly of her.

It was a fine, sunny day and the vicar welcomed the party
with his usual vague smiles and nods, and then ran through the
service very quickly. Unromantically, he poured water into
the font from an enamel bathroom can, and let it out, when the
baptism was over, by pulling out the plug, as if it had been a
scullery sink. However, nobody except myself seemed to
notice these things, and after it was over and young Winston
Churchill Potter had been admired, there was to be a fine party
at the Rous cottage; and Bessy told me next morning that they
had beer and cider and an iced cake and jellies and pastries and
gallons of tea, and "it was a rare do and lasted right up to
dark", when, presumably, Winston Churchill retired for the
night.

On our early-closing day this week we took Barbara to the
dentist. Her disgust at this waste of time was tempered by the
pleasure of travelling in the "Tram", a delight which so far
never palls, partly, I think, because of its slight resemblance to a
hearse which she and young Roger Blade—who came with us
on this occasion—both find hilariously funny.

When the dentist visit was over, we all went to the cinema
where there was luckily a slapstick farce, which suited the

children exactly. Bumble had been left to take care of the "Tram" and, on our return to it, we found that he had relieved his boredom by carefully opening a parcel which I had left on the seat. He had also eaten the contents—a pound and a half of best grilling steak, price 12/6.

I refused to buy more and we went home to an excellent supper of eggs and bacon.

9 May

I am often surprised when I think how well we know everyone here after only seven months in the village. I suppose it is because we see most people every day that the most trivial events in their lives are part and parcel of our own. For instance, last night there was a sharp frost and when H. Potter reported that every bit of peach blossom in the Vicarage garden (*his* garden) was caught—"and 'tis a damned shame, for vicar won't get no fruit at all this year"—I felt personally distressed.

Incidentally, our own early potatoes, just through the ground, are blackened; though old Mrs. Crabtree says, " 'Twon't hurt they. Maybe 'twill make un a bit slower—but ee'll have plenty."

I hope she is right for, if we go on using the "Tram", potatoes will be about all we can afford to eat this summer.

The month started badly with Miss P. Brown's usual morning visit. When she had collected her newspaper she leant over the counter and said that she was surprised to hear I had allowed Barbara to be up at the farm alone with John Carrick.

When I asked why on earth she shouldn't go there and re-marked that it was good for her to learn about the animals, she said, "Surely you've been told about his dreadful drinking during the last few years—although," she added, "I *have* heard that he started it before his poor wife died."

Staring at her, I asked—in what Jim afterwards described as my "ominous voice"—how she could possibly know whether he drinks or not and said didn't she think it silly to spread that sort of very unpleasant gossip.

"Gossip, my dear lady," she retorted, "why, ask anyone— ask his own men!"

"I don't believe a word of it," I began hotly, and only Jim's intervention prevented my blazing at Miss Brown; but it didn't prevent her looking at me in a very shrewd and knowing way.

"So that's how the land lies, is it?" she said, and she went out sniggering.

I felt absolutely furious; and although Jim said, "Calm down, calm down. Nobody listens to that old fool," I know jolly well the kind of rumours she will send creeping through the village, and I still feel helplessly angry and upset.

Miss Emily Brown came to fetch their newspaper this morn-ing but I left Jim to look after her, for I felt so angry with her sister that I just couldn't be friendly. I was sorry about this afterwards, for I think she is nice and I should like to know her better.

As it was, I went out into the garden at the back and found poor Kate Beery weeping on the other side of the wall.

A travelling fox had killed eight of their hens in the night and she was naturally terribly upset. The henhouse had been moved into their orchard only the day before, and Kate was so in-terested in some parlour game on the television that she had forgotten to go out after dark and shut the door.

I resolved to check the fastening on the gate of our own chicken run and told poor Kate how sorry I was for her.

" 'Tisn't only the money and the eggs," she said, wiping her eyes with a large and rather grubby handkerchief, " 'tis Oliver.

They fowls is like children to him, coming up to the kitchen window to take scraps out of his hand. He's fair broken-hearted, poor man, though he doesn't *say* anything."

Alas, I couldn't think of any practical way in which to comfort her, so I patted her shoulder sympathetically and thought it best not to *say* anything either.

Eleanor Halahan came to tea a day or so ago and thanked me for my support last weekend. I only wish I could have helped her more—but certainly I now know her much better because of it, and I realise how lucky we are to have the Halahans as neighbours. One can't expect, in a tiny village like this, to find anything more than friendly acquaintances; but, in fact, Geoffrey and Eleanor are real friends to us both and, if we were in any trouble, I know we could turn to either of them.

On this subject, the vicar's wife said to me the next day, "It's so nice for you to have made such friends with the Halahans. Charming people and, of course, as you know, fantastically rich. They could be very useful to Barbara I expect later on. One has to think of one's children and, frankly, I don't blame you for cultivating them."

I didn't feel particularly annoyed at the implication of these remarks because it was so wildly unjustified. In fact, I had had no idea that the Halahans were at all well off until we first heard of the Chalk Manor scheme. Their house is comfortably 'shabby, they have a five-year-old car and they live very quietly. Anyway, they are both dears, and if they are rich it can't be helped and I certainly shan't let it interfere with our friendship.

Barbara goes off to school tomorrow, and today there has been the usual last minute panic. Every holidays I try to avoid this but always on the last day it is, "Mummy, I can't find my ruler and I must have a new pencil box—I shall get into a frightful row if I don't . . . I can't find more than twenty-two handkerchiefs . . . have you remembered to sign my health certificate . . . I forgot to ask Bessy to wash my games jersey . . . what on earth shall I do?" And this usually ends in tears, really only because the holidays are over and school looms, uncomfortable and boring—though, when she is actually there, she seems to find it enjoyable on the whole.

When her packing had at last been completed, Barbara announced that she had an appointment with Evans to feed the calves. "And I can stay to tea if Mr. Carrick asks me?"

Remembering Miss P. Brown, I said quickly, "Yes, of course —but don't hang about and hint to be asked."

Barabara naturally scorned to reply to this very necessary warning, and went off with an air of tolerant resignation.

Barbara has gone and Jim took her to the station in the "Tram"—but it is a shame that the holidays ended today, for this morning the hen who has been brooding our duck eggs refused to leave her nest at feeding-time and, after tea, we found seven little golden fluffy balls with button eyes and shallow, pinkish-yellow beaks—and two cold eggs pushed out on to the floor. The little mother hen is very proud and so are we.

I asked Jim what he intends to do with seven grown ducks, for kill them he never shall.

"I *had* thought of duck and green peas," he replied wistfully, "but I suppose we can always sell their eggs in the shop."

He had just said this and I was getting ready to go to bed when the telephone rang; and, unexpectedly, it was Mrs. Frobisher-Spink, asking us to a cocktail party tomorrow night —at least, "Do come in both of you and have a drink . . . not a party, just a few people from the village and round about."

I accepted—but with some reluctance, for I had nothing to wear and also it would be a struggle to get Jim tidy.

Luckily, the next evening was cloudy and cool, and so I was able to wear my little dark-blue thin wool frock with the silver buttons, my only passable hat which goes with it and *very* nice blue shoes, bought with a cheque sent by my Mama last summer. Jim has only two good suits and I persuaded him to wear my favourite—a thin, hard Irish tweed—and, now that he is not such a skeleton, even I thought he looked rather nice.

We arrived at Mrs. Frobisher-Spink's, a big, square, Queen Anne house, at about six forty-five and found the drive and forecourt thick with cars. If this is her idea of "not a party" it is not mine, for the cars had disgorged at least sixty or seventy people and there were two hired waiters, her own butler and two maids in attendance.

Mrs. Frobisher-Spink looked very elegant in a dark green frock and pearls which suited her red hair and rather ripe good looks down to the ground. She was very friendly, and I could see for the first time what Eleanor had meant when she said that she *could* be a very nice woman. After she had left us I reflected that this party is probably her challenge to the neighbourhood after the undignified gigolo incident.

To begin with, we saw no one else we knew, but presently, as we stood drinking excellent sherry, a large woman in thick tweed and an unbecoming red hat parted the crowd with her bulk and joined us.

"I know who you are," she said, beaming, "don't tell me. I understand we're to be related one day, for my son intends to marry your daughter—in eight years' time I think he said . . . when he comes down from Oxford."

For a moment I was a little nonplussed but then realised that this must, of course, be the mother of Barbara's Marlborough boy, and I was soon amazed to discover how much she knew about us. She knew that Jim has a bar to his D.S.O., that he was a prisoner of war, that he nearly died in hospital when he came home, that he has a tin leg and that he recently bought an ancient Rolls Royce. She knew that my husband was the literary editor of a rather intellectual Right-wing publication, that I am obsessed with a passionate love of the country, that Barbara is at a far more expensive school than we can afford and that I add occasionally to my income by means of short stories and articles. I shouldn't have been surprised if she'd known what we had had for breakfast that morning and for dinner the night before; but she was so friendly—I can think of no word to express her personality except "jolly"—that nobody could take offence.

"You must be very kind and go and see my father-in-law one evening," she said to Jim, before she turned away. "He may have been a famous general, but he's a very lonely old man. We live in Cornwall and it's seldom I can get away to see him."

As she pushed her way back into the crowd, I caught sight of John Carrick coming over and, looking round frantically, saw Eleanor and hurried to her side. "Say anything," I babbled, "say anything you like—only please engage me in conversation. I'll explain another time."

She did as I asked, and out of the corner of my eye I saw J. Carrick talking to Jim. Then Eleanor introduced a nice old man, who said he had known my father, and presently I found myself sitting on a window-seat with Miss Emily Brown.

Whether it was due to the absence of her sister or to the very large champagne cocktail she was sipping, she seemed quite different, not shy, and full of dry humour. We had a comfortable talk about Barley affairs and about West Somerset, which we both knew very well, and eventually about Jim and the "Tram" and Jim's health and the shop and about Jim again. I liked her very much.

Then Jim himself was standing in front of us with John Carrick at his elbow.

Really, my brother can be the most tactless idiot. He knew perfectly well that Miss Phyllis must by now have told everyone that I am running after J. Carrick, and yet he deliberately brought us together in public—the one thing I had been trying to avoid.

"Carrick's asked us up for a drink on Sunday evening, Mary," he announced coolly. "We'd love to go, wouldn't we?"

It was impossible to say anything but, "Thank you—yes, we'd love to,"—but wild horses (as people so often unaccountably say) would'nt drag me to the farm on Sunday or on any other day.

The mother hen has brought her babies out into the grass—little fat, golden Easter egg things, scuttling in and out of the shelter of her wings when she sits and darting among the long grasses as she pecks and scratches for grubs.

Most of the trees are full out now, our orchard is pink with apple blossom, the sticky chestnut buds have burst their sheaths and the chestnut candles are nearly lighted. I am woken early each morning by the birds' chorus, the cuckoo calls off and on from dawn to dusk, H. Potter's wallflowers in the front garden are in full sweet bloom and the sun shines warmly. How lucky we are to live here!

Jim says (and I want to believe him) that we can quite well afford to employ Lucy for three afternoons a week, Monday, Tuesday and Wednesday. Since Thursday is our half-day anyhow, it would mean only Friday and Saturday in the shop most of the day. Nearly everyone in the village deals with us and we are always busy; but now that we have got the hang of it we don't find the work hard. It is just being indoors in fine weather that I hate. Usually, though, the door is open and the sweet country smells (as well as dust and an occasional stench of artificial manure) come into us.

Jim was annoyed—but I refused to go to John Carrick's with him. I said, "You can apologise nicely and say I've got a headache—and you'll probably enjoy it more without me." But Jim went on grumbling and said I must be half-witted to take any notice of that old fool, Miss P. Brown.

There is a small paved yard in front of the Red Lion, and in the middle grows a giant chestnut tree, now ablaze with thousands of white candles. Many years ago an oak bench was built round its massive trunk, and in the evenings the men sit there and talk and drink until the sun is level with their eyes and the old inn is gilded and beautiful.

May is the month of sweet smells, lilac and laburnum in nearly every garden, early honeysuckle and wallflowers and now—the may! The hedgerows are more than speckled with the heavy sweet blossom, they are smothered; and the green verges, where the dandelions showed golden a few weeks ago, are now frothy with cow parsley. Pansies, aubretia and purple flags decorate our front garden and there are some lupins showing yellow and palest blue in the border.

When April comes, I think that it is my pet month, but when May is here, I am not so sure. The sun is hotter, the days are longer, there are bluebells in the woods, all the curtains have been washed and ironed and today Bessy finished spring-cleaning the kitchen. Spring is a lovely time, and although this fact has been recorded in a thousand ways and in many thousand words—fact it is, and one does not need to be a poet to discover it.

Mrs. Crabtree scolded me today for missing the W.I. meeting again last Wednesday. "But 'ee'll have to come next time, missus, for there'll be a real argy-bargy—there always is."

"What about?"

"Why, a-fixing of the outing, of course. Some wants one thing and some t'other and some won't say. The vicar's wife she brings out some new notion every year; but the seaside's what we likes and there ain't no use really in thinking of aught else—though I mind we *did* go to London one time."

"To London? What did you do?"

"Oh, us had a motor-coach same as usual—only going the wrong way like instead o' to Southampton."

"Did you enjoy it?"

"Middlin'. Us went to the Zoo, and while the rest was traipsing round the monkeys and lions and such, me and Lucy went to one o' they places wi' little tables out o' doors and we sat down and had a right good tea. When the others came back wi' the vicar's wife ('twas his first as I'm speaking of and a real lady *she* were) they was that tired they couldn't hardly stand and your Bessy's Auntie Flo, she fainted right off. 'Twas the heat, you know, and her weighing nigh on twenty stone. But her come round all right and then they starts their tea and Lucy and me had a second go. 'Twas very enjoyable—but I thought

London smelly wi' all them cars and jabbering people. I'd rather have the seaside any day."

"Will they go to Southampton this year?"

"Not if the vicar's wife has her way they won't. She's all for going to Reading to see round the biscuits for a change. But I reckon it'll be the sea."

I did not say so, but I have considerable experience of meetings to "discuss the outing", and I intend to avoid this one at all costs.

As I talked to her I marvelled at Mrs. Crabtree, whom I now know to be eighty-seven, and I cannot think how she managed to get through and to survive her New Year's party. But she seems always to be the same, reads without spectacles and is only a little deaf; although once or twice lately she *has* accused me of "muttering, like everybody do seem to nowadays—too lazy to open their mouths, I suppose."

Last time little Mrs. Lacey came in I asked her how the dramatic society was getting on, and she said that if they could get one single rehearsal with everybody there it would be getting on very well indeed. She added that there "are a lot of wheels within wheels to be thrashed out" at the meeting to-morrow night, and she hoped that Miss Phyllis Brown would be there for she hadn't turned up at the last two.

Remembering that Miss Phyllis was not at Mrs. Frobisher-Spink's party either, I asked Mrs. Lacey if she knew why.

"Oh, something to do with her rats," she said vaguely.

"I suppose you mean her little dogs."

Mrs. Lacey smiled. "Dogs then—but we always call them rats, nasty snappy little things."

This reminded me of Bumble's unfortunate mistake when I called at The Weavers last winter, and when I had described the scene and we were having a good laugh, we were interrupted abruptly by the arrival of Miss P. Brown herself.

She looked pale and drawn, and, as she waited for Mrs. Lacey to finish her shopping and go, she drummed impatiently on the counter.

If she was yearning for Jim, I knew that she was wasting her time, for he was out in the shed opening a huge packing case of groceries; but, "You've heard, I suppose?" she asked dramatically, when at last the shop was empty.

I had no idea at all what she meant, and when she saw my blank expression she drew a pale green georgette handkerchief from her raffia bag and dabbed her eyes.

"My little Fairy Frivolous," she whispered, "I've lost her."

"Lost? You don't mean dead?"

"Yes, I do—poor, sweet, tiny little heart."

"Is it the old one you brought in here some time ago? Do you remember, I grumbled because you put her on the counter?"

"Yes—yes. . . ."

"But, Miss Brown, she must have been very, *very* old."

I am absurdly fond of dogs myself and realise that a toy dog can be just as appealing to some people as a bigger one; but Miss Brown has at least twenty of them and this old matron was nearly blind and had next to no teeth.

"No, she wasn't. My little Fairy was only eleven—but she'd always had poor health."

I felt that this exchange was getting us nowhere, and I looked doubtfully at Miss Brown, wondering why she had come, for I felt sure it couldn't be only for my sympathy.

"I'm dreadfully sorry," I said at last. "I know how awful it is to lose a dog—but, perhaps, if she wasn't well, I mean—perhaps it's a good thing really."

"She's to be buried at the bottom of the garden," said Miss Phyllis (how suitable for a Fairy, I thought flippantly), "and I wondered, I just wondered if the Commander would come round and dig her little grave and put up the stone. I can't bear an insensitive village person to do it and"—she fluttered her hands,—"my sister and I are so upset. . . ."

For a second I felt like retaliating with, "So that's how the land lies," for I hate insincerity and I was sure that all this was only an elaborate excuse to get hold of him; but my better nature took charge for once—and, "I'll ask him," I said gently. "I dare say he will. I'll ring you up."

A gleam came into her eyes, and I believe she had almost forgotten about Fairy Frivolous as she tripped out of the shop.

Later, I explained all this to Jim. He can't bear Miss Phyllis, but he has a very kind heart; so he said, grudgingly, "Oh, all right," and went off soon after lunch. When he returned I asked him how he had got on.

"Terrible," he said gloomily. "The old fool wept on my shoulder and I cleared off as quickly as I could."

"How about the sister? Was she upset, too?"

"Emily? She opened the door to me and I thought she looked particularly cheerful. She said it was very good of me to come—and then the old hag rushed in and I never saw her again."

(I thought at the time there was something odd about this report of Jim's—but I couldn't somehow place it.)

On Saturday afternoon, when the shop was crowded, old Mrs. Root dropped her loaded basket with a crash on the floor. It contained, among other things, half a pound of bacon, a pound of margarine, two pounds of sugar, a dozen eggs and a bottle of tomato sauce.

The mess was appalling, and Mrs. Root rounded on her nearest neighbour, swearing that it was her fault. As she shouted and stormed, I looked up into her flushed and angry face and was distressed to see that in fact her eyes were filled with tears and her stern old mouth quivering. She is, I should say, only in her early seventies and a big, upright, unyielding figure—but now Jim, too, seeing how near she was to breaking down, picked up her basket, and said firmly, "I'll clear it all out and give you everything fresh. You go on home, Mrs. Root, and the whole lot will be down at your house in about ten minutes. Don't worry—it won't cost us anything—we're insured."

I found myself gaping at this last ridiculous statement, but I quickly realised that he was right, for if she thought that we were doing her a favour she would have refused it angrily.

When we shut the shop at one o'clock I said to Jim, "That was very nice and understanding of you," but he was embarrassed and muttered, "Damned old fool. That little lot cost us nearly fifteen bob."

Yesterday was Rogation Sunday and a fine warm morning. The vicar and his choir (eight little boys, the blacksmith and small-holding Mr. Parker) beat the bounds and the crops were blessed. I consider this to be one of the most moving ceremonies of the country year, and I should have liked to join the little party of people who followed them—but I had no intention of walking round with J. Carrick.

Now that the flat racing has begun again, there is a lot of betting in the village. Our predecessor used to telephone people's bets to the Badgerford bookie; but Jim won't do it, for he says it only leads to trouble.

A local horse was second in the Lincoln and both the Upper Barley stables have been doing well since then. Now one of them has a colt running in the Derby and excitement is mounting; a chestnut called Thunderflash (by Rocket out of Lightning), he did well as a two-year-old, I believe, but was a fifty-to-one outsider at yesterday's call-over. The village is putting its shirt on him but I am not going to, for I can't afford to lose money—and I have not forgotten Barrabas.

I was summoned to a rehearsal last night, for the actors are now supposed to manage without their books.

Miss P. Brown alone had not attempted to learn her lines, and her muttered excuses about Fairy Frivolous cut no ice with the vicar's wife, who said, "How can one be expected to produce a play with no co-operation from anyone and not even an example set by the better educated." Miss P. Brown dissolved into near hysterics and resigned from the dramatic society; but her part was taken over by little Mrs. Lacey, who will certainly do it a great deal better.

The play is really extremely funny and the actors have begun to enjoy it, but the gentle temperament of the blacksmith is still a great problem. He is supposed to be a desperate character, but, try as he will, he cannot be even faintly tough and, indeed, last night he held his pistol as if it were a cup and saucer.

Mr. Parker too is a problem, and the vicar's wife has found her match in him, for even though he does value her occasional custom for his taxi, he stands no nonsense where his art is concerned. So she has had to let him go his own way and, except that he very much overacts, he is not at all bad.

The Badgerford Rural District Council is considering putting some kind of proper drainage in the village, and a parish meeting to discuss the matter was held last night.

Jim and I had had no strong feelings one way or the other, for our own apparently non-existent system seems to work satisfactorily; but the vicar's wife, with whom I walked across the Green, said that they thought the idea absurd and entirely unnecessary.

I asked her why; but she only tossed her head, thereby increasing her likeness to a morose van-horse, and said that when we got to the hall I should be able to find out for myself.

The meeting began at seven. It was a chilly evening, and only a few cottage people left their televisions to attend it—but nearly all the gentry were there.

The idea, I found, is to instal proper drainage throughout Lower Barley and to dispose of the sewage in a field which will have to be bought for that purpose. If such a field hadn't been available, the scheme would have been dropped altogether; but it seemed that Mr. Davenant had been persuaded to sell a piece of ground to the R.D.C., under the impression that the digging of which the surveyor spoke to him was for the purpose of archæological research. Although the mistake had now been explained to him, he is a man of his word and refused to go back on it.

The vicar' was physically (but his wife spiritually) in the chair, and the vicar vaguely outlined the general scheme.

The main contributions to the evening's discussions were then as follows:

Colonel Halahan: "Isn't there a danger of the county council's interfering and making us into a kind of dormitory for one of the Government depots, if we insist on having all the amenities?"

Mrs. Lacey: "If amenities means a bus to Badgerford every day, I'm all for it."

The vicar's wife: "Why more buses when we've got them regularly one day a week already? Surely that's enough (glancing rather sourly at me) when we've got such an excellent and up-to-date shop in the village."

Mrs. Root: "People what rides about in cars never thinks about them as has only got their two feet."

Kate Beery: "The bus is always late anyway—and you can't get on to Salisbury—not if you misses the connection like I did last Saturday week."

Mrs. Crabtree: "Who wants to go to Salisbury anyhow—dirty old place wi' all them pushing people. 'Tis nearly as bad as London."

Mrs. Root: "London? Now they 'as plenty o' buses there. Why, when my daughter, Ruby, what lives at East Ham, wants to go to——"

The vicar's wife (interrupting): "We'd all like to hear about Ruby another time; but meanwhile how about the drainage scheme?"

Mrs. Davenant: "As my husband has promised a field and it does seem as if it would really benefit the village, I'm wholeheartedly for it."

The Vicar's wife (contrarily): "The whole thing seems quite unnecessary. We've all managed very well up to now—and I quite agree with Colonel Halahan, we don't want the village spoilt."

Mrs. Frobisher-Spink (unintentionally putting herself on the side of the Davenants, whom she had believed to be away or she would never have come to the meeting at all): "No wonder the Vicarage isn't interested, seeing they've just had a new septic tank provided by the Church Commissioners."

Kate: "Won't it smell a bit ripe like when the wind's our way?"

The vicar's wife (ignoring Kate): "Whether or no we have a new septic tank would naturally not affect our judgment and (turning to her husband) we only want what's best for everybody, don't we, dear?'"

The vicar: "Naturally . . . naturally."

Mrs. Frobisher-Spink (quickly changing sides, as she realises where she has landed herself): "Kate's quite right and it seems most peculiar to have invited the council to use a field so near at hand for sewage."

Mrs. Davenant: "It isn't near at hand and the council wasn't invited."

At this point, *Mrs. Frobisher-Spink* did not actually say, "Liar!" but she might just as well have done.

Eleanor Halahan: "Are we deciding now or are we just recommending to the council?"

Mrs. Frobisher-Spink (making the most of her opportunity): "It's all been decided beforehand. People who sell their land at a huge profit to the council and then come to a meeting to discuss the idea are nothing more than hypocrites."

Kate: "About them smells, I was wondering——"

Mrs. Davenant, very red in the face, was about to say something, but *Nurse Ames* quickly intervened and said, "Smells there may be, Kate, but they'll be nothing but hygienic."

Mrs. Crabtree said: "A smell's a smell."

Jim came in at this juncture and whispered to me that he had put a hot bottle in my bed and it had leaked through to the mattress and what should he do. To his surprise, I smiled at him with the greatest pleasure and thankfully escaped from the meeting to deal with the mattress myself; but I was told next day that the discussion went on, with a good deal of acrimony, until 9.30 p.m. and that even then nothing was finally decided.

10 June

Haymaking has begun, and the smell of new-mown grass sweetens the air and comes in delicious waves through the open shop-door. It makes us long to be out of doors and wish even more passionately that we could have afforded a small farm.

It is Derby Day tomorrow and everyone who comes into the shop babbles on about Thunderflash. Even Jim admitted to having put five shillings on him, and at last I weakened and did the same. The odds were still fifty-to-one and by lunchtime I had already in my mind spent my winnings on nylons, new cushion covers and one of those huge dog-beds about four inches off the floor, which Bumble will love next winter. It seemed to me that I ought to get about £12, so I should be able to buy something nice for Barbara as well.

In my last letter to her I referred facetiously to her "engagement" to Master Blade and I had the following perfectly serious reply this morning:

"What rot about Roger. He's not good at anything and Madge Beeton whose brother is in his house says he's potty. I like Peter Davenant and George but I shan't get married before I'm thirty at least because I want to be an air hostess and I don't think they can be. So don't start getting silly ideas and looking for husbands like mothers always seem to. . . ."

H. Potter came in just before closing time and said that he'd heard that Thunderflash had strained a muscle and won't go; but I preferred not to believe this and decided not to say anything to Jim. H. Potter also announced that the doctor had been seen visiting one of the cottages and, "They do say as it's scarlet fever."

On Derby Day itself we were too busy in the morning to think about anything except work, and the vicar's wife came in to buy her weekly groceries just as we had turned on our wireless to listen to the race. Unselfishly, I left Jim poring over the list of runners and myself returned to the shop and duty.

The vicar's wife was very talkative and said, among other things, that she deplored the gambling spirit which is sweeping over the country and that, what with the Pools and racing, no one saves a penny nowadays. Look at today, even Mrs. Lacey, who ought to know better with that large family to bring up, and who usually works at the Vicarage on Wednesday and Friday afternoons, refused to come in until after she'd heard the Derby on the wireless. It's ridiculous and really a little alarming, didn't I agree?

I didn't agree at all and was longing to rush back into the house from which I could irritatingly hear the B.B.C. commentator but not what he said. However, I consoled myself with a clear vision of Thunderflash's being led in triumphantly by our Upper Barley neighbour and managed, I think, to seem pleasant and unhurried.

By the time the vicar's wife had left, the race was over and Jim came into the shop grinning broadly. "I've won two quid," he said and laughed.

"Is that all? I thought you put on five shillings? Mine comes to about £12. What a thrill for the village!"

"What *are* you talking about?"

"Thunderflash, of course. You said he'd won."

"No, I didn't. He was scratched last night—Potter said he'd told you." Jim smiled complacently. "I put something on the French horse and very nice, too."

I could think of no even remotely ladylike words to express my feelings—so I kept quiet and didn't *say* anything at all.

There are no cricket matches fixed for June and very little practice in the evenings, for as soon as haymaking begins, everyone is working over-time. The Derby has been forgotten and now, with June ten days old and the weather fine and steady, some of the hay is already being picked up. The baler went past our door this morning and I can hear the mower in the meadows behind us.

The scarlet fever rumour has been confirmed. It was the head cowman's son, "Toots" Evans, and I suppose this means that the father will be off work, too—which will make things pretty awkward at the farm.

The shop was empty just before lunch today, when the bell jangled and in walked John Carrick.

"I've come to ask you a great favour, Mrs. Braid," he said at once. "In fact, I hardly like to ask it."

I couldn't help warming to him as he stood there—shy, a little embarrassed and twisting his cap in his hands like a great silly child—and, of course, he couldn't possibly know the reason why I had been avoiding him lately.

"I expect you've heard they've got scarlet fever at Evans's house? The son's gone off to the isolation hospital and, of course, Evans can't have anything to do with the milking."

"You must be pretty shorthanded," I said, seeing clearly into his mind, "especially with the hay."

"We are. I can manage in the mornings, for we can bring in a couple of ordinary hands to help with the machines, but the awful problem is in the afternoons. I've got three of our best cows, including the old lady you liked so much, just within a week of finishing their lactations—they'll all do over 1,500 gallons if we can keep 'em going—but they're all three hand-milked. I remember telling you none of 'em'll stand the machine or ever have.

"It was the Halahans suggested it really," he went on. "They told me you'd worked on a farm in the war and were a first-rate milker. I wondered—just in the afternoons—just for a week—if you would think of it. I mean if your brother could hold the fort here...."

I wanted to say "yes" at once; but I remembered Miss Phyllis Brown.

"I'd like to help," I said, "but why don't you do it yourself?"

He held up his left hand and, for the first time, I noticed that three fingers were scarred and permanently bent.

"Can't," he said, half laughing. "Gallant hero—wounded in war."

I felt my face flushing and was overcome with shame. It was just the same situation as when strangers are surprised and slightly contemptuous when Jim refuses to do something he can't manage.

"What an idiotic thing to say," I mumbled. "I'm dreadfully sorry—I'd no idea."

John Carrick laughed outright.

"Good," he said, "now I've put you in the wrong. Will you help me?"

"Yes, of course," I said—and, to myself, "be damned to Miss Phyllis Brown."

A week of glorious weather has gone by and a good deal of the hay is in. Barley Buttercup, Butterpat and Bountiful have reached their 1,500 gallons in 305 days and, what with the shop, the farm in the afternoons, two rehearsals and the usual cooking and chores to do, I have had no time at all for this journal—at least I have been too tired to write it.

But now, John has got a relief milker, a fat, apple-cheeked girl from Devizes, and soon Evans will be back, for it looks as if "Toots" is to be the only victim.

I enjoyed going to the farm every day although my hands ached abominably at first; and it was particularly satisfactory because the cows there are superb and the whole place is beautifully run.

I know John very much better, too, for I stayed each day to help clear up, so that the men could get away to the fields, and had a cup of tea with him afterwards. He is such a nice person and it is really a tragedy about his wife; for he must be lonely and unhappy, and the house, which is old and rambling, has a neglected kind of air.

He has two farm women who come daily to do for him, but although the house could be comfortable, as well as old and beautiful, it seems only half lived in. Whether or not he minds this, it is impossible to tell.

We had several long talks and we seemed to agree about farming affairs and about most other matters—but he never mentioned his wife, nor did he give any hint at all as to his feelings about his present everyday life; and it would have been an impertinence for me to have questioned him. He *did* reveal though that he has a quick and intelligent mind and a keen sense of humour: and when he laughs, which he seems to do much more often lately, he looks ten years younger than when I first saw him. I am glad that we are friends now—and when his father and mother come to stay in a week or two, I have promised to go there with Jim to meet them.

Jim is a good-natured old thing. He went to see General Blade about a week ago and described him afterwards as a "monumental bore"—but the old man is almost bedridden and I find that Jim has arranged to go and play chess with him every Wednesday evening.

I have a wonderful feeling of well-being these days. I suppose it is the lovely summer weather. The hedgerows are sprayed now with wild roses, to me the most lovely of all flowers—and today Mrs. Davenant brought us a punnet of strawberries from the Manor garden, the first strawberries we have had this year.

Also Miss P. Brown told us that her invitation to the U.S.A. has been repeated and she expects to go at the end of June.

The village is beginning to get ready for its annual jollification. This is called Barley's Glory and it happens on the last Saturday in June. It is the only occasion on which the two Barleys combine—or indeed have anything to do with each other if they can help it—and I understand that it is the one day in the year when the village really lets itself go.

Mrs. Crabtree says that there was much more to it in her young days, when there were stalls set up all round the Green (with fairings to be bought for a few pence and gilded gingerbread houses and so on), and merry-making until midnight . . . "But not a minute after, for the old vicar were very strict—and quite right, too. It wouldn't do at all to offend the dear Lord."

But it seems to me that they don't do so badly nowadays, for the occasion is a general holiday. The little fair pays its summer visit, there is a fancy dress parade for the children, sports (including a grand tug-of-war across the stream between the two Barleys), a free tea provided by the squire, a show in the village hall and, at night, a grand drinking and dancing outside the Red Lion.

It is for the sports that the village is now practising, and there are long jumping and high jumping and skittles out on the Green every night while, in their doorways, the women sit making elaborate fancy dresses for their children.

When I first heard all the plans for the Glory, I thought at once how dreadful it would be if the whole thing were spoilt by rain and wondered what the village would do; but I was assured that it is invariably fine on the last Saturday in June and has been for as far back as anyone can remember. This statement was confirmed by Mrs. Crabtree, who has herself seen well over eighty Glories.

John's father and mother have put off their visit; but this evening Jim and I went to his house for drinks. The Halahans were there and also a very nice young couple who farm about ten miles from here.

It was a friendly little party and I enjoyed it; but Jim said stupidly on the way home, "I think Carrick's got rather a thing for you," which annoyed me, because I'm sure he hasn't.

Most people in the village lost money on the Derby—but not old Mrs. Rous. Rumour said that she had netted a hundred pounds, but our Bessy, who is usually to be relied on, denied this and told me it was only forty and "she be going to buy a smashing telly on the h.p."

Apropos of this, I asked our Bessy what she thought the Pools winners of last winter did with their money—except, of course, old Mrs. Crabtree who, we know, blew most of hers on the party.

"'Tis difficult to be certain," said Bessy cautiously, "but I reckon I've got a pretty good idea. There's Tom Crabtree for a start. He's close, you know, and I bet he ain't spent a penny. They say he's got a tidy bank account in Badgerford, and there's a plenty of Barley girls as would like to get him—although he's gone sixty—but he never seems to have fancied a wife like; though maybe he'll have to when his old Ma goes.

"Then, of course, there was our Bert. He put every penny of it in the Post Office for when we goes away . . . and I reckon it'll come in handy enough, too, down there."

"How about the blacksmith, Amos Rous?"

"Oh, he's a quiet one, you know, and there's no telling exactly what he's up to—but he's soft really and I wouldn't be surprised but what he's given most of it away."

"And old Mr. Root?"

Bessy laughed. "He's done a lot o' betting with his—I know that for a fact. He's always fancied having something on a horse; but she wouldn't never let him when he'd only got his week's wages."

"I suppose he's lost most of his money by now then?"

"No. The funny thing is he keeps on winning. I bet he's got a tidy little pile in his old teapot."

"Bessy, you don't really mean a teapot? That's just an expression?"

Bessy laughed again. "Why, everybody knows his old teapot! Ain't you never seen it?"

"No."

"They say his dad bought it in a sale somewhere. 'Tis big enough for ten—sort of creamy china with roses—and he's kept his money in it ever since I can remember."

"But, Bessy, if everyone knows this, surely it might get stolen. I should have thought it was a mad thing to do."

"Ah, you don't really know Mrs. Root, m'm," said Bessy, giggling. "If anybody was to come after that dough she'd half kill 'im first and then ask who he was. I remember once, before I left school it was, a stranger come badgering at her door and wouldn't go when she asked him civil-like—and she hit him wi' a hammer before he had time to explain he were only the Insurance. . . . Four stitches Doctor Baker put in and Ma Root never said she were sorry nor nothin'. Just said he shouldn't have come bothering."

"But Mrs. Root goes out sometimes. What then? Her husband doesn't look a very tough customer."

"'Im? You're right—he ain't much good at anything, tough or no, but he be that frightened o' his missus I reckon he'd stand up to a bloody great giant before he'd let her come back and find the money gone. . . . But," Bessy added with calm assurance, "there ain't anybody in Lower Barley what'd touch a person's savings—not even Lofty. I don't say as I'd trust him half an inch outside the village—but that's different."

What with the milking and the Derby and one thing and another I forgot all about the W.I. meeting this month; not that I meant to go—but I never heard what they settled about the outing.

I asked Mrs. Crabtree last time she came in—but she was feeling crochety and only muttered, "Southampton, like I told 'ee," and she wouldn't even let Jim carry her basket.

"What's the matter with her?" he asked, as the door banged.

"Rheumatism, I should think. Poor old thing, did you notice how bent she was?"

The door opened again and Mrs. Crabtree looked in.

"Not so bent as what I can't 'ear," she said, "and if you likes to carry me basket, Commander, you can; for, if you wants to know, 'tis too heavy and now I've put un down I can't pick un up."

"She told me," said Jim, when he came back, "to say that they had a rare do at the W.I., just like she forecast. The vicar's wife was all for going to Huntley and Palmers and having tea in Reading, but most of them wanted to go to the sea—and that was that. Personally, I can't imagine anything more unpleasant than a bus load of women going to Southampton, with the children yelling and being sick and not getting back until nearly midnight."

"You wouldn't like it," I said, "but they do. The sea's an excitement when you've hardly ever stirred from Lower Barley. Not that anything would ever drag me there. . . ."

We were interrupted at this moment by the entrance of Miss P. Brown, who had come to tell us that, after all, she still couldn't make up her mind whether or not to go to America.

"But I thought it was all settled," said Jim quickly.

Miss P. beamed at him. "So it is, I've booked my passage and everything but I *could* still cancel it. Three months is a long time to be away from one's friends."

"Absence only makes the heart grow fonder," he said—but he was paid out, for she lent forward and patted his hand.

"Do you mean that?" she asked intensely, and she gave him an arch look.

"Of course he does," I said, "and, anyway, the invitation must be a great honour. I'm sure you oughtn't to turn it down."

Miss P. Brown gave a rather pathetic little simper.

"Oh, it is," she agreed, "and I suppose it would be silly of me —but the trouble is my little Fairies. Emily *won't* take charge of them while I'm away. It's so selfish of her."

"What will you do then?"

"I shall have to send them all over to Miss Pethick's, near Salisbury. She has a kennel there—in fact, I started her off with my little Fairy Famous years ago. And that reminds me, I want a very special name for Fairy Fuchsia's little son. Now, Mrs. Braid, you're a booky person . . . think of something really appropriate."

But before I could speak, Jim said, "Why not Fairy Fertiliser?" and poor Miss Phyllis, who is not very quick on the uptake, was so delighted at his helping her at all that she gave herself no time for reflection but almost danced out of the shop, singing "Fairy Fertiliser! Fairy Fertiliser! Thank you so much," to the usual accompaniment of her bangles' jangles.

A moment later, she came back. "That was rather *naughty* of you," she said to Jim and, giggling, shut the door.

"I suppose it was," he said thoughtfully, "though as a matter of fact I didn't mean it in that sense at all."

The vicar, who is as vague in his way as Mr. Davenant and through sheer absentmindedness has had no less than eight trivial mishaps with his car since we have been here, was sitting in it outside the shop this morning and talking through the open window to Dawn. They chatted for some time and then, blowing a kind of papal kiss to Winston Churchill, the vicar pushed the self-starter and backed his car smartly into the milk van which was standing close behind it. The milk van is one of those electrically propelled things with tiers of milk bottles on each side and, unfortunately, at the moment of impact, the driver was balancing a full crate on the edge. The result was spectacular! There was a crash of breaking glass, the driver slipped on the kerb and fell on his back, fourteen bottles of milk broke or rolled into the road, Winston Churchill howled and Mrs. Frobisher-Spink, who drives fast and seldom looks where

she is going, came rushing round the corner and swirled by
with a satisfying but ominous scrunch of glass.

"My!" said Lucy Rous, with unusual understatement, when
she and most of the women who live round the Green ran
out to see the fun. And "Whatever you been up to, sir?"
asked our Bessy, as the vicar opened his car door and stepped
out.

Luckily, the milkman had only a few scratches, but he bled
freely and made so much fuss that Nurse Ames had to be sent
for.

"Glory be to God," she exclaimed, exaggerating her natural
brogue as she plastered his hand, "by the way they all came
tearing up for me I thought there'd have been a real accident."

The vicar, looking very distressed, said, "Oh, dear! Oh,
dear! My poor boy—I'm so dreadfully sorry. You must let me
pay for the milk." And forgetting his car entirely, he walked
hurriedly home.

There was another rehearsal last night. The cast really do
know their words now, and since Miss P. Brown's resignation
things have gone pretty smoothly—though smallholding Mr.
Parker is still troublesome. Unfortunately he has a craze for
adding to his part and slipping in little bits and pieces, so that
the others' cues are lost and the rest of the players are driven
mad. But there is no hope of replacing him should he cut up
rough, so the vicar's wife, for once, is helpless. I tried myself to
explain to him that he was confusing the others, but he had the
bit between his teeth and said airily and optimistically, "Oh, the
audience likes things topical—I only puts in a piece here and
there to make them laugh. Don't worry, Mrs. Braid, mam, it'll
be all right on the night."

Poor Kate next door has had the most dreadful toothache for
two days and nights but won't go to the dentist and just sits, so
Jim told me, in their bar parlour rocking to and fro and holding
a hot-water bottle to her face; which if she has an abscess is, in
my experience, the worst possible thing she could do.

As soon as I heard of her affliction I sent word by Jim that I would see to her chickens for her; but Fanny, Miss Grogan's little hen, quickly took advantage of Kate's absence and this afternoon, when we were busy in the shop, hopped over our garden wall and scratched up most of our two rows of young peas. I discovered this when I went out to the shed to get paraffin, for there was a tremendous commotion going on—with Bumble trying to send Fanny home and Fanny squawking and flapping all over the kitchen garden. Her private scrabbling had done enough harm already and now their combined rushing about had created hideous havoc which I rather nervously reported to Jim; but although he is terribly proud of the garden, he took my news with comparative calm. Lately nothing seems to upset him, and he was in fact rewarded today for his good temper by the welcome information brought in by Miss Emily Brown that her sister is really definitely going on the 30th of this month and will be away nearly three months.

Things are beginning to warm up now for the Glory at the end of this week. There is an air of excitement over the whole village. The Red Lion is stocking up with crates and crates of beer, Kate's toothache has subsided and the dramatic society's dress rehearsal is only two nights away.

Nothing more has ever been heard of Mrs. Frobisher-Spink's young man, and I learn that her chauffeur kept his job after all. Lately she has started coming to the shop almost daily, but unfortunately Jim finds her very good company, and, although I have warned him that if he isn't pretty careful there will be trouble one day, he only laughs and says she is not a bad sort. She annoys me personally, not only because she usually ignores my presence altogether but because she wears such lovely, if rather too-grand-for-the-country, clothes. I should not at all like to change places with Mrs. Frobisher-Spink but her wardrobe makes me bright green with envy.

The elder Lacey boy fell out of a tree yesterday and spiked himself on a sharp stake which was sticking up from the ground.

The child was in great pain and had to be whisked off to hospital, and before nightfall I had been informed positively by three separate cottagers that his mother had been sent for and he was not expected to last the night.

In fact, it was not a very serious matter, but naturally Mrs. Lacey was anxious to go to see the child this afternoon and Jim offered to take her in the "Tram".

The dress rehearsal was due to begin at 7 p.m. and at six-thirty they had not returned, and it seemed as if the whole affair would be ruined. However, the "Tram" swept up to the hall at six-fifty-five exactly, to the relief of everyone and especially the vicar's wife who, for the past half hour, had looked as if she *must* have a stroke at any moment. Jim reported that they had not only had a puncture but it had taken ages to change the wheel which, he said, cannot possibly have been removed since about 1930.

The rehearsal itself started badly due, once more, to the irrepressible Mr. Parker. It is his job to come on alone in the first scene and quietly to put a gun he is carrying into the corner by the stage fireplace; but, in fact, the whole of the cast and hangers-on were almost frightened out of their wits by a deafening explosion as he laid the gun down. When calm had been more or less restored, he explained that he thought the audience would think it funny, and it was perfectly safe because he only pointed the thing at the ceiling.

This was the last straw for the vicar's wife in her then state of nervous tension and, risking the complete collapse of the show, she told Mr. Parker exactly what she thought of him. But, had she only known it, she could (I have now discovered) have safely taken this risk long ago, for he is an ardent admirer of Mrs. Lacey's and it would have taken far more than harsh words from the vicar's wife to have torn him from her side, even as a stage husband. As it was, he took his scolding very meekly and promised not to load the gun on Saturday and not to insert any unrehearsed gags either. Myself, I doubted his sincerity and so I think did the rest of the company.

The blacksmith, though, has come to life—and on Thursday night, suddenly realising at last that he is supposed to be a tough guy, he charged about the stage like a buffalo and, with his huge bulk and grim expression, he was quite terrifying.

Nobody can think of anything now except tomorrow's Glory—and the tales of past Glories which the older villagers bring into the shop reveal them as pretty hectic affairs.

At three o'clock this afternoon two Rural District Council lorries arrived and started to unload a mass of gear on to the Green. They were soon followed by a couple more and, presently, two loads of sand and gravel and a stack of drainpipes were emptied on to the very site on which tomorrow's sports are to take place.

The village men were all at work when the lorries arrived but several of their wives came out to see what was going on; and at last old Grannie Rous stepped forward and asked the R.D.C. men "what they think they're a-doing of and don't they know 'tis the Glory on the Green tomorrow?"

The R.D.C. men, two of whom were those who got into trouble over H. Potter's leg, were surly and said that they "don't know nothing about that but we've been told to dump the stuff and we ain't going to take it back not for no bloody Glory nor nothing else"

Mrs. Rous, old, tough, enormously fat and shaped more or less like an egg, stood her ground. Her old black felt hat was dusty, her legs swollen and her feet pushed into very old bedroom slippers—but she is the matriarch of the village, mother of fourteen—most of them married and with children of their own—and she is someone to be reckoned with.

"'Ee'll take them things back," she shouted, "or we'll have the law on 'ee. Cluttering up our Green wi' your old rubbish the night before Glory. Go on—get it back on yer lorries before I clouts 'ee."

The young man at whom this speech was directed grew very red and muttered, "It's no good you carrying on like that, Ma.

We got our orders, see?" Mrs. Rous now had a crowd of supporters behind her and he looked round uncomfortably. "Pipe
down, Ma," he went on, "I tell you, we *got* to leave the stuff
here."

"Oh, 'ee have, have 'ee? We'll see about that. Best come up
to Vicarage wi' me right away—vicar be on council and he'll
tell 'ee what to do."

The stuff had all been unloaded by now and the young man
backed away from the angry woman and looked over his
shoulder at his mates.

"Better clear off, boys," he said, "we don't want no more
argument."

The other men got into their lorries and he tried to do the
same but Grannie Rous caught hold of him by the collar and
pulled him back.

"Will 'ee come up to Vicarage like I tell 'ee—or do we chuck
'ee in pond?"

The young man hesitated, and at that moment the vicar himself appeared at the churchyard gate.

"There's yer blinkin' vicar," cried the youth and, with great
presence of mind, he jumped into his cab as the women turned
to look across the Green. The driver already had his engine
running, and although Mrs. Rous grabbed at the man's coat he
managed to push her away and the lorry lurched forward and
bounced down the road after its fellows.

The women were still shouting after it when the vicar came
up and asked mildly what was the matter.

"Dear me," he said vaguely, when all had been explained,
"what an unfortunate thing—most unfortunate—but I dare say
we'll manage somehow."

"Manage?" echoed Grannie Rous, giving a dramatically
harsh laugh, "yes, we'll manage. Don't 'ee bother, Vicar, we'll
manage all right."

And she stumped off to her cottage, leaving the other women
to chatter and gape and the vicar to raise his hat and wave uncertainly before he turned away.

I watched this scene with fascination and presently asked Jim, who had been mowing the orchard and had seen none of it, what he thought would happen. "Oh, I dare say they'll chuck the stuff somewhere out of the way," he said; and he was not in fact far wrong.

Soon after six o'clock the men began to stroll down to the Red Lion, and presently old Mrs. Rous, Mrs. Root and a few other women joined them at O. Beery's.

All was quiet until about an hour later and then suddenly the pub door swung open, there was a lot of confused shouting and a crowd of excited people spilled out on to the Green.

In a few moments they were all milling round the offending pipes and heaps of sand and, above the din, we heard H. Potter yelling, "Come on, lads, get to work! Come on, come on!"

Spades and shovels seemed instantly to appear from nowhere and, as the sand and gravel were scattered over the road, Mrs. Rous, who—like Mrs. Root beside her—had clearly had a stimulating drop or two, screamed, "Chuck the pipes in the pond, boys! What you waiting for?"

The men needed no more urging and very soon the air was filled with the noise of splashing water and cracking earthenware. Then someone set light to the workmen's canvas hut, and as the flames flew upwards the whole mass of people seemed to go crazy. The men roared with laughter, the women screamed and the shrieking children rushed about throwing sand at everyone.

Then, suddenly, it was all over, and the Green emptied as quickly as it had filled. The whole affair had been quite good-tempered but the people had known their minds and done what they wanted and not cared a toss for the consequences! I was astonished and faintly shocked—but it certainly has given us some warning of the kind of mood the village will be in tomorrow.

Barley's Glory turned out to be all and more than we had been promised. A soft, misty-pearl morning heralded the hot summer's day which everyone was expecting, and at 6 a.m. the fair people were already doing their chores and setting up on the Green their red-and-gold swing-boats and the little blue-painted roundabout horses.

The day was a holiday for everyone, but we opened the shop from nine until ten to allow the punctilious fat postman (whose turn of duty it is this week) to collect the morning's mail.

The Glory proper started at ten-fifteen and had a most touching and decorous beginning, for the vicar, followed by the choir, came out on to the Green and blessed the assembled people and the village itself and Barley's Glory Day. The choir sang a short hymn, their voices rising thinly on the soft summer air, the people (or some of them) murmured "Amen", —and, "May it be a day to the glory of God," said the vicar gently.

Then the music from the fair blared out, the little blue horses were set prancing and the Glory continued on a rather more material note.

The children's sports were in the morning and Jim was one of the judges, but I decided that as everyone else was having a holiday so should I—for as long as possible anyway. So I retreated in peace to the garden and didn't stir out of it until it was time to see to lunch—cold ham, new potatoes and peas.

Jim, when he came in, reported that the sports had gone off well, with few tears and not much obvious cheating; but, as we watched the children's fancy dress parade at two o'clock, we agreed that the awards are bound to lead to trouble after it is all over, for the women are madly jealous for their offspring.

My job for the day was to help with the tea, and a tremendous undertaking it was, for the spread was magnificent and people could eat at any time between half-past three and five o'clock. As the day was so perfect it was agreed to have the whole thing out of doors and everything went smoothly until the collapse of the trestle table which bore all the tea urns. Luckily no one was scalded and only thirteen cups and three saucers were broken—but "it was quite a do" as, of course, somebody said.

After tea came the "dramatics" and at five o'clock I had to rush away from washing up the former to making up the latter.

The play went well, from the point of view of the audience: but Mr. Parker broke his word and let off his gun at the beginning, its shattering crash in the crowded hall bringing screams from the women and children and delighted roars from the males. This success went to Mr. Parker's head completely and, sailing through the performance on a sea of broken promises, he gagged to his heart's content and to the utter confusion of the rest of the company. The audience certainly loved him and, although I don't think he will be asked to join the dramatic society next year, he had his hour.

The men's sports, beginning at about seven o'clock, are the great event of the day, and as the hall emptied the Red Lion opened and O. Beery and Kate were worked off their feet in preparation for the men's efforts.

The village was crammed with people by now, for Upper Barley was there in full strength, and it seemed odd to us to be surrounded by strangers, most of whom were known to everybody else. There is a strong and, on the whole (but not always), good-tempered rivalry between the two villages, and as the evening wore on I noticed particularly an enormous man called "Bobby", from Upper Barley, who seemed to win everything. He must have been six foot four and was broad in proportion, and when he was not running somewhere or throwing something he was either teasing and kissing the girls or rolling across to the Red Lion and shouting to Kate for more and more beer.

At half-past nine the sports finished except for the tug-of-war—a tremendous pull across the stream—just where the water breaks under the little stone bridge and for a dozen yards runs freely until it joins the pond. This contest is in fact the climax of the whole day and is taken very seriously, the winning team getting medals and keeping the little silver cup in their own village for a year. For the last three years the cup has stood in the bar of the Crown at Upper Barley, but Kate told me that our men are sick to death of the indignity of being pulled into their own stream and they had sworn to set it up in the Red Lion tonight.

The scene was very gay—and brilliant with colour. The hot sun slanted through the trees; and the men's bodies, as they stripped off their shirts, showed milk white in contrast to the brick-dust red of their arms and faces; the women's and children's coloured frocks and the boys' washed-out jeans crowded together in a mass of blues and yellows, reds and pinks and white; the little pale blue horses leapt up and down behind the red gold of the swings; and, backed by green canvas, the hairy coconuts sat securely on their red-painted stands. Behind it all rose the church tower, not grey now, but bone white against the fading blue sky.

H. Potter was our caller and I saw him whispering last-minute instructions to the blacksmith, who was at the end of our line. Amos was still wearing his make-up, and his blue-shadowed eyes and lipsticked mouth gave him a grotesque air as he wrapped the rope round his middle and spat on his hands.

Colonel Halahan was the umpire, and at the first possible second he shouted, "Ready!" and fired his pistol.

It was a terrific struggle and the noise made by the crowd was worthy of it. H. Potter stumped up and down, screaming, "Heave! Heave!" and the Upper Barley caller, a wizened stable lad with a very deep voice, roared against him. I recognised Dawn's husband and our Bessy's and Albert Lacey and Lofty, the thief, among our team, and out of the corner of my eye I saw Grannie Rous, magnificent in scarlet, banging the ground with her stick and yelling encouragement.

The pull seemed to go on for ever, the men's backs were glistening with sweat and the blacksmith looked as if at any moment he would burst—when, as the noise became even more deafening, our men began very slowly to move backwards.

Then something seemed suddenly to give way and, with a tremendous splashing, the Upper Barley team were in the water and ours were lying in a confused heap on the ground.

When the excitement had died down a little I realised that I was being devoured by midges and I decided to go home; and I am glad that I did, for Jim said afterwards that the tug-of-war was followed by a free-for-all scrap, in which "Bobby" from Upper Barley was ducked several times and half the men (and a sprinkling of girls, too) were in the stream and soaked to the skin before they all calmed down.

After this I felt that I had done my duty by the Glory and I did not venture outside again until the singing in front of the Red Lion was over and the dancing on the Green, under a brilliant moon, had nearly finished. Then I stood at the garden gate for a little while as the bandsmen from Badgerford worked themselves up to a last frenzy and stopped—punctually at eleven fifty-five.

There were shouts of, "Go on you——! Chuck the bloody drum in the water!"—but nobody took any notice and gradually the crowd began to drift home.

There were a lot of drunks about and Jim advised me to go in—which I gladly did; but it had been a wonderful and exhausting day and an experience which I wouldn't have missed for anything.

Until the two or three old regulars shuffled out of doors and draped themselves as usual over the seats on the Green, everyone in Lower Barley might have been dead this morning—and these old men are half dead anyway. Kate, who is usually so chatty, fed her birds quickly and dashed back into her house, banging the door behind her, and even the children walked quietly and sedately to Sunday school—no scuffling on the pond's edge, no pulling off of hair-ribbons . . . oh, no! The whole village has got a hangover and everyone may as well know it.

Miss P. Brown telephoned in a panic after breakfast because she can get no answer from Mr. Parker, whom she wants to drive her to the station. She had *such* a lot of luggage—could she *possibly* beg Jim to take her—of *course*, she'll pay.

Rather surprisingly, Jim said "yes", as a favour—but there is to be no nonsense about paying. I can't think why he is so grand (and said so) when, with Barbara and the "Tram" and one thing and another, we are so dreadfully hard up. I had, in fact, forgotten about Miss P. Brown's going off tomorrow and thought, unkindly, how nice it will be without her.

This afternoon we went over to see Barbara, whose birthday it is, and took her, by request, a special fountain pen—the request having been made, I think, in the hope that she may share the publicity given to her favourite film and television stars who, according to the advertisements, seem to spend a large part of their time giving one to each other. Jim took her a box of chocolates and also shared in the cost of the pen, and Lucy Rous had made her a very fine iced cake into which we stuck the necessary thirteen candles.

Unembarrassed by her uncle's rather unusual car, she insisted on our driving her back to school after tea—but I feel that she may very likely regret it.

Workmen from the Rural District Council arrived at half-past eight on Monday morning, stood and stared for some time and then drove away. Most of their pipes have sunk but a few have drifted revealingly to the shallow edge of the pond; and I should imagine there will be the devil to pay, particularly about the burning of their hut; but I cannot really see how any single person can be proved to have taken part.

Gradually the village is returning to normal. The fair moved out soon after dawn and "Badger" is grumblingly engaged in clearing up the iced lolly sticks, sweet papers and general mess which is disfiguring the Green. People began, during the morning, to do their shopping, and the usual Monday morning washing is flapping gently in the cottage gardens.

Mrs. Root has a black eye and we long to know the reason but she was out of humour and came in only to complain that her bacon last week was short weight. This is possible but very unlikely, for in spite of Jim's tinkerings the scales which we bought with the shop are inclined to stick and we usually add a bit on to be on the safe side.

Miss P. Brown is staying the night in London, so she had to leave by the 5.50, and Jim put on a tidy suit for his taxi job, though I can't think why. Miss Emily went to the station with them to see her sister off and then actually suggested a drive round on this lovely summer evening—her first sign of emancipation, I suppose.

11 July

The R.D.C. row has begun and Kate tells me that our police-man was in the Red Lion last night questioning all the men—but for all he got out of them he might as well have stayed at home.

He was rushing about the village again this morning, fol-lowed at the trot by a portly man from Badgerford; but the only person against whom they could possibly have anything definite is old Mrs. Rous—and, naturally, the village is solidly behind her.

No one knows anything about the pipes or the hut or the sand and gravel—and everybody is ready to swear that it was not Grannie Rous who led the attack on the lorry driver. It couldn't have been, they told our policeman, for she's in bed now with a bad leg and has been since last Thursday. Bessy will allow no one into the cottage, and, blocking the doorway, says firmly to all visitors, "Gran's not fit to see nobody. She were took real bad last week and I ain't going to have her upset now"; and, to my astonishment, Nurse Ames, in a roundabout way, confirms this. She is, now I come to think of it, almost a native of Barley, having lived here for twenty-five years, and of course the villagers can count on her to stand by them.

"Yes, indeed, the old lady's in bed," she told the policeman, "and you certainly can't see her, for I ordered her there myself. Poor soul, her legs is swollen up like the full moon. No one says they've seen her, do they? The poor creature! 'Tis a dull time she's had, with the rest of the village gallivanting to the Glory and her missing the sight of those pipes and stuff running off by themselves. The wonder to me is, with the lie up she's had, that her legs is no better."

Unfortunately the council official, after listening to this speech, had the bright idea of interviewing the vicar—and this might well have ended in disaster; but before the vicar could say anything unsuitable, little Mrs. Lacey, who was helping him at the time to make a list of parishioners to do the church flowers, flew gallantly to the rescue.

"Good gracious, sir!" she exclaimed, in a shocked voice, "you know quite well poor Mrs. Rous took to her bed two days before the Glory. She missed it all and could only lie there in agony, poor thing, listening to us enjoying ourselves. These gentlemen must be crazy."

The vicar looked worried and uneasy, she told us afterwards, for he had a hazy recollection of having talked to Mrs. Rous quite lately—but he is so vague that he thought he must be mistaken and accepted Mrs. Lacey's statement absolutely.

"Dear me," he said, "I should have been to see her. It's most remiss of me—most remiss." And then Mrs. Lacey clinched the matter by telling them all, in disgusting detail, the exact state of Grannie Rous's legs which, she said, "have holes in them the size of your fist, sir, and she could no more come capering down to the Green than fly."

After this, the policeman and his companion drove away— followed by catcalls and whistles from the lads and boys and by an almost audible sigh of relief from their elders.

But I doubt if we shall get away with it, and Jim says that the parish will certainly have to pay for the damage. If that is all and no one gets hauled up in court, I think we shall be lucky.

John Carrick came in this afternoon and asked if I liked honey in the comb and, if so, would I swap a comb of honey for half a pound of bacon. I thought this a very generous offer, and I was just going to say so and that honey doesn't grow on gooseberry bushes but bacon does, when it occurred to me that the exact opposite is true. What I really meant was that you can buy bacon at any grocer's but comb-honey is a luxury.

"Come and fetch it this evening," said John, "and you can give me your opinion of young Barley Brigand, a bull calf I think it may be worth keeping."

I couldn't resist this invitation and, after tea, spent a very happy hour at the farm and returned with John carrying two combs of honey and half a pint of cream—"as a peace offering for the past".

He came in for a drink and then stayed to supper, and I was very pleased to see that he and Jim get on well.

Incidentally, whenever John or the farm is mentioned in the shop, I find myself scanning the villagers' faces for some signs of Miss P. Brown's gossip—but I have never seen the smallest sign; and either she didn't spread it after all or our villagers have beautiful manners—which, in fact, country people basically have.

Since we first came here there has been a small empty house on the opposite side of the green—the one bit of property, other than the council cottages, which doesn't belong either to the Carricks or the Davenants. I have asked about it occasionally, for it is a nice little Georgian house, known as Farthings, and it seemed sad to see the garden overgrown and the paint peeling from the doors and windows. Nobody could tell me exactly why it was empty but it apparently belonged to some relation of the vicar's first wife and I was told, "Oh, 'tis the lawyers and the deeds or summat. They been arguing the toss for years and no one can't live there till it's settled."

Now, it seems that "it" must have been settled, for strangers were seen there a few days ago and today a Badgerford builder's lorry arrived with ladders and bags of cement.

Speculation and rumour ran wild as usual but nobody knows anything and we can only wait and see. Meanwhile, they have started to strip the old tiles from the roof.

There was a heavy thunder storm yesterday. It started at about tea time and went on all evening with the thunder prowling round the hills and returning again and again—and I remembered Mrs. Crabtree's first husband, the shepherd, and his collie, Nell.

A tree in the park was struck by lightning and the three little Boot girls, who had gone up to the Manor with a message and were sheltering under an elm, saw it with their own eyes.

"They burst into the house," Mrs. Lacey told me this morning, "their little pink faces shining with wet and their eyes bright with excitement. Their hair was plastered and streaming and their clothes clung to their bodies as if they'd been bathing. They looked like kind of water fairies or something, dancing about with the rain dripping off them on the floor. (I cannot better her description and put it down in her exact words.) "But fairies or no," she went on, "I didn't half give it to them. I've told them time and again not to go near a tree in a storm . . . just think what might have happened."

Mrs. Davenant (who encountered Mrs. Frobisher-Spink in the shop this morning and murmured an automatic "Good morning" before Mrs. F.-S.'s cold stare reminded her of the permanent status quo) told me that her husband is at present torn between extreme misery at the probable drowning of his young partridges in the torrential rain and utter rapture at the finding at Saxon's Plate last week of a small pot, believed to be over two thousand years old.

I could not decide how best to comment on this information
—but there was in fact no need for me to say anything, for
Mrs. Davenant laughed and remarked cheerfully, "Sometimes
I think men are really *most* peculiar."

The village has settled down to its usual quiet, and nothing
exciting has happened lately. It is as if everyone needed to
convalesce after the Glory.

The storm has cleared the air but it is still exceedingly hot
and, even with the shop door open, we find that the butter and
margarine turn soft and the bacon flabby. The far end of the
shop is cool and dark, but we can't keep everything there all
the time; and Jim said madly yesterday, as he spooned half a
pound of butter from its glass case, "There's only one thing for
it—we shall have to get a fridge. It would pay for itself."

All the week it has been too hot to walk with Bumble, too
hot to cook or to do anything but sit in the garden after the
shop is shut. Jim takes the "Tram" out most evenings, for he
says he must get some kind of change. Eleanor's mother is ill
and she has been away for ten days, so I suppose he goes over
to Chalk with Geoffrey Halahan.

Occasionally I think of Miss P. Brown and wonder how she
is getting on in the U.S.A., and hope unkindly that they will
keep her there a long, long time.

A heap of ominously purplish-red tiles has been stacked in
the garden of Farthings, and I was just considering how easy it
would be to ruin that nice old house when the vicar's wife
came in to ask if I was going on the W.I. outing to Southampton. She said that she would have to go herself and it would be
so nice to have someone to talk to, and although I told her
that it would be impossible for me to leave the shop all day, I
felt rather flattered. In fact, after she had gone, I thought that
she was not so bad really and certainly she must think better
of me than she used to—but my self-esteem was rather dashed
when presently Mrs. Lacey told me that they've hired and
paid for a bus but haven't managed to sell all the tickets for it.

On the day of the actual outing the bus left at half-past six in the morning and I heard it return only just before midnight.

Our Bessy told me next day that "it was very enjoyable". And then she went on, "We'd have got back sooner only some of them went paddling and Kate got a chill in her stomach and were fair doubled up wi' it and went into a great flashy pub down on the sea front for a drop of brandy. Most of us followed her in—to keep her company like—and, well, it was nearly dark when the driver and the vicar's wife got us all collected.

"And Ma Root, well, I don't want to *say* anything—but when she were climbing up into the bus, she missed the step somehow and sat back pretty heavy on the kerb. She wasn't hurt nor nothing, but she began to sing and we couldn't move her till she'd been right through 'Annie Laurie' and 'Rule Britannia' and 'The Soldiers of the Queen' . . . and then she began to cry because she said the last one reminded her of her long-lost brother what never come back from South Africa or somewhere. But we got her up in the end and Kate gave her another drop or two of something she'd got in a bottle from the pub and she slept like a baby all the way home.

"Vicar's wife weren't half fed up though, and sour as gooseberries, till Mrs. Crabtree asked her if she weren't thirsty too in all that heat, seeing as she'd been sitting in the coach while we was all enjoying ourselves. And Mrs. Crabtree gave her a drop o' lemon cordial what she brought with her . . . and the vicar's wife tossed it straight down and nearly coughed herself out of the bus—for Mrs. Crabtree told me afterwards that it were neat rum! But it did vicar's wife a power of good, and she were quite jolly and sang with the rest of us and let little Boosey Lacey sleep in her lap all the way back to Barley."

The glorious weather still goes on and it looks as if it will be a very early harvest, for the corn is turning fast. We had a nice bit of rain earlier in the summer and now the sun has been blazing for a fortnight.

John came in to buy stamps for the fourth time this week and said the binder would be in the oats at the end of our orchard tomorrow. He has two combines but he uses the binder in the smaller fields—and I think he dislikes combining as much as I do, but he says it has come to stay.

Our Bessy, who in spite of having enjoyed the outing, seldom speaks now of anything but their departure to Australia—and is generally rather tearful about the whole business—told me today that yet another sister is to be married—Pearl, aged nineteen, who is in service at the Rectory at Upper Barley.

" 'Tis to be bridesmaids and all," said Bessy grandly, "and do you know how many of them sequin things is going into her dress? Eleven hundred! 'Tis pale cream colour with red roses for Pearl and sweetpeas for the maids."

I asked when the wedding is to be and why I haven't heard about it before.

"Saturday week's the day and you'd have know'd that if you'd been to church lately."

Bessy grinned, as she bent to her work, and the pale blue jeans, which have lately replaced her black satin, stretched alarmingly across her round behind. "Not that I often goes meself," she added. " 'Tis young Tony Root she's wedding—him that drives the baker's van—and it'll be a real posh do."

"That's a grandson of Mrs. Root's, I suppose."

"That's right. 'Tis two of the oldest families in Barley getting together like. . . ."

Bessy looked superiorly at the sweetpeas in our front garden, which are a mass of colour and have been greatly admired. "We be going to get ours for the wedding from Badgerford Nurseries—big show blooms, you know, with maidenhair. I reckon they'll look pretty with the little maids in pink silk."

I asked her if the "little lad" would be coming and she nodded. "Oh, aye," she said. "Grand-dad never misses. And 'twill be a big do altogether, for there's Rouses all over hereabouts and they likes a wedding."

I thought, as she said this, of poor Dawn and how hers was "quiet like, seeing as how things are"—but Dawn looks happy enough now and Bessy told me that there is another already on the way to join Winston Churchill.

John's father and mother are staying at the farm and on Sunday Jim and I went there for drinks before lunch. I was a little alarmed by old Mr. Carrick, for he seemed rather formidable and slightly disapproving. He is tall, thin and white-haired—with black brows and blue eyes like his son—and I heard him telling Jim bluntly that he is wasting his time running a village shop and ought to find something better to do. To which Jim retorted warmly, "Tell me a worth-while job in the country for a man over forty with very little capital and I'll take it." I suppose he would, but they don't seem to exist.

Mrs. Carrick was kind and friendly but, embarrassingly, she took me aside and talked to me about John as if I had known him for years, when in fact I hardly know him at all. She said that his marriage was a double tragedy for not only did his wife die of cancer but, long before she was taken ill, the whole thing had failed dismally and there would almost certainly have been a divorce. As things turned out, John absurdly blamed himself for everything. She also said that he was reserved and sensitive and had been the same as a small boy, and she added that he was devoted to children and had taken a great fancy to my young daughter.

I began to be afraid of what she might say next—and, I think rather brusquely, said that we must go.

Mrs. Crabtree bought three pairs of thick black woollen stockings this morning, "for 'tis past the longest day and summer's going"—although it is so hot that the sweets melt in their jars, and my hands always feel sticky.

I had hardly seen Mrs. Crabtree since the Glory and she confessed directly she came in that her "rheumatics have been that bothersome I can scarce get out of bed."

I asked her how she enjoyed the Glory.

"Oh, 'twas pretty fair," she admitted, "but the lads ain't got the guts they used to have. I remember the time when they'd a' throwed they lorries and the drivers, too, into the old pond *and* chucked the chaps back again when they come creeping out."

I reminded her that our men were in fact away at work on the afternoon when the lorries arrived and said that perhaps the law is stricter now than it used to be, so maybe it's just as well that nothing worse happened.

"Laws!" she exclaimed scornfully, "when I were a girl we never worried about they; I mind the time when me uncle got the sack for a bit o' poaching—just a couple o' pheasants like anybody might a' taken out of a tree by night and nothing said—and his two sons (cousins o' mine they was and big up-standing lads) broke into the Manor just before dawn and took all the squire's guns and chucked 'em in the pond. Ruined they was but nobody could prove nothing."

She chuckled as she tucked her stockings into her basket alongside her cheese and bacon and half a pound of brown sugar.

"That little old pond," she said, "could tell you some pretty tales."

She had begun to tell me a grim story about a sleep-walking child who was drowned in the pond, when the vicar's wife, whom she detests, came in; and, with a very pointed, "Good-day to 'ee, dear," to me and a brief nod to the vicar's wife, she went out, banging the door behind her.

"It's nice," said the vicar's wife insincerely, "how well you get on with the village people. But, of course, you have to or you wouldn't sell your things. That's a disagreeable old woman if ever there was one."

"Oh, no!" I protested and was about to add, "not when you know her properly," but remembered in time that there are few things more irritating than to have a newcomer tell you about your own village—and shut my mouth.

I was not rewarded for this good behaviour though, for she

said patronisingly, "Of course you haven't been here very long. You'll get to know in time what people are really like."

As she spoke, I remembered Mrs. Crabtree's gift of chocolates to Barbara, her generosity over the New Year's party and her courage when she scalded her old hands with her pudding —and I could not resist saying, "I shall be pleased if I'm anything like her when I'm well over eighty."

But the vicar's wife was offended and bought her postal order and left the shop with only a very formal "Good morning, Mrs. Braid".

Two large furniture vans from London were outside Farthings all yesterday and I have been told (a) that Captain Fox is a rich gentleman from India who is going to settle in the country, (b) that they're people from London what's just coming down for week-ends, and (c) (by Mrs. Frobisher-Spink, unconsciously using Barley's pet phrase) "I don't want to *say* anything—but I should be a little careful if I were you."

When I asked Mrs. Frobisher-Spink what she meant, she said darkly that Captain Fox was in her husband's regiment for a short time and "I wouldn't give him too much credit until you know just where you are".

I was glad that we were alone in the shop when she gave me this well-meant warning. Otherwise it would have been all over the village that the newcomers are thieves and swindlers and probably that Captain Fox is only just out of jail.

When I told Jim, he said, "I dare say she may have meant well but she'd better look out or they'll have her up for slander."

I decided, all the same, not to let the Foxes run up a big account.

It doesn't look as if we shall have the opportunity of allowing them to run up an account big or small, because Mrs. Fox came in later to buy a book of stamps and said, smiling sweetly, "I *do* hope you won't mind if we get our groceries in Badgerford. I always think it's so difficult for little shops like this to have things really fresh. You know what I mean—one always thinks of a village shop with faded dusty packages in the window that have been lying about for months."

I do know what she meant, but, as it happens, Jim and I take particular pains to keep our window newly stocked and attractive looking—but I didn't *say* anything and merely expressed the vague hope that the Foxes would like the village.

"It's adorable," gushed Mrs. Fox, a dark, petite woman, very well made up and dressed in clothes which would look extremely nice in, say, Maidenhead.

She then asked if I could recommend a daily maid and rather reluctantly I suggested one of Bessy's many married sisters; but when Mrs. Fox learnt that she was unlikely to find anyone who would work more than part-time she gave a little pout and said she'd thought that out in the wilds like this the poor people would have been glad to earn something extra.

Barbara is home for the summer holidays, and directly she arrived she said that the "Tram" needed new paint on the wings and bonnet and could she do it? I said, "Ask Uncle Jim," which was simply a cowardly way of saying "no".

But I had a boiling fowl from Kate's, new potatoes and peas from the garden and ices from the shop as a "welcome home" dinner that night. Barbara was very pleased, ate like a horse and exclaimed, "How marvellous to have some decent food after three mangy months."

On Pearl's wedding day the sun shone from dawn till dark and no bride at St. Margaret's, Westminster, could have looked prettier than she did as she walked shyly across the green, her eleven-hundred-sequin dress glittering in the sunshine and her bunch of red roses held very tightly.

Our Bessy had dressed herself in bright blue satin and Grannie Rous had on a lilac-coloured toque (rather like royalty used to be seen in) and the scarlet dress which she wore for the Glory. At least thirty Rous sons, daughters and grandchildren followed the bride, and beside her walked the "little lad" in his usual frock coat and bowler.

The Root party had reached the church well before them and had made themselves as smart as the Rouses—Mrs. Root, massive and upright, was tightly encased in purple nylon, and the bridegroom wore a very pale grey suit, rather cut in at the waist, and a white carnation.

The walk to the church was a quiet and sedate business on both sides, but the return journey was very different and there was a great deal of laughter and confetti-throwing and encouragement from the rest of the village before the party disappeared into the hall. Bessy told me afterwards that they had a wonderful time there and that young Mr. and Mrs. Root had such a grand and dawdling send-off that Mr. Parker, who was one of the guests and had done himself very well, had to drive his taxi as if the devil were after him to catch the 6.40 to Southampton.

Bessy said that Pearl chose Southampton for the honeymoon because, "You see, going there so often with the W.I. she wouldn't feel so strange like."

Barbara said, as she watched them drive off, "I do hope you understood my letter, Mummy. I couldn't bear to get married for simply *ages*."

I must be mad not to have realised about Jim before now. Of course, bless his silly heart, he is "courting" Emily Brown, and why I never thought of it I can't imagine.

We went to the Halahans'. for lunch today and afterwards Jim and Geoffrey left us to go over to Chalk Manor.

It was only when I said something about their having gone there every evening lately that Eleanor gave me a very straight look and began, "I think it's about time I said something, Mary——"

I felt momentarily alarmed, wondering if we had somehow done something to offend them, but she went on gently, "Perhaps I'm being interfering—but I don't mean to be. Jim hasn't been near Chalk, except on Sundays, since Phyllis Brown went away. He's very taken with Emily, I think. I do hope

I'm doing right in telling you—I wouldn't hurt either of you for the world."

For a few moments I was staggered and then, of course, completely delighted. I said as much, and Eleanor kissed me warmly.

"I knew really it would be all right," she said, "but I was so afraid you might be hurt at his not telling you."

"Good gracious, no!" I said, "but will she have him, do you think? Has he asked her?"

"I've no idea," said Eleanor, "but if he had and she'd said 'yes', I'm quite certain he'd have told you at once. He's devoted to you."

And so, I feel sure, he will; but now, I suppose, I shall have to pretend to know nothing until he does tell me—and it will be pretty difficult.

The more I think of it the less I can understand my having been so blind. I can recall now all sorts of small signs—his using her Christian name a little while ago (I remember I couldn't think what was unusual about the way he spoke of her), his smartening himself up so very uncharacteristically, his excessive annoyance when he thought Miss Phyllis had changed her mind about going away—and then all these evenings out in the "Tram". Dear, silly, comfortably familiar Jim—she'll be a fool if she doesn't jump at him.

I feel very happy about all this and have decided not to consider any further implications until the whole matter is settled.

Barbara has been helping in the harvest field for the last two days, taking her lunch with her and coming home tired, dirty and happy for tea. Yesterday she told me that she had asked John to take her on properly during the holidays; and later he looked in to say he'd like her help "on a business basis", but suggested that half a day's work at a time would be plenty.

I agreed gratefully, so long as Barbara is really useful, but explained that I am taking her away to the sea for three weeks in August.

"That'll be good for you, too," he said, with a very friendly smile, "but don't stay away any longer."

Barbara was delighted when I told her that she was to be taken on as a real paid hand, and she announced tonight that she had changed her mind about being an air hostess. "I did think, Mummy, that when I got tired of it I could pick up one of the millionaires who are always travelling by air and marry him and give you a lovely time—but, as a matter of fact, I believe I'd really rather work on a farm and marry a farmer. I hope you don't mind very much, because, of course, it won't be so nice—for you, I mean."

The Foxes have put some little gnomes with red hats in their front garden and I learn from our Bessy, one of whose sisters has started to work there, that they have built a cocktail bar into a powder-closet and have also a gigantic television. Bessy's sister covets the latter, which she says is so big that it's as good as being at the cinema, "Only," she says, "the pictures is more private like if you're courting."

Speaking of courting, Jim has said nothing at all to me, and it is only two days now before Barbara and I go away; so I suppose he hasn't yet asked Emily—but why ever not?

Barbara and I are going to Somerset and taking one of her school friends, so that they can amuse each other and I can have a chance to relax.

Lucy Rous and Bessy between them are going to help Jim in the shop while we are away, and he seems quite happy about our going—but I should feel much happier if I knew that everything is all right between him and Emily.

12 August

Jim took us to the station in the "Tram" and I longed to speak out and wish him luck with Emily; but I managed to keep quiet and instead (rather to his surprise) kissed him an affectionate "Goodbye" and begged him to send for me if he should get into the *least* difficulty about anything.

I took this journal away with me and read it over; and I can see now that anyone else who looked it through would perceive at once that I have been gradually getting more and more interested in and fond of John Carrick. And it is true that I have, for a long time, been trying to shut my eyes to my own feelings, for until this business of Jim and Emily Brown, I believed myself to be securely and irrevocably tied to our present way of life. Jim was and, indeed, is—until Emily accepts him—my first responsibility, and he has been through so much and suffered so deeply that I would die rather than let him think that I could even want to desert him. But suppose Jim marries? What will he do? Will he run the shop with Emily to help him, or will he try to get a real job that will keep them both? Whatever he decides, it means that I myself will be free, and that is a new and exciting (and perhaps frightening) idea.

Now that I have started writing about this in my diary, I had better be honest and have done with it. Of course, I am deeply in love with John and, unless I force myself to concentrate on ordinary things, I am always thinking about him. I feel a kind of relief even to have written these words—but what will become of me, God knows, for I have no reason at all to think that John feels as I do.

We are home again after three weeks of hot, lazy days which Barbara enjoyed to the full but which seemed long to me.

I feel very, very happy to be back again, for many reasons, and dear Bumble was hysterical with joy at my return . . . and even the cat was quite demonstrative.

The village was sun-baked and sleepy and the Green deserted as we drove up to our gate, for there was a cricket match in progress in the park, and I observed, as we passed the Foxes' house, that they have added tomato-coloured sunblinds to their yellow paint.

The shop looked even smaller than usual to eyes which had not seen it for three weeks and smelt pleasantly of cheese, bacon, Beauty of Bath apples, tea and soap.

Our Bessy had crammed flowers into every vase and jam-jar she could find, and Lucy Rous had made us scones and a ginger cake.

Only Jim, in spite of giving us a warm welcome—with the "Tram", cleaned and polished, waiting at the station—seemed not to be as usual, and it did not take a very acute eye to observe at once that something was wrong. He had an air of half-hidden excitement but at the same time seemed nervy and depressed. I longed to say something but I usually find it best when I hold my tongue and, therefore, reluctantly did so. But surely, surely Emily has not refused him?

Yesterday I started work again and was really enjoying a very busy morning when we had a most unwelcome visitor. The shop was crammed with people, half of them children buying ices and starting to eat them from the wrappings while still on the premises; Jim, in his shirt-sleeves, was sweating over the undoing of one of our huge cheeses, and I myself was carrying a smelly can of paraffin from the back of the shop —when suddenly I saw our Aunt Grace standing in the doorway.

She is a huge woman with a massive presence, and she wears Edwardian clothes and very high, florally decorated hats set straightly on top of her piled white hair. She is not, in fact, particularly grand, being the daughter of a Yorkshire wool merchant, and she married my great-uncle when he was a very young soldier stationed in York; but she assumed an air of grandeur, I believe, when she first married, and has maintained and magnified it ever since.

She was annoyed with Jim when he left her so-called land-agent's job and did not at all approve when she heard that he and I had taken a shop. In fact, she wrote to me angrily, at the time, saying that it was a pity I had dragged Jim into this sort of thing and it would have been much better if I'd taken a post with a decent family and sent Barbara to the local school and let Jim go his own way.

So far as I really dislike anybody, I dislike Aunt Grace—but Jim still has expectations from her (for she has no children) and I should hate to upset them.

Now, I could do nothing but wait until the shop cleared, thinking frantically as I worked if we had anything suitable to offer her for lunch—and remembering that it was to have been only cold sausages.

"Do come in, Aunt," I said, as the place gradually emptied, and then added insincerely, "How very nice to see you. Have you come all the way from Bath?"

"I have," she answered, "and I must say you took a great deal of finding."

She came slowly right into the shop, and little Boosey Lacey, whom the other children had left behind and who was staring up at her, unfortunately dropped the ice he was licking on to her foot—a foot encased, naturally, in long, narrow, rather pointed glacé kid.

Out of the corner of my eye I saw Jim staggering in from the back, almost hidden by his cheese, and I was afraid that, probably, he hadn't observed his aunt's entry. He had not.

"Clear the decks, Mary," he shouted, "and make room for this bloody great thing!"

"Jim!" exclaimed Aunt Grace, genuinely horrified by his appearance, "what on earth are you doing?"

With difficulty he dumped the cheese on the counter and then peered round it. His face grew very red.

"Welcome," he said at last, with a kind of sham heartiness. "It's just closing time. Come in and see round—though I'm afraid there isn't much room."

Aunt Grace sniffed, for the weather was warm and the cheese fairly ripe; and, as she moved forward, the child Boosey began to howl. She looked down at him and, at the same time, caught sight of her shoe.

"You disgusting little boy," she cried, and shook her foot ineffectively.

"Jim," I said, torn between laughter and annoyance, "Boosey's dropped his ice. Give him another while I mop up the mess."

Luckily, Aunt Grace didn't stay long—but long enough to see everything and disparage it, to ask us out to luncheon, for which we couldn't possibly get away, to moan at the squalid and useless manner in which Jim was wasting his life, to tell me that I had put on weight and it was a pity I was dressing and getting to look like a cottage woman, and to say that it couldn't be very nice for poor little Barbara to be sent to an expensive school (absurdly unsuitable) and to have to admit that her mother kept the village shop.

After she had gone I thought of many clever and appropriate

things I could have said in return, but at the time I found myself simply flushed and tongue-tied; and Jim was no help to me, for he soon became surly and very nearly rude.

The visit was of no importance really except that it added to the already uneasy feeling I have that Jim is indeed wasting his time and it is my fault. Didn't old Mr. Carrick say the same thing? And I have let him put his money into this place and what on earth is he going to do about that if he married Emily?

Today, smallholding, amateur-dramatic, turkey-breeding, gun-letting-off Mr. Parker looked in just before one o'clock and asked, "Was that *your* relative's Daimler I found in the ditch the other side of Badgerford, Mrs. Braid?"

"When?" I asked, alarmed. "Yesterday, about lunch time? I haven't heard anything about it—but I expect it was."

"Aye, 'twas Mrs. Frobisher-Spink done it—flying along with her head in the air as usual."

"My aunt wasn't hurt?"

"No," he said, half laughing, and added, "but the old lady didn't half tell Mrs. Frobisher-Spink off."

"When I come along in me taxi your relative's posh chauffeur, with the little thing stuck in the front of his cap, was standing there looking daft and doing nothing, so I thought I might as well make the most of it. She ain't a favourite of yours, Mrs. Braid?"

"No, not exactly," I said faintly. "What did you do?"

"Took her to Bath in me taxi and got little Joe Wilson in Badgerford the job of pulling out her car and mending the axle—and he'll stick the price on, too, I shouldn't wonder."

"But why?"

"Oh, I just didn't take a fancy to the old girl. Stuck-up airs don't suit me, not when they treats you like dirt."

"Oh, surely not, Mr. Parker. She's an old lady, you know——"

"Not so old but what she can't look after herself. Wanted to

know what I'd charge to take her to Bath in me dirty little car
—and it's not dirty—not really, for I brushed it out meself
after Miss Brown's little dogs was in it last time. 'Eight
pounds,' I said, 'take it or leave it,' I said, 'for there's not
another car to be hired hereabouts and I got plenty to occupy
me without traipsing off to Bath.' So then I took her home.
Posh place she lives in, don't she? I wished I'd asked her more
really, for I had a job to get me money and they never even
give me a cup of tea."

"I should think you had enough money to buy one on the
way back," I said drily.

Mr. Parker looked at me with a rather anxious expression.

"No offence meant, Mrs. Braid," he said. "I didn't think
you'd mind me sticking it on a bit, for she hadn't a good word
to say for you nor the Commander nor Barley nor me taxi. I
hope I ain't done wrong?"

"No, of course not, Mr. Parker. She was lucky to get home
so soon, I expect. How about Mrs. Frobisher-Spink?"

"Oh, just mucked up her off-side wing a bit. When she got
out and saw it, she swore like a man. Your old relative didn't
care for that at all and she began telling her off again—but she
didn't take no notice. She just said something off-hand like
about the insurance would pay and got back in the old Buick
and whizzed off."

When, presently, I reported all this to Jim, I said that, after
all, Aunt Grace must be well over seventy and I hoped she
wasn't too badly shaken up.

But, "Serve her damn well right," he retorted. "What did
the old fool want to come snooping over here for anyway?"
Which just shows how unfair life is—in that I, who felt
genuinely anxious about the old woman, will never see a fourpence from her, and Jim, who was heartlessly indifferent, will
almost certainly be left a few thousands one day.

Kate remarked over the wall this morning that it's lucky the
Foxes have come to Farthings.

"The Captain come over the first night," she said, "to ask if we'd got a spirits licence—and, when I said 'yes', he took two bottles o' Johnny Walker and two o' gin and, since then, he's sent over for a lot more. Oliver was saying just now 'tis a pity there ain't more like him in Barley."

This information made me wonder rather anxiously whether or not I ought to pass on Mrs. Frobisher-Spink's warning and I decided to compromise.

"What do you do, Kate, when people want to run up accounts? My brother won't let me give a lot of credit."

"Oh, we don't bother about that," answered Kate complacently, "not wi' the gentry. We keeps a slate for the rest, of course, and they has to pay up Saturdays or Oliver won't serve 'em."

"I believe my brother's right, you know; it's better not to give too much credit to anyone really."

Kate stared at me with her mouth open. "You don't think as them Foxes won't pay? You ain't heard anything? Why, 'tis over twenty pounds already."

"I don't know anything about them—and, if I don't know anything, I'd rather not give credit, that's all."

I tried to speak pretty cautiously, but I quickly realised that I had, in fact, said too much, for Kate darted into the pub, shouting over her shoulder, "I must tell Oliver—I must tell him right away."

Jim says that my half-warning will be all over the village in no time, probably greatly exaggerated, and may lead to trouble. But I think that anything is better than the Beerys' being done.

Later in the day I found it quite impossible to carry out my own advice, for Captain Fox came into the shop and said he'd like after all to open a small account, as his wife seemed always to be running out of little things.

He is a short, plump little man with protruding eyes, pale, smooth cheeks, a much-too-large moustache and thinning hair, brushed straight back without a parting. He wears quite good, but rather too new, tweeds and usually a duffle coat with a hood.

I agreed, with inward reluctance, to his opening an account, and he immediately bought three pounds of chocolate biscuits, a pound of cooked ham, a cucumber and fifty cigarettes. I felt certain, at the time, that I was really making him a present of these things—but I hadn't the courage to refuse him, although I did just ask if they would mind paying weekly, as we ourselves have so many bills to meet.

"Of course, of course, dear lady," he said at once, pulling out his notecase. "I'll pay now if you'd rather."

"No," I said foolishly. "Weekly will be quite all right." And his wallet was back in his pocket before the words were out of my mouth.

I feel greatly relieved about Jim's affairs, for Eleanor came over on Sunday with comforting news.

She confided to me that Geoffrey is going to offer him the job of Warden at Chalk Manor, and said that they will consider themselves very lucky if they get him. It is he, of course, who is lucky, for it is a wonderful job and exactly what he would like.

I promised Eleanor to say nothing until Jim himself tells me, but Geoffrey is seeing him about it one day next week and she thinks he will then definitely ask Emily to marry him. "She's a dear, you know, and full of character—and, from our point of view, exactly the right woman to be at Chalk."

I tried to tell her how grateful I felt, but she said again that it is they who are lucky and she added, "Whatever happens, it must be all settled before that dreadful sister gets back."

I asked her what she thought Miss Phyllis would do—and she said at once, "Join up with a Miss Pethick at Salisbury, who has a whole kennel of those horrid little dogs. I should think they'd suit each other exactly." Then she looked at me very seriously.

"It's you, Mary," she said, "who is going to get the rough edge of all this. Have you thought about that?"

In fact, I am determined not to think about it yet. I know that if things don't go right with me—and why should they, for I have nothing to offer him, I am forty-two and not very pretty—I shall be desperately lonely running the shop without Jim. But I shall manage somehow; and I said so to Eleanor.

"I suppose you will," she said evenly, and she kissed me and went home.

13 September

Barbara has gone away for a week to stay with a school friend in Dorset. I have seen very little of her since we came home, for she is absorbed in the farm and evidently John and the men have been very kind to her.

She looks brown and well but is always grubby and I had rather a job to make her presentable for her visit; but I am glad, really, to have her away just now; for I know that I am moody and irritable, even if I try not to show it.

A letter came today from Aunt Grace, warning us against the scoundrelly taxi-driver who blackmailed her into hiring his filthy old rat-trap when her car was deliberately rammed by one of our neighbours: "A most unpleasant woman—and I've instructed my insurance company to take the matter up with the police."

I thought myself that Mr. Parker had really behaved very badly but decided that Aunt Grace's letter had best be left unanswered.

Mrs. Frobisher-Spink came in during the morning and said she hoped my aunt was none the worse and called her "a most tempestuous old party, if you don't mind my saying so". And this is the first time I have ever found myself in complete accord with Mrs. Frobisher-Spink.

Mrs. Davenant arrived as Mrs. F.–S. was leaving and said loudly that she was horrified to hear one of my relations had been crashed into by that dreadful woman. "She's nothing but a menace," she went on fiercely. "She ought to have her driving licence taken away. Only yesterday she came tearing round the corner by the forge and nearly killed my husband. I dare say he *was* walking in the middle of the road but he has every right to walk where he likes in his own village."

She also said that some of her grandchildren were arriving today and would love Barbara to go up to the Manor, and that she'd heard some very peculiar people had taken Farthings and did I know anything about them.

I replied regretfully that Barbara was away and discreetly that I didn't know anything about the Foxes.

I have seen nothing at all of John since we came back from Somerset, but I like to think that this is only because he is working in the fields all day long and even after dusk until the dew falls. This has been the easiest and quickest harvest I can remember, and I think that it must be almost finished. I walked up the Downs with Bumble yesterday afternoon and saw pale gold stubble nearly everywhere and only one unfinished field where the combines were at work.

Now that the corn is nearly all in, we need rain badly, for the meadows are brown and hard and there is very little keep. Even our little garden looks burnt up, and the apples drop before they ripen.

Old Mrs. Root came into the shop when I got back and began a long argument about her weekly bill. Like most cottage women, she not only says things twice but she usually repeats herself three or four times; and, when she had said over and over again that we'd charged her elevenpence for a piece of slab cake she'd never had, and her husband doesn't like cake and he'd said he wished she wouldn't keep buying it, and she'd told the Commander herself to leave it out of her basket and if he'd put it in 'twas his own fault, and she didn't mean to pay for what she hadn't asked for and if I asked the Commander he'd tell me himself she'd said she didn't want it—I would willingly have given her half-a-crown just to go away.

This would never have settled the matter though, and it was only when I said, absolutely untruthfully, that I remembered all about it and my brother had told me but I'd forgotten to alter the bill, that she at last took herself off, turning back at the door to say, "I thought I'd better get it straight, for I don't like paying for what I ain't asked for, and I told the Commander I didn't want it. . . ."

I felt at this stage that I *must* scream—but luckily Mrs. Root was pushed aside just in time by Mrs. Fox, who asked, "*Do* you keep olives, because we've run out and it's *so* tiresome?"

I said we don't keep olives, for there is no demand for them, and Mrs. Fox looked pained.

"Oh, I felt *sure* you would," she said wistfully, "just for yourselves and people like the Manor I mean."

I suppose I should have been flattered at being bracketed with the Manor by Mrs. Fox, but I had again to say, "No, I'm afraid we don't keep olives."

She then lingered for a few moments, looking round the shop and picking up one thing and another, and at last she said, "I hear your brother was in the Navy—I'd no idea. Do bring him over for a snort one evening . . . I'll get Lance to ring you up."

It was my turn to look pained, but I tried not to do so and said instead that we'd love to come in some time—but, in fact, I have no intention whatever of visiting the Foxes.

John looked in later and said he hoped he hadn't overworked Barbara. I told him she'd enjoyed herself enormously and thanked him for being so kind to her . . . and he was just beginning to ask me when I was coming to the farm again when

Mrs. Frobisher-Spink came in and he cleared off at once. As the door shut behind him, she said she thought he had a charming smile and was a most attractive man, didn't I agree?

I had a horrible and frightening experience today.

The shop was very quiet, as is usual on a Monday afternoon, and the village utterly deserted, for the men were all at work, the children playing in the cornfields and the women indoors. Even the old men had found it too hot to loll on the Green and there was not a soul in sight.

I had the door open and was reading, when I became aware of someone looking in at the window. He was a man of about fifty, unshaven, dirty and bald. He was a big man and in his left hand he carried a small, cheap, sham-leather suitcase. As I stared at him he looked up at me through the glass, wiped his nose with the back of his hand and spat in the roadway. He was, in fact, a very nasty-looking tramp.

Jim had gone to Upper Barley to borrow something or other from the grocer there and I was alone. Bumble was shut out into the garden in the shade and I remembered uneasily that we had not yet banked our Saturday's takings, so that there was a good deal of money in the till besides the stamps and postal orders. I am not a very timid woman, but as the man came in at the open door I began to feel frightened. For a minute he stood there, looking round the shop saying nothing, and at last I asked him briskly what he wanted.

He didn't answer but, instead, picked up a meat pie from a tray on the counter and began to eat it, the pastry flakes sticking to his bristly chin and dropping to the floor.

"That'll be fourpence," I said. "Do you want anything else?"

The tramp still said nothing but he took a couple of packets of cigarettes from the shelf beside him and stuffed them into his pocket and then some apples and a bar of chocolate.

"Please don't help yourself," I said. "Tell me what you want and I'll get it for you."

He gave a kind of smile, showing his rotten teeth, and then he began to lift the flap of the counter. I snatched at it and banged it down, but a very nasty gleam had come into his eye and, ignoring me completely, he swept a lot of stuff off the counter with his elbow to make room for his case and started to cram it with everything he could lay his hands on.

By now I was really afraid, and I looked desperately out on to the empty Green. The tramp was, of course, between me and the door and it was no use running back into the house, for I felt certain he would follow.

"Stop that!" I shouted at him, trying to sound convincing. "My brother'll be back in a moment. Go on, get out before he makes you."

The man took no notice at all—but, leaning forward, he pushed his face close to mine; and his breath smelt horrible.

"Hand over the dough," he said hoarsely—and his filthy hand grasped my wrist.

I don't think I had ever in my life really screamed until then but, although it was unlikely that anyone indoors on that hot afternoon would hear me, I screamed as loudly as I could.

Then the tramp pulled me half across the counter and I could feel sickly that he was going to shove his sweaty hand over my mouth—when suddenly the little shop seemed full of men and, all at once, the beast was lying on his back in the dusty road outside.

Bill Evans, his son "Toots" and John were all there.

"Get up," roared John, giving the tramp a kick, and the others roughly pulled him to his feet, marched him across the Green and, with a mighty swing between them, threw him into the pond. The splash he made was terrific.

John picked up his case, emptied it and threw it to "Toots".

"Chuck that in after him," he ordered, "and run him out of the village, will you? Tell him if he ever sets foot in Barley again, he'll find himself in jail."

He came back into the shop. "Are you all right, Mary?

What a beastly thing to happen, my dear. Where's Jim and the dog?"

I nodded and he took my hand, but before he could say any more I heard the "Tram" draw up outside and a moment later Jim was standing in front of me.

"The men shouted there'd been some trouble," he said—and then, seeing John, "Oh, you're here, Carrick. What's going on?"

At last I found my voice. "A filthy tramp," I said, "tried to steal the money and frightened me out of my wits."

"We were just coming back for the milking and heard you screaming. You frightened *us* out of our wits, I can tell you."

"Quite a rescue," I said weakly; but I felt rather sick.

John looked anxiously at me and then nodded to Jim. "Better have a cup of tea or something," he said. "I'll leave you to it. Your sister's had a nasty turn. Let me know if I can do anything."

Jim thanked him and he went out.

This was something which might not happen again in fifty years, for we are not near a main road and it is very seldom that there is no one in the village; but for the moment it has taken my nerve and, privately, I dread the idea of being left alone when Jim goes. If I do keep on the shop I think I shall *have* to get someone to help me.

I wept with self-pity when I went to bed last night. It was shock, I dare say, from the afternoon's upset—but I felt utterly miserable. I had been determinedly shutting my mind to the future, but now the whole thing seemed altogether too much for me. I ought, of course, to have foreseen that Jim might marry some day—but he had been ill for so long and was so dependent on me that I had never thought seriously about it. Naturally, I am delighted, truly delighted for him, but I don't much care for the lonely prospect in front of me. I am grimly sure, too, that John does not care for me, for he is simply cool and friendly (very friendly—but that is not what I want), and even in yesterday's crisis he showed no sign of anything but kindness.

I felt a little better this morning when Mrs. Crabtree hobbled into the shop the very moment we opened the door. Her kind old face was even paler than usual and her eyes anxious, for she had heard, about my horrid encounter with the tramp.

"Are you all right, dear?" she asked fearfully. "They tells me he struck 'ee wi' his fist, the brute, and no one within call. You poor thing, he might have murdered 'ee."

"So he might," I answered laughing, "but he didn't—and he didn't hit me either; but I don't mind telling you I was very frightened."

"Now listen," said my old friend, "I brought 'ee something. 'Tis the old school bell what my mother used to ring when she were the teacher. Her got cracked somehow or other and when they gets a new one, Mother takes her home and rings her to call us children into dinner. I minds how we used to hear her right down the meadows."

Mrs. Crabtree fumbled in her leather shopping-bag and pulled out a big and tarnished hand-bell. "Now, you keep that by you, dear, and ring her loud if you wants anything. I shall hear 'ee."

As I thanked Mrs. Crabtree and put the bell on the shelf behind me, I decided that she is not only a true friend but one of the very nicest people in Barley.

"That's right," she said, as she went out, "don't 'ee let her out o' sight. And keep that big good-for-nothing dog with 'ee. There's some funny things you reads in the papers, wi' folks getting battered to death and such. We don't want that in Barley."

During the morning John rang up to ask if I was all right and said oughtn't I to have a day in bed after a beastly experience like that and if there's anything I want he'd come down right away. (I know exactly what I want—but it was not for me to tell him!)

Then Eleanor, Mrs. Lacey, the vicar's wife, Mrs. Davenant, Mr. Parker, Lucy Rous (who is now shapeless and expects her baby next month), Kate, Grannie Rous, Nurse Ames, Tom Craddock (whose wife has not had a single fit since last Autumn), H. Potter and a lot of other people all came in to sympathise—so that the little shop was crowded all morning; and old Mrs. Root actually brought me a present of a Victorian policeman's truncheon, painted in black and gold. It belonged to her uncle, she said, who was a constable in Salisbury; and she brandished it fiercely at Jim and told him that he ought to be ashamed of himself leaving me alone, for the place might get on fire and no one know till I was burned to death.

Mrs. Crabtree has spread the news about giving me her bell, and I dare say if I were to ring it now the whole village would come running—a tempting and rather comforting thought.

Jim ate no dinner last night and went moodily to bed at nine o'clock and this morning he said he wasn't particularly hungry. He has behaved oddly ever since I came back from Somerset but early today he looked really wretched—and I didn't know what to do for him—except to think out a very nice lunch of cold tongue (from the shop), salad (from the garden) and raspberries and cream (from John).

It was our half-day and by noon the shop was empty, so I started clearing up; but Jim kept following me about, saying nothing and getting in the way until I couldn't bear it another moment and turned on him in desperation. "What *is* the matter?" I said. "Can't you tell me, my dear?"

And then, at last, it all came out and he told me he'd been thinking for some time of asking Emily to marry him.

"I'm sorry I didn't tell you before, Mary, believe me. The fact is I've been awfully worried."

"That's all right. I'm delighted with the idea—I think it's wonderful, honestly I do. But what's wrong? Surely she hasn't refused you?"

"No—no, she seemed pleased when I asked her—but——"

"But what?" I said a little impatiently.

"Now, don't get het up, Mary. I'm trying to tell you. You see, at first I didn't like to ask her, because I'd got nothing to offer. Well, then Halahan asked me if I'd like the job of running Chalk Manor with Emily and, of course, it's marvellous of him and a grand job, well worth doing—but——"

"But *what?* Doesn't Emily want to go there?"

"Yes, of course—only the thing is I feel I'm treating you abominably. You and I took on this job together, and we both put our money into it and I think you did it really to give me something to do and to give us a home together as much as anything else—and now I'm proposing to abandon it and leave you on your own and . . ."

He stopped and looked at me helplessly.

"Oh, Jim, don't be such a silly, damn silly fool," I said, bursting into tears, and, presently, with his eyes shining and a silly self-satisfied grin on his face, he dashed off in the "Tram" to fetch Emily back to lunch.

Myself returned to the shop and recklessly took a chicken in glass, which we were recently bounced into buying, and added it to the cold tongue. I also opened our last bottle of sherry.

When Barbara returned from her visit, I told her Jim's news and she was at first rather disapproving.

"I should have thought Uncle Jim was a bit old for that kind of thing," she said—but, when she heard about Chalk, her mood changed. "Do you think they'd let me run the farm there?" she asked eagerly. "When I'm a bit older I mean?"

Emily *is* a dear. Everybody kept telling me so—until I began to feel she couldn't possibly be—but it's true and I like her very much; and Jim is quite off his head with happiness and perfectly useless in the shop.

It has been decided to say nothing (except, of course, to the Halahans) until the end of the month, in fairness to Miss Phyllis who returns then. I do not envy them the job of telling her, and I am appalled at the idea that she will now be my sister-in-law; but if Eleanor is right, and she joins up with the dog woman in Salisbury, perhaps we shan't see much of her.

Barbara got up early on Sunday morning—at about six—and, having bought the stuff with her own money, set about painting the "Tram's" wings and bonnet pure white. Not only is it highly unsuitable but B. has had no experience of painting and the result, which she showed me after breakfast, was terrible; for she had got her paint too thin and blobs and trickles had run down the wings and dripped on to the floor. She herself didn't seem too satisfied and she asked me rather nervously if I thought Uncle Jim would be pleased.

"I meant it for bridal white," she said, her mouth trembling ominously, and, at that moment, Jim himself appeared.

"My God!" he exclaimed, as he saw the havoc which Barbara had made of his darling "Tram"; and B., howling with shame and disappointment, rushed into the house.

"Damn the child," said Jim, "she's ruined the 'Tram'—ruined it."

"Oh, no——" I said. "It's still wet. Let's wipe off what we can and you can get Mr. Parker to spray it properly. You must admit it wanted doing. Poor Barbara! She bought the paint with her own money; she thought it looked bridal."

Jim's heart is as soft as butter. "Poor kid," he said. "All right, I'll go and put it right with her. But if you think I'm going to use the 'Tram' until it's done, you're mistaken. Bridal indeed!"

And then he began to laugh (for he is very happy just now) and went indoors to comfort his well-meaning niece.

After this, Jim and Emily and I lunched with the Halahans; and Barbara, who is very resilient, went off to the Manor and spent a hilarious day with the Davenant children until nightfall.

Ours was a very gay party, and Geoffrey told me that he would have offered Jim the Chalk Manor job long ago, only it was essential to have a married man there, so Emily had done them all a good turn.

It has been very difficult to keep news of Jim's affairs to ourselves, but we have resolutely said nothing to anyone for Miss
Phyllis's sake; and I have tried very hard to ignore my own
anxieties and to concentrate on everyday village doings. So I
paid due attention to Kate when she told me over the wall
that she and O. Beery are worrying about the Foxes' account.

" 'Tis nigh on thirty pounds now," she said gloomily. "He
said as he'd give Oliver a cheque last week but nothing ain't
turned up. He comes in every night for his doubles, too—but
I don't like to *say* anything."

"If your husband doesn't say something pretty soon, he'll be
very silly," I told Kate. "We don't know anything about these
people. Honestly, I should be firm if I were you."

Kate went off, muttering that she supposed I was right, and
she'd told Oliver a fortnight ago that I'd said not to trust the
Foxes an inch—but he didn't like losing a good customer and
he reckoned I might have got it wrong somehow.

Outside Farthings this evening were a Bentley, a Jaguar, a
Riley and two large red sports cars, brand unknown to me.
No doubt their owners were enjoying O. Beery's spirits, and I
wish the Foxes had settled elsewhere.

Mrs. Fox appeared in the shop this morning and said that
she'd encountered an "absolutely marvellous old character,
exactly like a witch" and did I know her name?

By a process of elimination we at last settled on old Mrs.
Weller; and Mrs. Fox said, "We thought her so quaint and it's
really rather lucky because she says that she and another old
crone will do most of our personal laundry. I can't bear these
steam laundries which absolutely wreck your clothes."

I fully agreed with her about steam laundries but did not
think it necessary to tell her that Mrs. Weller and "the old
crone" who lives with her are well known to be two of the
dirtiest and least honest inhabitants of Lower Barley. After all,
if Mrs. Fox thinks Mrs. Weller "quaint" and "a character", she
is probably getting value for her money.

The vicar's wife was here soon afterwards and asked if I thought Mrs. Fox would join the W.I. I have no idea, and said so, but I should think it very unlikely.

"It'll be a great asset to the village to have nice well-off people at Farthings," continued the vicar's wife, "and I expect your brother and Captain Fox will have a lot in common."

I made no comment; and, looking at me severely, she said that when I've been here longer I shall realise how important it is to be friendly with everyone in a small place like this.

The weather has broken at last, a wet wind blows from the west and the rain sweeps in gusts against our shop window, whips the pond into waves and drips from the raincoats of our customers as they stand making pools of water on the floor. The apples are falling and the garden flowers, brittle from the drought, are dashed to the ground.

H. Potter said he knew it was going to rain, for his wooden leg "hurt him something chronic"—and Mrs. Crabtree's rheumatism is so bad that Tom has had to stay home from work to do their cooking.

As the time for our Bessy and her family to leave England draws nearer, she seems more and more depressed.

" 'Twas always Bert as always wanted to go down there," she said to me today, "and now he's turned round and said he done it for my sake—and he's as miserable as me. And I've been against it from the start, as you know, Mrs. Braid, m'm, for it'll never be the same as Barley."

I could not honestly contradict this statement, and when I tried to comfort her with highly-coloured pictures of Australian life all she said was, "I know all that, m'm, but I don't want to leave my Grannie nor Granddad neither (though I think she sees the 'little lad' only at weddings anyway) and Dawn and Pearl and Joe and the rest of them . . ." She began to cry. . . . "And I'll be that lonely. . . ."

"Not with Bert and the children——"

"I tell you, I don't want to go down there."

But go I'm afraid they will some time this winter, for Bert

has already given in his notice to his "nursing home" and is going to help Mr. Parker with odd jobs at the garage until they are ready to leave.

Barbara went back to school this afternoon, but as they drove to the station she ignored the sober grey paint with which Mr. Parker has obligingly replaced her attempt at bridal decoration.

Emily went with Jim to see her off and was formally shaken hands with by Barbara, who said politely, "Good-bye, I suppose you'll both be married and have started a lot of children before I see you again—so the best of luck."

Emily is not far off forty.

Fox has not paid our small bill nor O. Beery's big one, and Jim was told in Badgerford yesterday that so far he has not paid anybody. It looks as if Mrs. Frobisher-Spink was right for once—though she is going to get a shock when she hears about Jim and Emily; for she is always making excuses to come in here and keeps inviting him to go off racing with her.

For the first time, it is believed, in nearly forty years, O. Beery emerged from the Red Lion and was seen this morning crossing the Green. His face is terribly disfigured, poor little man, and greyish white, too, from being so much indoors, but he ignored both stares and greetings as he stalked up the flagged path of Farthings and gave a tremendous pull at its wrought-iron bell. He was in the house about a quarter of an hour and, when he came out, he hurried back to the Red Lion, without a word to anyone, and slammed the door behind him.

Unashamedly, I lingered in the garden this afternoon, hoping to hear the latest news from Kate, and I was not disappointed.

"Ah, he's a rare temper when he's roused has Oliver. Mind you, it takes a lot to upset him, but when he's roused—crikey, he's a terror I can tell you. 'Captain Fox!' he says to me this morning, 'Captain Fox! We ain't in the Army now and I be going to get me money.' And out he goes—and, honestly, Mrs. B., you could have knocked me down with a feather, after all these years.

"Well, when he comes back I asks what happened and, for answer, he just flings a bunch o' pound notes down on the bar.

" 'So he paid you then,' I says, 'he'd got the money on him like?'

" 'Aye,' says Oliver, 'them's the kind what has notes or nothing. Smart, that's what he is—and I wouldn't be surprised if he ain't got no bank account at all. I told him I'd see he didn't get another thing on tick hereabouts and we didn't want his sort round Barley—and then I picks up a girt stick what was standing in the hall and told him straight, if he didn't pay up I'd bash him. *Captain* Fox! He started making a lot of excuses and saying he didn't want no violence—and then he give me the money.' "

"I *am* glad," I said—and Kate began rattling her chicken bucket and calling her hens and shooing Fanny away.

When her birds were fed she strode up the garden path and disappeared into the house—but she put her head round the door a moment later and shouted morosely, "I reckon we lost a good customer, you know—I reckon Oliver done wrong."

Miss P. Brown (no, I suppose I shall have to call her Phyllis) returned two days ago, and Jim and Emily decided to get it over quickly and went down to Southampton to meet her.

Directly they got back I asked Jim anxiously what happened and he said, with obvious relief, that she took the news surprisingly well. He said that Eleanor was right and she will probably set up with the Salisbury dog woman, and it seemed to him, from the way she talked, that she'd really been wanting to do it for some time.

He also reluctantly admitted that she kissed him when they parted. "She smelt of moth-balls," he added, "at least I think it was moth-balls; and she was much more excited about getting back to her beastly little dogs than she was about seeing Emily—so I don't think there's anything to worry about."

I expect he is right and I am thankful she did not make a scene.

Miss Phyllis spread the news everywhere yesterday and so now Jim and Emily are officially engaged and they will probably be married in November.

Kate told me that, of course, the village had known all about it for ages, but they didn't *say* anything, and she hoped the Commander would be very happy; for Miss Emily was a nice little thing—and she and Oliver had never had a cross word between them in nearly fifty years and she hoped they'd be able to say the same.

She is perfectly right about the village's having known of Jim's intentions, and I now learn that for the last six weeks the affair has been discussed in nearly every cottage.

"Surely you didn't think, Mrs. Braid," said little Mrs. Lacey, "that anyone could go courting in Barley and nobody know about it?"

(I had in fact thought so, if the parties were reasonably discreet, and now I wondered uncomfortably what kind of rumours about my own affairs might be floating across the pond.)

People have been in and out of the shop all day, congratulating Jim and, when they get me by myself, saying whatever will I do and won't I be dreadfully lonely without him? . . . until I am sick to death of their well-meaning sympathy.

And I have no intention of being lonely, for after all I shall have Barbara for the holidays, the Halahans are close at hand, and if I stay here, I shall get someone to help me in the shop. "If I stay here"—Jim is so absorbed in Emily and Chalk that, since the day when he told me about her, I don't think he has thought about my future at all. It is only twelve months since we came here, and, while I remember the chaos we found and how painfully difficult it all seemed at first, I am as at home now in the little shop as if I had been here for years; and in this short time I have become so mixed up in and so absurdly fond of Barley that I don't feel I could bear to leave it.

This has been a strange Sunday and when, waking, I looked at the rain-streaked window and pushed Bumble's mop face away, telling him that it was nothing like time to get up, I had not the slightest premonition of how the day would end.

Jim and Emily went off to Chalk after lunch, looking very happy, with even the "Tram" splashing light-heartedly through the biggest ruts and puddles; but I decided to stay quietly at home, for the afternoon was still wet and gusty and our fire-side seemed very attractive.

Instead of having a quiet time I had a steady trickle of visitors.

Mrs. Davenant came first, friendly as usual and delighted about Jim, and said, "Thank goodness, my dear, we're not going to lose *you*." And she did not add, "but I'm afraid you'll be very lonely without him," for which omission I could have embraced her warmly.

Then the vicar's wife came in to say that she did hope poor Phyllis was not too upset and did I think the vicar ought to go and see her? Of course, my brother and Emily must be very set in their ways and she was never sure it was wise for older people to marry, unless they had been widowed, and she couldn't help thinking it a pity they'd rushed into it behind Phyllis's back; but, naturally, we all knew our own business best.

H. Potter arrived, smelling strongly of beer, to say that he was really looking for the Commander to tell him to think twice about what he was doing, for he (H. Potter) had kept clear of the wedding-bells all his life and glad he was to be free now. Women was all right in the right place—but not in church, "if you gets my meaning—and no offence meant to you, Mrs. Braid, mam."

Mrs. Crabtree came in and said she knew she wasn't as young as she used to be but she could still write a good hand—and she didn't mean backwards neither—and if ever I wanted a bit of help with the books, when the Commander went gallivanting off with his lady, I'd only got to ask her; "For figures always come easy to me, you know, easy as kisses when I were a young girl."

Mrs. Fox tripped over to say they'd run out of oranges and she knew it was *awful* of her to knock me up on a Sunday . . . and she really must remember to settle up her account to-morrow.

Then John came in, without knocking, and shut the door carefully behind him and stood looking down at me. He seemed tall and big in our little sitting-room, and his face was set and serious.

"Is this true about Jim and Emily Brown?" he asked.

I said, "Yes."

And he smiled and said, "Good—and thank God it's happened at last."

And I said, "Why 'thank God'?"

And he said, "Because I'm sick of hanging around, and much as I like Jim he's been in my way."

I stood up and faced him and tried to say something sensible —but I couldn't get out any words at all.

"Because," he went on, "I want you—and I haven't dared say so, for I knew you'd never leave him in the lurch—that's why."

Then he put his arms round me and held me to his heart and kissed me.

Presently, he asked me to marry him and, when I had said "yes" (trying not to say it too readily—but I expect I did), he looked about ten years younger and laughed like a boy.

"This is a kind of fairy-tale ending to the village shop business," he said, "with you and me and Jim and Emily living happily ever after—and young Barbara, too. Now I come to think of it, I'm not at all sure she isn't even nicer than her mother."

This is the last time that I shall write in my journal, for our shop venture is nearly over and tomorrow everything will be different.

But, before I finish, I want gently to stir the ingredients that go to make our Barley Brew.

Late tonight I walked out on to the Green, round which the

village lay silver-grey and beautiful in the mellow light of a full harvest moon . . . and the moon's reflection, like a great pale coin, stared up at me from the still, deep waters of the pond—the pond which has witnessed the whole of Parley's history.

And as I stood there a kind of sixth sense took me behind the shut doors (and often tight-closed windows) so that, unseen, I entered each house in turn.

All was quiet and dark in Grannie Rous's cottage, for she slept too soundly to miss the "little lad" after all these years or to bother with her huge family; but there was a lighted window at Mrs. Crabtree's, where the old woman, stiff with rheumatism, had at last called to Tom to help her turn in bed and to make them both a comforting cup of tea.

The Red Lion too was lighted up, for its doors had closed only an hour since, and Kate and her Oliver were eating a fine hot supper by the kitchen stove. Kate didn't *say* anything but she looked fondly at O. Beery, whose poor, twisted face was as handsome to her now as when they first set up house together.

Under H. Potter's smart new thatch the old sailor had hung his wooden leg from a nail on the bedroom door, his auburn wig was packed away against next winter's cold and his reefer coat and blue trousers lay, folded with naval precision, on a chair beside his bed.

Next to Mrs. Cobbett's, where Lofty was examining two silver cups and a pair of candlesticks which he had taken from a sack, old Mrs. Root, her sparse grey hair screwed into metal curlers, lay breathing heavily—and her husband, starting up suddenly in his sleep, felt under the bed and, reassured, fondly touched his precious tea-pot.

By his fireside, Amos Rous, the gentle blacksmith ("soft he is—and I reckon he'll have given most of his Pools money away"), dozed in his chair, for there was no one to urge him out of it, and dreamt of scrolls and beautiful intricate patterns for his wrought-iron gates; and, at the garage, Mr. Parker's turkeys drooped despondently among his bolting lettuces or roosted dustily on the bumpers of his taxi.

At The Weavers, so soon to be deserted by its famous Fairies, Miss Phyllis lay awake and staring into the darkness, her poor starved body yearning for the love she would never have, and little Fairy Fuchsia snuggled closer to her side as if in understanding. Emily, too, was awake; and, small, soft and brown as a bird, she sat at her open window and looked serenely across the silvered fields to Chalk and her life there with Jim.

In his wretched bungalow, old General Blade, deaf and nearly blind, who had struggled through another day (with only sixteen medals in a black velvet case to comfort him), prayed for the end which would soon set him free to march out into that lovely, exciting world in which he had believed unswervingly since he was a little boy.

In a room at the Manor (a beautiful room with linen-fold panelling and a huge stone fireplace), while her husband peered through his microscope at minute slivers of flint, Mrs. Davenant was writing a letter—a letter, perhaps to her daughter, to say that it was high time to let bygones be bygones and how wonderful it would be if she should come home to visit them on her father's seventieth birthday.

Up at the Vicarage, the vicar's wife, gaunt and unrelaxed, her plaited hair tied with tape and her big body shrouded in thick calico, turned and tossed in discontent; but her husband, the moon shining on his child-like face and silver hair, stirred in his sleep and, taking her hand, held it gently in his own.

In the Old Mill House, Geoffrey and Eleanor were still up and working contentedly on their plans for Chalk Manor; and at Mrs. Frobisher-Spink's, the telephone was ringing as, undefeated and in a black lace night-gown, she sat up in bed to take the long-distance call she had put through to Mexico.

In the little house where Mrs. Lacey's jars of jams and pickles weighed down the cupboard shelves, five small Boots and Laceys slept sweetly in preparation for another riotous day; but, from Dawn's cottage, a light showed in an upstairs window and Winston Churchill, his little jaws aching, fluttered his eyelashes, clutched tightly at his father's finger and wept.

And, last of all, behind their close-pulled curtains, our Bessy was crying in her husband's arms and the tears were wet on his cheeks, too—for they were wretchedly unhappy. They were as much a part of the village as were Grannie Rous and Mrs. Crabtree, and for them to leave Barley was like tearing a great branch from a living tree.

But, suddenly, I realised that, by accident, Jim and I had solved their problem for them—and there was no smallest need for them to go "down to Australia" to find their independence. Someone must take over the shop when we leave it, so why not Bert and Bessy? She will love it and he will be "his own master"—and I could hardly wait until tomorrow to tell them of this wonderful idea.

And so, leaving our Barley Brew to simmer, I walked away from the green and along the ancient track which leads to Saxons' Plate. Half-way up the sloping Down I turned and, as I looked back to the roofs and chimneys of the village, a great wave of happiness swept over me.

Barley is more than a collection of houses and people; it has a deep, strong, stirring, bubbling life of its own, and at that moment I knew that we had truly become part of it—Jim and Barbara and me and even Bumble, stretched out on the cool grass at my feet.

In just a year, I thought, Barley has given happiness to Jim— and to me, my heart's desire; and secretly—although I didn't actually *say* anything—I promised to serve my dear John and his village very faithfully for the rest of my life.

Lightning Source UK Ltd.
Milton Keynes UK
UKHW010727140223
416966UK00007B/102